GARY ARMS

Jack DeWitt is an Idiot

Advantage | Books

Published by Advantage, Charleston, South Carolina.
Member of Advantage Media.

ADVANTAGE is a registered trademark, and the Advantage colophon is a trademark of Advantage Media Group, Inc.

Printed in the United States of America.

10 9 8 7 6 5 4 3 2 1

ISBN: 978-1-64225-926-1 (Paperback)
ISBN: 978-1-64225-925-4 (eBook)

Cover design by Beatrice Schares.

This publication is designed to provide accurate and authoritative information in regard to the subject matter covered. It is sold with the understanding that the publisher is not engaged in rendering legal, accounting, or other professional services. If legal advice or other expert assistance is required, the services of a competent professional person should be sought.

Advantage Media helps busy entrepreneurs, CEOs, and leaders write and publish a book to grow their business and become the authority in their field. Advantage authors comprise an exclusive community of industry professionals, idea-makers, and thought leaders. Do you have a book idea or manuscript for consideration? We would love to hear from you at **AdvantageMedia.com**.

For Susie

Contents

Acknowledgement

A lot of kind people read the early chapters of this book. When I finished writing a chapter, I would ask if anyone wanted to read it. Eventually, I had a crew of loyal readers. It is impossible to exaggerate how much their praise and encouragement helped me to continue. Special thanks to Scott Gurman, who suggested I write this book, Geoff Klein, David Rash, Glenda Nelson, Lenelle Freeman, Robert Cox, Rebecca Hamm, Joe Arms, Darrell Arms, Craig Arms, Carol Ryan Sullivan, Ken Love, Colin Morton, Bob Pelelo, Lisa Steinle, Jenn Sill, Jim Butler, Maureen Butler, and Madison Rhymes. I am grateful to Mary Wente for connecting me to the publisher Megan Drake, to Evan Schnittman and Kevin Kane for their advice, to Bea Schares for designing the cover, and to Michael Knock for his friendship.

1

Baritone Boy 1966

The week before fall semester started, West High School sent me a letter. My friends Calvin and Michael got the same letter. It welcomed us to high school and told us our schedules. It assured us West High was a wonderful place, very welcoming. According to the letter, our high school years were going to be the greatest years of our entire lives. While attending West, we were going to become Adults.

The letter asked us two questions:

If you were going to describe the JACK DEWITT you are in a word or a phrase, what would it be?

There was a space where you could write down your answer. I wrote: *Bookworm.* Then I crossed out *Bookworm* and wrote *Brain.*

If you were going to describe the JACK DEWITT you aspire to be in a word or a phrase, what would it be? That's the JACK DEWITT we want to meet! All of us here, the administrators, the teachers, the staff, and students are eager to help you become exactly the adult you want to be!

I thought about it for a long time and finally wrote: *Cool.*

I was a Brain who wanted to be Cool.

I drew a big triangle on a blank sheet of paper. I drew horizontal lines across the triangle. Beside the top part, the pinnacle, I wrote *Jocks*. I thought about sub-dividing the pinnacle. At the tip-top would be Rich Jocks Who Are Also Good-Looking. Underneath the tip-top would be a category called Ordinary Jocks Who Aren't That Good-Looking (or Rich).

I was never going to get into any part of the tiptop of my triangle.

In the slice of triangle beneath the pinnacle I wrote Hoods. Then I put a question mark beside the word Hoods. One of my coolest friends Ray Kavanaugh was a Hood. You better believe it, baby. He was big and dangerous. He even had tattoos on his hands, homemade ones that he got when he was in reform school. Not to mention the fact that his daddy Red Kavanaugh got murdered (with a hammer, no less) and to this day no one knew who did it. Not to mention all Ray's girlfriends. Not to mention his motorcycle, an old Harley held together with wires and duct tape. Not to mention the fact he was a drummer in a rock and roll band called Brain Damage. Unfortunately, my friend Ray had no intention of going to West High or any other school ever again. He was a dropout. Probably all the truly dangerous hoods like Ray were dropouts, so did that suggest the hoods that were left were second-rate? Not all that scary? Mere wannabe hoods?

There was still a lot of space left in the lower part of my triangle. Underneath *Hoods?* I wrote *Brains*. I looked at the word for a while. Probably I could subdivide the category into two parts: *Ordinary Brains*. And *Cool Brains*.

There was still plenty of space at the bottom of the triangle, so I wrote *Nobodies*.

According to the letter, before the semester got going, I should create a Plan for Success. My plan was to make sure I did not slip down into the Nobodies Category and, if possible, climb into the top of the Brains Category. I aspired to be a Cool Brain. That was my Plan for Success.

I imagined myself walking down the halls of West High School with my friend Calvin beside me. Calvin was clearly an Ordinary Brain. A pretty girl (perhaps Cathy Ryan) would walk by. Naturally she would glance at us but only for a moment and then her eyes would flick away. In her head, she would be thinking, "OK, one Plain Ordinary Brain. Yuck. But that other one? There's something about him. Something cool." Probably all day long she would be trying to figure out what it was, Jack DeWitt's secret but unmistakable cool quality.

On the bus on the first day of school, I showed Calvin my triangle drawing and explained the categories to him – JOCKS, BRAINS, NOBODIES — not mentioning that I was in the top tier of Brains, the Cool Brains, but he was stuck at the Ordinary level. He took my piece of paper away from me, studied it for a moment, pulled a pen out of his pocket, crossed out Brains and replaced it with the word Nerds. He handed the piece of paper back to me.

I looked at for a while and then said, "I like the word Brains better than the word Nerds."

Calvin looked out the bus window. "Who cares? You're a nerd. We're both nerds."

Unfortunately, I did not feel cool because I had a baritone in my lap. It was the first day of school and I had my baritone with me because according to the letter West High sent me, I was going to need it for band practice. I was officially enrolled in the West High Marching Band. We had a practice the very first day of school. The letter said: *Bring Your Instrument!*

It is impossible to feel cool when you have a baritone case containing a baritone on your lap and you are riding on a school bus with a bunch of – let's face it – Nobodies. The reason the baritone was on my lap was because when I got on, the driver – a young guy – looked at me funny and said, "Don't you dare put that thing in my aisle."

I looked down the length of the bus. There were kids in almost all the seats. I could see Calvin toward the back, acting as if he didn't know me. "Where'm I gonna put it then?"

The driver said, "You can put it in your lap." Then he closed the door behind me, released the brake, and started rolling down the street, which meant I had to find my way back to Calvin while carrying a baritone. Kids were leaning away from me for fear my big instrument case was going to sideswipe them. *Great, I thought, now they are all gonna call me Baritone Boy.*

Cool high school kids don't ride the bus. They have cars of their own. If they are rich, their parents buy them a car. If they are poor, they have an after-school job and buy their own car, a junker. Kids who are only mildly cool catch a ride with one of the kids who owns his or her own car. Uncool kids get a ride to school from their mom. My mom couldn't give me a ride because she was now a qualified teacher with an official teaching certificate. She had just got a job at one of the Catholic schools in town teaching History and Geography. She had to get up early before I was even out of bed, put on a dress, and drive herself to her job. My dad could not give me a ride either. We only had one car and my mom needed it. My dad was in a carpool. For two dollars a week, this guy nicknamed Fat Ernie picked him up every morning and drove him and two other guys to the factory.

I knew this kid who was called The Nazi because of his obsession with World War 2 and Adolf Hitler. He had read about a thousand books on this topic. His parents owned a motel, so by the standards of my neighborhood, he was a rich kid. He didn't have a driver's license though, so his mom had to drive him to school every day. They offered me a ride, but no way did I want to arrive at high school every day in a car with a kid called The Nazi. First impressions matter.

A boy named Dennis lived two blocks behind us. Dennis was two years older than me and had his own car, a rusty Chevrolet, but when I approached him about giving me a ride to high school, he said, "Yeah, maybe I would...if you weren't such an asshole."

My reputation in my neighborhood was not high. I was considered a la-di-dah snob, a brain, and a pimple-face. In short, bad news. Everyone preferred my little brother Dean. He was now about to enter the ninth grade, and he was still the size of a sixth grader. I was pretty sure he had not yet experienced puberty. No one cared. He was cute and funny and daring. He was an excellent shoplifter and knew a lot of dirty jokes. He drew funny cartoons (also dirty) and was excellent at flattery. What was not to like?

We made several twists and turns on the way to school. Occasionally, the bus driver yelled at us for making too much noise and throwing things. It seemed to me he got angrier and louder than was truly necessary. I told Calvin, "I bet it's his first day on the job."

As we neared the high school, we got into heavy traffic. Four blocks from the school, we approached a red stoplight. Our driver waited too long to put his foot on the brake. A long bus full of kids won't stop on a dime. He stood on his brake and the kids up front started yelling. He slammed into the back of a car in front of us.

Lots of screams. And then quiet.

No one was hurt.

The kids up front could see the car we'd run into. A junker. Its door flew open and two guys got out.

The Hulk. "Oooh," people said. The Hulk was my age but appeared to be at least 30 years old. He was enormous and stupid. If you took a huge bull and magically transformed it into a 16-year-old boy, it would probably look exactly like the Hulk. Kids said the high school football coach had personally gone to see him over the summer and begged him to be on the football team. The Hulk was in the passenger seat. In the driver's seat was his brother, his older brother who had been in prison. He was out now, on probation or supervised release or something like that, and was giving his little brother the Hulk a ride to school.

"Oh, wow," the kids on the bus said, when they realized who we'd hit.

The driver got on the radio and told the dispatcher he had been in a slight accident. A fender bender, he said. Nothing really.

"You know what?" Calvin said. "We're going to be late. On the first day!" Calvin was the sort of person who hated being late. He was always five minutes early to everything.

Kids were looking at their watches. In a few more minutes, we were supposed to be in our homerooms.

The driver opened the door and left the bus.

The kids in the seat in front of us started talking. They had heard that the Hulk's brother had killed someone, not just anyone. "He murdered a cop! I know for a fact!"

I was pretty sure the Hulk's brother never killed a cop or anyone else. All he did was damage a cop.

The kids in front of Calvin and me were hoping we might see a murder. If the Hulk's brother killed a cop, what was he going to do to the bus driver?

The driver was out on the street talking to the ex-convict. The Hulk was standing there too, sort of like a gorilla standing beside two normal-size men.

When everyone realized there was not going to be a murder, or even a beat-down, a wave of disappointment passed through the bus.

The driver came back and told us another bus was on the way. We should remain in our seats. Or we could walk the rest of the way to the high school. "It's only four blocks."

No one wanted to wait on the bus. We all grabbed our stuff and paraded down the sidewalk to the high school.

That was how I managed to be late for homeroom on my first day in high school.

So far as I was concerned, West High School was magnificent. As I walked toward it, I compared it to my last school, Poe Junior. West was better in every imaginable way. Poe Junior High School was old. West had been built after the war, and then five years ago, a big addition was added. The entire high school looked new. Modern. Clean and shiny. And it was big. Two large junior highs sent their graduates to West. It was roomy enough to house 3000 students.

I was an incoming sophomore. In other words, I was a frightened little mouse, a near-sighted mousy mouse who refused to wear his (uncool) glasses, walked around in a fog, and got lost easily. Other refugees from the bus told me how to get to my homeroom. Still lugging my baritone, I got there only minutes before the first period bell was going to ring.

To my happy surprise, the homeroom teacher, a man, did not get mad at me for being late. He had already been informed about the bus accident and knew that one of his students might be late. When I entered the room, and all the other kids looked up at me, the only thing the teacher wanted to know was my schedule. He told me I did not need to sit down. "When the bell rings, go back the way you came. Teachers will be out in the hall helping everyone. If you get lost, just show them your schedule and ask for directions. You better take that," he indicated my baritone, "to the band room. Tell your teacher what happened. All the teachers know about the bus accident. You'll be OK."

"Thank you," I said.

The rest of my first day went like a happy dream. Everyone was nice. No one yelled at me. Every time I got lost, some helpful person showed me where to go.

After school, I went to the proper location and got onto the correct bus. It was not driven by the young bus driver.

We never saw that guy again.

West High was the result of the merger of two large junior highs, so I thought kids I was used to seeing in my smart kid classes at Poe would make up half the class, and the other half would be strangers from our rival junior high. In fact, the Poe Junior contingent was dwarfed by the group that arrived from the other junior high. Two thirds of the students in my talented and gifted classes were complete strangers to me. They were the sons and daughters of professional middle-class people, doctors and dentists and lawyers, or it would turn out their dad owned a store, or he was a supervisor at the factory.

I thought of them as rich kids. Every one of them had his or her own room, a luxury beyond my imagination. I shared my bedroom with my two brothers. In their rooms, rich kids had their own phones. When they turned sixteen, their parents gave them a car. Sometimes the car was brand-new. They went to nice restaurants, the kind where you sit down at a table and a waiter attends to your every need. They went on family trips to the Caribbean, to Paris and London. At Christmas time, they went to Colorado for "the skiing." Rich kids were better dressed than the kids from my neighborhood. They seemed better looking. They had an air of confidence I was not used to, as if they were already adults.

I decided I would resort to secrecy. I didn't want any of these smart rich kids to realize how woefully ignorant I was about nearly everything, or how pathetically poor I was compared to them.

My parents were never going to buy me a car. We had only one car. My parents shared it, and it was not new. My dad had told me many times that only rich men buy new cars. It is much more responsible financially to buy a low mileage used car. If I ever dared to ask my parents if I could have my own phone, they would have laughed in my face. Our idea of an excellent restaurant experience was stopping by McDonalds after church and buying a sack of hamburgers. Paris? London? Our idea of vacation was to go visit family members, either in Oklahoma or northern Michigan. My parents would never dream of wasting money on a motel. Our relatives would force a couple of their kids to evacuate a bedroom so my parents could sleep there. My siblings and I would sleep on a floor somewhere.

Rich kids had opinions about clothes. I had never thought five seconds about what I was wearing. Rich kids had opinions about fabric, about brand names and style. I did not even know what the word "style" entailed. When I got too big for my mom to make my clothes on her sewing machine, she started obtaining them for me at a discount store. I was never consulted. "Here," she would say, "I got you a new t-shirt." I would not even bother to look up from whatever book I was reading. "Thanks, Mom."

Up until I set foot in West High, I had felt that, because my mom was now a teacher at a little Catholic school, my family was becoming prosperous. My parents were no longer fighting all the time over nickels and dimes. Our gravel driveway had been replaced with a new one made of cement. We now had sidewalks. Our neighborhood was a no-frills neighborhood. No one had a cement driveway or a sidewalk. If you wanted frills like that, you had to pay for them yourself. My parents were saving up for a garage.

I was pretty sure all these rich kids had double garages and more sidewalks than they could possibly need. They probably had swimming pools in the back yard. Their parents were probably saving up to buy a chain of islands somewhere.

One thing I learned to do was skip lunch. Lunch cost 50 cents. If I never ate lunch, at the end of the week, I would have $2.50, almost enough to buy an entire (monaural) album or two singles. Or a paperback book.

None of the rich kids had to worry about money. They got substantial allowances.

My mom once attempted to give me a small allowance. This happened when I was in eighth grade. We had a family meeting. Each of the five kids in my family would get an allowance of 25 cents per week. An entire quarter! There were strings attached. We would be docked a nickel for insubordination or failure to do a chore. My mom would make up a list with specific chores for each kid. When we finished each task, we would put a checkmark beside the name of the chore. Then my mom would inspect our work. If we had done our work properly, she would add the letter M (for Mom) beside our checkmark. If we had done the job sloppily, the M would be withheld until we did the chore right.

When the weekend arrived, I was greedy for my 25 cents. For exactly that amount of money, I could purchase a comic book and a small plastic squirt gun. My mom dispensed quarters to my siblings. They had accomplished their chores satisfactorily and had not once committed any disobedience. Then she came to me. Mom looked at me sadly and made a clucking noise with her tongue. My siblings clutched their quarters and watched. Mom observed that my chore sheet included blank spaces because I had not done all my chores. Twice, although I had done the chore, I had not done it satisfactorily. As a result, I did not receive an M. Also, there was that time at the dinner table when I threw mashed potatoes at my little brother Ron and made him cry. Mom informed me my allowance for the week would be exactly one nickel. She dropped the nickel into my extended hand.

I thrilled my siblings by uttering a forbidden word and flinging my nickel across the living room. I uttered more forbidden words and stomped out of the house. My mother told my siblings that whichever one of them found my nickel first could keep it.

I was certain that nothing remotely like this ever happened to any of the rich kids.

I decided I would never eat lunch. In effect, I would give myself a weekly allowance of $2.50, an allowance that could never be docked. I would never reveal one word about my family's relative poverty, our house, our neighborhood, our church, or the fact we had never visited Disneyland.

There was a bright side to all this. I met a lot more book readers. And I met atheists. Three of them! Until I arrived in high school, I had imagined I might be the only teenage atheist in my entire town.

Because I did not go to lunch in the cafeteria, I spent my entire lunch period in the student lounge. West High School was provided with a lounge, just for students. The lounge was carpeted and full of armchairs and sofas that looked brand-new. There were little round tables with stools. The walls were covered with framed photographs of the Class Presidents.

It was in the student lounge that I met Epstein and Rothstein. First, I eavesdropped on their conversation. They were discussing the new TV shows: *The Monkees, Mission Impossible,* and *Star Trek. The Monkees,* said one of them (Epstein), was an insult to civilization, a mockery of all that was good and decent. It was the crass attempt by American corporations to turn the Beatles into a commodity, to create fake plastic versions of John, Paul, George and Ringo, and turn them into simple-minded clowns. Why did these corporations want to turn the mind-blowing Beatles into mildly talented buffoons? To sell toothpaste and deodorant!

Mission Impossible (said Rothstein) was a clever, well-made show about a troop of American spies who travelled around the world wearing disguises that no foreigner ever managed to see through. The Mission team would target a hapless dictator or corrupt aristocrat and make a fool of him, frame him, and then get his wife to murder him.

Or something. There was plenty of suspense. Rothstein approved of *Mission Impossible.*

Epstein agreed *Mission Impossible* was fun to watch, exciting and suspenseful, but since it presented all foreign dictators as if they were morons, was it also a bit racist?

Rothstein said that sort of thing would not be racism, it would be xenophobia. It took me a week to find out what exactly xenophobia means because I could not find it in the dictionary. Finally, a kind-hearted librarian explained to me the word meant prejudice against people from other countries and was spelled with an X and not a Z.

Star Trek, said Epstein, was by far the greatest of the three new TV shows. It was nothing less than an immense cultural achievement, a leap forward, a breakthrough and a treasure, the best show of its kind since *Twilight Zone. Star Trek* was well made, intelligent, socially progressive science fiction – on TV!

I had so far not seen any of these shows. Despite my mom's job, my parents continued to resist my pleas that they purchase a TV set, even a black and white one. They had a list of expensive stuff they were saving up to obtain, and a TV was not even on the list.

The fact that I was so culturally deprived I had no TV in my house was another item I intended never to reveal should I ever be fortunate enough to convince Epstein or Rothstein to be my friend, but I agreed with their opinions. If the *Monkees* program was an attempt to demean and rip off the Beatles, I hated the show. On the other hand, *Mission Impossible* sounded pretty cool. I loved the idea of characters who wore artificial faces and tricked dictators. Of course, I agreed that science fiction in any form was an important and highly valuable asset to civilization.

I soon found myself parroting the opinions of Epstein and Rothstein to Michael and Calvin. Michael and Calvin probably wondered how I had become so much more knowledgeable than usual about TV shows, but if so, they did not say anything.

After the first week of school, I wanted to be the friend of Epstein and Rothstein. After the second week, I wanted to be them. I told myself that, in a way, we were spiritual cousins already. Atheist bookworms are a kind of tribe. I wanted to be as good as they were at sarcasm and irony. I felt I already sorta kinda looked like them, as if I spent too much time indoors, as if I did not participate in any sport. Like them, I carried around books no teacher would ever assign. Like them, I used certain unusual words, words I was not certain how to pronounce, words I found only in the books I read. Like them, I was very hard to please, more likely to criticize than praise.

So, how to befriend them?

It turned out Four Point Levine was the answer. Epstein was in love with her.

2

High Maintenance Girls

When I arrived in the student lounge, Epstein and Rothstein were discussing Jewish girls. Rothstein said he didn't like them, too high maintenance.

Epstein said he was deeply and hopelessly in love with Janet Levine.

That name rang a bell in my head, but I couldn't place it. Then I remembered. Four Point. At my previous school, no one had ever called her Janet.

Rothstein said, "There are three kinds of Jews."

Epstein said, "Do they walk into a bar?"

"Why do I even try to talk to you?" Rothstein said.

"Conservative, reform, and atheist?"

Rothstein said, "Ugly Jews, Beautiful Jews, and Golden Jews."

"Would Albert Einstein be your best example of an Ugly Jew?"

"A classic example, but he is also a Jew blessed with a golden brain."

"So, he's like a crossover?"

"Other examples of Ugly Jews: Walter Matthau."

"The Marx Brothers."

"Bingo."

I felt uncomfortable listening to this conversation because I felt they sounded like racist white people discussing black people. I said, "But they aren't all Jewish, what about Chico? Pretty sure he's Italian or something. Or maybe Mexican."

They burst into laughter.

Rothstein said, "That could be a new category, Invisible Jews. Jews nobody realizes are Jews."

I said, "Chico's Jewish?"

More laughter.

Epstein said, "Invisible Jews: Sandra Dee. Eddie Fisher."

Rothstein said, "My favorite is Yul Brynner."

Epstein said, "Yul Brynner is not Jewish."

Rothstein said, "Sure is, baby. Also, Kirk Douglas."

Epstein said, "I think I knew that."

"Know what Kirk's real name is? Issur Danielovitch Demsky."

I was amazed Rothstein knew all this weird stuff about celebrities and wondered if he was just making it up.

Epstein said, "John Wayne's real name is Marion Morrison."

I couldn't help myself. I said, "The Duke is Jewish?"

"Of course, he is. *Oy vey, pilgrim. A man's got to do what a man's got to do.*"

I thought for a moment that maybe John Wayne really was Jewish, and then realized Epstein was teasing me and got irritated, but at the same time I was impressed. That was a darn good John Wayne impression. I abandoned Epstein and Rothstein and walked over to a couch where this guy named Cooper was reading a book. I sat down beside him and accused Epstein and Rothstein of being anti-Semitic. Cooper had known Epstein and Rothstein since he was five years old.

Cooper looked up from the book he was reading. "You think Epstein and Rothstein are anti-Semitic?"

"You should hear the kind of stuff they say about Jews. I think they're prejudiced."

To my embarrassment, Cooper waved them over and tattled on me, "Young Jack here says we have a couple anti-Semites at our school. Yeah, anti-Semites."

Rothstein narrowed his eyes, "Who, pray tell?"

"You, Epstein, and you too, Rothstein. Jack feels you fellows may be just a wee bit anti-Semitic."

"Me and Rothstein?"

I weakly attempted to defend myself, "You are always talking about Jews. Ugly Jews and all that. I even heard Rothstein say he doesn't like Jewish girls because they're too high maintenance."

Rothstein and Epstein looked at each other and burst into laughter.

I stuck to my guns. "You really did say that. I heard you."

Rothstein said, "Jack, do you realize that Epstein and I are in fact Jews? Epstein is an Ugly Jew. Aren't you, Epstein? While I am a Beautiful Jew."

Epstein said, "In your dreams maybe."

"What?" I was so flabbergasted I turned red. How was I supposed to know?

Epstein said, "That's great, Rothstein, you made poor Jack here blush."

I felt my face turn a deep shade of red.

"Rothstein didn't mean any harm, Jack. It's just that darn Jewish humor."

For some reason, after I made this gaffe, Rothstein and Epstein liked me more, not less.

Epstein said, "You should not imagine poor Cooper here is Jewish. He is... what are you again, Cooper?"

"I was born into a proud family of Presbyterians, but alas I have lost my faith."

In hopes of salvaging a tiny drop of dignity, I told Epstein, "That girl you like, Janet Levine. I know her. I went out with her once. She took me to an anti-war rally."

It turned out Epstein and Rothstein were regular customers at my favorite record store downtown and knew Four Point's big brother Jimmy Levine, who worked there. I could see they were interested, so I described the anti-war rally that Jimmy and Four Point took me to at the university and the college boy who thrilled the crowd by burning his draft card. I suggested if Epstein really wanted to impress Four Point, he should burn his draft card. Epstein said he would gladly burn a thousand draft cards for one kiss from Janet Levine. Unfortunately, none of us could obtain a draft card until we turned 18.

I suggested Epstein should try talking to Four Point about the recent race riots in Atlanta. She would probably be into that. "She's pretty political." I thought for a second and then added, "Hey, you know what? She loves professional wrestling."

"You can't be serious?"

It turned out Epstein also loved professional wrestling. I suggested he take Janet Levine to a professional wrestling show, maybe one that included her favorite wrestler, Big Moose Jolack. He could take her backstage to meet the Big Moose, get his autograph or something.

I am not sure I ever fully won the friendship of Cooper, he was a cold-blooded sort of person, but after that conversation in the student lounge, Epstein and Rothstein liked me. For the next two years, until they graduated and went off to college, I learned as much from them as I did from my teachers. More probably.

I sometimes sighted my own high maintenance love interest, Cathy Ryan, in the hallways of West High. She was usually with a pretty girl named Mary Ellen, who I assumed was her best friend. They were often carrying big art notebooks and I remembered that Ray once referred to Cathy as "the artist." Ray knew her father Big Bill Ryan, who owned a bunch of businesses in my neighborhood. He owned the bowling alley, where Ray had a job. He owned a bar and a grocery store. He owned a bunch of low-end houses that he rented out to poor people like Ray's mom. Everyone said Big Bill Ryan was probably the richest guy in our entire town. His daughter Cathy was so far above me on the social ladder, she was practically another species. But last winter, more or less by accident, I had met her mother, Mrs. Ryan. Mrs. Ryan and I became friendly. Mrs. Ryan would go to the bowling alley during the day and read a book and then she would come by the junior high in her Cadillac and give me a ride home. Unfortunately, Mrs. Ryan had died in a tragic car accident. That was how I met her daughter. One time I was visiting Mrs. Ryan's grave and Cathy was there too. She even gave me a ride home. Now, I had a crush on her.

Cathy Ryan and her friend Mary Ellen were always talking and laughing as they walked. I envied girls for the way they loved each other so intensely and cracked each other up. Sometimes, Cathy and her friend would make each other laugh so hard, they would bend over and stagger and bump into the walls. I tried to think of even one example of me making any of my male friends laugh like that. I could not think of a single example.

The unfortunate thing about my crush on Cathy Ryan was that my interest in her was not returned. In fact, that time she drove me home from the cemetery, she told me I should not get my hopes up because we were not friends. She told me not to expect her even to say hi to me when we encountered one another at West High.

This fact had not totally demoralized me. Pretty girls like Cathy Ryan were constantly being hit on by boys. It came naturally to them to tell us to back off. And then there was the fact I was not a jock or even a hood like Ray. Calvin said nerds like us could not expect to be liked by girls, especially pretty ones. We were lucky if they even talked to us.

As she had warned me, Cathy Ryan did not accept me as one of her friends. It was as if we had never met. When I saw her in the halls, she would look in another direction and just keep walking.

Those first few weeks of high school, I met one other person who interested me. In the entire high school student body, almost 3000 students, there was only one black kid, Eugene Masterson, and he sat beside me in my English class.

My friend Calvin explained to me how Eugene Masterson was even possible. He was adopted. Two infertile white people who lived out east in New Hampshire or someplace like that adopted him. In their state, white babies were in short supply at the orphanages, so they adopted a black one. Mr. Masterson was an engineer. He got hired by the factory where my dad and Calvin's dad worked. Before he moved his little family to our town, Mr. Masterson arranged to buy a house in a nice neighborhood on the west side of town. When his wife and kid arrived, the white people living on that street found out they had a little black kid living in their neighborhood. When Eugene got old enough, he became the only black kid in his elementary school. In due course, he became the only black kid in his junior high, and now he was the only black kid in our high school.

Eugene Masterson was in the school orchestra. He played the cello. To be in the orchestra, you had to be talented.

This was not the case with the marching band. The marching band was happy to accept even the most untalented musicians, a group that included me. I was the worst baritone player in the marching band. There were only three of us and, talent-wise, I was in last place. Talent-wise, I may have been the worst baritone player in the entire history of the West High Marching Band.

Eugene Masterson wore a bowtie and glasses. One could forgive him for wearing glasses, but the bowtie? I was convinced his mother must be buying all his clothes, and that she was ruining his life by making him look peculiar. My mother bought my clothes too, but at least she didn't make me wear a bowtie.

I kept thinking I could use Eugene as an excuse to call up Rose White. I had not talked to her in a very long time, and in my idle moments I wanted to talk to her. When I was in elementary school, Rose and her brother Tommy were the only black kids in my school. Their family, the Whites, was the only black family in my entire neighborhood. People said this was because of Tommy. Even when he was a little kid, he was a phenomenal athlete. Cathy Ryan's dad Big Bill Ryan loved sports; he was a big booster of West High football. To make sure Tommy White was on the West team, he bought the White family a house on my side of town.

Unfortunately, a lot of the neighbors objected to having a family of black people living on their street. One night, when the entire White family was out of town, visiting relatives, their house burned down. Arson. The cops never solved that crime, but it wasn't as if the cops put a lot of effort into it. The Whites wound up living in the North End, where all the other blacks in my town lived.

Even after she moved, I kept in touch with Rose because like me she was a bookworm. She was two years older than me, so it was totally impossible for me to catch up with her in terms of reading. Like me, she read everything she got her hands on. Also, she had good taste in music. Because of Rose, I had opinions about great singers like Marvin Gaye and Aretha Franklin. Rose had a leg situation which to my way of thinking was similar to my pimple situation. She had had polio and was often stuck in a wheelchair. She had a prickly personality and did not suffer fools gladly. Most of the time, I liked that aspect of Rose White, but it did mean that fairly often she told me I was stupid and hung up on me. Our friendship had a lot of ups and downs. She was now a senior at East High School, a school that was half black and half white.

I figured the fact that I was becoming friends with the only black student allowed to attend West High might interest Rose, so I kept talking to Eugene Masterson.

Not only was Eugene an interesting person to talk about, so was our English teacher, Miss Pross. She and Eugene had something in common. He was the only black student in our school, and she was the only black teacher. Wasn't that intriguing? I wondered if Rose would find it as fascinating as I did. Before her house was burnt to the ground, Rose too was one of those black kids in a school full of white kids. I wondered if she knew about Eugene. Was it possible all the black people in our town knew each other? There were more than 10,000 black people in my town, so probably they did not all know each other.

I had learned somewhere that there was such a thing as an Oreo person: black on the outside, white on the inside – like an Oreo cookie. Possibly Eugene was an Oreo. There was also something called a Snowball, black on the inside and white on the outside. Snowballs were little cakes sold in gas stations, coconut on the outside and chocolate in the middle. I wondered if I might be a Snowball. If a white kid loves James Brown records and listens late at night to the soul station, wouldn't that person be a Snowball?

I wondered if Rose White might be willing to help me answer these important questions, or would she just get mad at me for asking them, and hang up on me?

I thought if Rothstein believed Jewish girls were high maintenance, he should meet Rose White.

I wondered if Rose White considered me a nerd, but for her was that a plus or a minus? When we had been on speaking terms, she too had been a nerd. Now, she was semi-famous, The Girl Who Desegregated Junior Prom. She had led a protest at East High, first a protest and then a walk out against the no biracial dating policy. Her photo had been in the paper. She had been elected Prom Queen, for god's sake. Rose White had transcended her former status and left me far behind. But I had always lagged far behind Rose White anyway. She was cooler and smarter than me. And yet, for a while we had been friends.

I wondered if Rose White knew Miss Pross. Maybe they went to church together or something. I thought Miss Pross was the sort of woman who probably went to church every Sunday and wore white gloves. She was stiff and proper, prissy. I was pretty sure Miss Pross was an Oreo. Miss Pross was totally in love with dead white authors like Shakespeare and Dickens. She adored the English poet William Wordsworth. How could any sensible person, black or white, adore the poet Wordsworth? According to Miss Pross, Wordsworth had a lot to teach us about Nature. I wondered if Miss Pross ever went camping. It was hard to believe she ever smelled of bug repellent and camped out in a tent. Normally, she smelled like perfume.

Eugene and Miss Pross reminded me of one another. They both had a high opinion of Great Art created long ago by white men. I once eavesdropped when the two of them were talking about a classical music concert they had gone to see at the university. Mozart for god's sake. Who cares about Mozart? Miss Pross and Eugene Masterson, that's who.

Obviously, both of them were Oreos.

I also wanted to talk to Rose White about marching band, which was the bane of my existence. I decided to call her up.

Rose's brother Tommy answered the phone and startled me by recognizing my voice. "Hey, I know you. You're that white kid, aren't you? Jack... somebody?"

"Jack DeWitt. I go to West High now."

"Hey, know what? My team's gonna play your team in a couple weeks. We're gonna kick your little white asses. Seriously. Know what I mean?"

"I'll be there."

"Whoa. On the team? What position you play?"

"I'm in the marching band."

Tommy laughed loudly. "I'm sorry. We all have a cross to bear. You want my sister? Rosie, it's for you! It's that white kid Jack Dimwit. Want me to tell him you're not here?"

Rose took the phone and astonished me by telling me she was glad I called. She told me she had the blues, and it was my job to get her out of them.

"Right," I said. "What's wrong?"

"There is only one reason anyone gets the blues."

I thought: *Oh, my god, Rose White is in love!*

My plan to tell her about Eugene and Miss Pross evaporated. Rose wanted to talk about unrequited love. It was as if our long period of not talking had been forgotten, and we were friends again.

Rose said, "It has come to me, what I hoped to avoid, and it's worse than I thought."

I said I had endured a few cases of love myself, but only the mild kind.

Rose said she did not care to hear about my mild cases. "If it's mild, it ain't love."

"OK," I said. "Start at the beginning."

Rose said she had the love-sickness so bad, sometimes she took a great notion to jump into the ocean and drown.

"Don't do that. That is not a good idea. Can I ask a question? Who is this guy?"

Rose said, "From a white man's point of view, is a black girl an untouchable? What if she is also in a chair? And wears glasses?"

"A white man? You're in love with a WHITE man?" Then and there, I decided Rose White had lost her mind. "How OLD is this white man?"

It turned out Rose White was in love with her English teacher, a forty-year-old white man who was married and had three children.

Before I could find out more, my mother entered the living room, and looked straight at me, narrowing her eyes and wrinkling her nose as if she smelled something stinky.

I told Rose, "I gotta go. But take care of yourself. Stay safe. Feel better."

"Who was that?" my mother demanded when I hung up.

"Calvin," I lied. "He's sick. A bad cold or something."

3

Mission Impossible

I will reveal the thing about Rothstein soon, but first I will explain my problem with marching band.

As I have already indicated, I had no musical talent. None. In an ideal world, a kid like me would never be forced to participate in any kind of band. That kid would be left alone to read books.

The only reason I was in a school band was because of my mother. She felt I should be in one. There, I would learn discipline. She was not alone in believing I sorely lacked discipline. Also, I would learn to be part of a team. Teams, according to my mom, are the building blocks of civilization. All the grand activities of human beings involve them. Individuality is all very well in principle. In practice, to have any real worth to our societies, we humans need to realize it is our destiny to become cogs in Large Machines. What had been the great crisis for my mother's entire generation? World War 2. How had they survived that crisis and conquered the world? By participating in Teams!

My mother when young and poor had been on a basketball team (so she claimed) and felt it had done her a world of good. Even my dad had been on a basketball team though he mostly just sat on the bench. Unfortunately, I hated sports. My parents had accepted the fact I was never going to be part of a basketball team or – God help us — a football team, but that just meant it was all the more important I be part of a band. A band is also a kind of team. One plays a position. The band director is the coach. Like sports, band requires its participants to practice. Practice, practice, practice!

I was forced to practice my baritone for one entire hour every evening. This practice could not be faked. I could go into my bedroom and shut the door, but the baritone produces loud noises. It is an instrument that demands attention and knows how to get it. No matter where she was in the house, my mother could easily determine if I was practicing. If all she heard was silence, soon she was pounding on my bedroom door, opening it (without my permission), and invading my privacy. "Why aren't you PRACTICING?!"

My discomfort grew exponentially when I arrived in high school. The first week of school, I learned that all band members were required to participate in marching band. Nothing like this had been required at Poe Junior. In junior high band, we sat on hard wooden chairs and played our instruments. No one expected us to march around like idiots. At West, we were given dorky uniforms and hats – tall, ridiculous hats with plumes and chinstraps. Our jackets included rows of buttons. Our trousers had vertical stripes. On our feet and ankles, we wore spats. Let me assure the reader that in the fall of 1966 no teenager wore spats unless that kid was in a marching band.

The band had a new director, a young ambitious person named Mr. Angelus. He wanted to lift the West High Marching Band to new heights. He wanted us to win regionals. That was our semester goal. Win Regionals!

Mr. Angelus would begin every practice by yelling, "What is our Semester Goal?!"

The band would yell back. "Win Regionals!"

On a specific night, at halftime during a football game, judges representing our region would be in the audience watching us march. On that night we had to be perfect!

One aspect of winning regionals was that the band members were not allowed to read music while playing. Our instruments contained little mounts where one could attach a tiny music stand. That was where, in previous years, the sheet music was clipped. The student could march along like a robot tooting or tweeting and reading the music as he or she went. Now, the music had to be in our heads. Why? Because, said Mr. Angelus, no band had EVER won regionals unless they memorized all the songs.

My head refused to cooperate. No matter how often I practiced, my mind refused to memorize any song. The failure of my head to do its job was ruthlessly exposed in baritone sectional, a once-a-week humiliation when each baritone player was required to stand in front of Mr. Angelus and play all our songs without any helpful sheet music.

When it was my turn, I would recall the fiasco of that long-ago Mother's Day, when I had tried and failed to recite a poem in front of everyone at our church. I had frozen up. Every word of the poem simply vanished from my brain. Something similar happened when I attempted to play songs for Mr. Angelus. He stared at me, and I began. I played the beginning measures correctly – almost correctly – and then the notes began to swim inside my head. Strange unearthly noises emerged from my baritone as if it had been possessed by demons. This embarrassment went on until Mr. Angelus could not bear it and shouted, "Stop! Stop! For the love of God!"

Mr. Angelus attempted various pedagogical techniques to help me. Sometimes he was kind to me, sympathetic. Encouraging. Sometimes he simply ignored me. Sometimes he sighed heavily. Sometimes he yelled at me. Once, he offered me a candy bar for each correctly played song. I did not manage to earn a single Baby Ruth.

Since the school policy was that no student, no matter how musically inept, was to be expelled from marching band, Mr. Angelus was forced to allow me to participate in all our shows. Mr. Angelus bowed to necessity, but he made it clear to me that I was not to play my baritone during the show, or even during our outdoor practices. I was to hold my horn to my lips and PRETEND to blow.

The actual marching was less of a problem. All I had to do was march in rhythm behind the other two baritone players, both of whom were able to memorize the songs and always knew where we were supposed to go next.

I will pause for a moment and say that in my humble opinion marching is a peculiar and bizarre and stupid activity. I am unable to understand why it has gained so much popularity. Marching is an angular, jerky activity – a type of dancing invented by men who hate real dancing. Long rows of marchers are trained to do exactly the same thing at the same time. They march forward, backward; they turn left; they turn right. They halt.

The crowd watches and listens, and at the appropriate time claps politely. Everyone involved becomes a cog in the Machine. And in this way Society benefits.

Mr. Angelus spent a great deal of time working out our formations. The band director thinks of the uniformed bodies of his students as mobile dots of paint. He arranges the dots in pleasing patterns. Squares, circles, triangles, hexagrams. These geometric shapes form and then dissipate. A square turns into a circle, and then the circle becomes a five-pointed star.

For the East-West football game, Mr. Angelus chose a topical theme; our band would perform the easily recognizable theme songs of popular TV shows like *The Beverly Hillbillies* (poor hicks from the sticks strike it rich and move to Beverly Hills but continue to dress like yokels). We performed other theme songs too, in the middle of the show, but I forget what they were. The exciting climax of our show was going to be an eye-popping performance of the theme music from the popular new show, *Mission Impossible.* Half the band would form a giant rectangle. The other half of the band would form two enormous circles inside the rectangle. A narrator would read lines from the TV show, famous words that were instantly recognizable.

"Your mission, Jim, should you choose to accept it ..."

The wheels inside the rectangle would revolve.

The crowd would realize what they were watching. A giant Tape Recorder!

At the end, the announcer would recite the famous phrase, "As always, should you or any of your I.M. Force be caught or killed, the Secretary will disavow any knowledge of your actions. This tape will self-destruct in five seconds. Good luck, Jim."

One Mississippi, two Mississippi, three Mississippi, four Mississippi, five Mississippi. Woosh! A fire extinguisher would create the impression of the tape going up in smoke. It would be beautiful. I have zero doubt that Mr. Angelus was darn proud of himself when he thought of this climactic touch because it would cause the judges to award us extra points for showmanship.

What is our semester goal?

Win Regionals!

But what kid should operate the fire extinguisher? Mr. Angelus remembered his third-chair baritone player, a tenth grader named Jack DeWitt. That poor kid seemed intelligent, but he simply could not memorize songs. He could operate the fire extinguisher!

It was a shock to me when Mr. Angelus introduced us to our drum major, and it turned out to be Rothstein. It will seem odd that I had seen our drum major before, at every outdoor practice, and of course hung out with Rothstein nearly every day in the student lounge but failed for so long to realize they were the same person. This is because, when we were outdoors in the early mornings practicing our marching, my mind was occupied, trying to remember the formations. The grass was marked with chalk lines, and I was trying my best to make sure my foot hit those white lines at the exact same moments that the feet of everyone else hit them.

Meanwhile, the drum major was doing his drum major things. There were several rows of people between us. Until I found out he was Rothstein, I had no reason to pay any attention to him.

Drum major motions are difficult to describe. The drum major turns into a wind-up toy. He blows his whistle, loud abrupt bleats, and makes sudden angular movements with his feet and arms. He flings his baton high up into the air and catches it. To tell the truth, drum majors are a little frightening to watch. They are on the Scary Spectrum. When drum-majoring, they no longer seem entirely human.

There were aspects to Rothstein that surprised me. His friend Cooper told me that Rothstein's mother had made him take six years of tap dance lessons. As a result, Rothstein was an amazing tap dancer, like Fred Astaire or Gene Kelly. Also, in the summertime, he was in a Drum and Bugle Corps.

When the night of the East-West football game arrived, Mr. Angelus was in a state of high excitement. The regional judges, he reminded us three times, were in the audience. Also, we had a last-minute replacement. A new drum major was going to substitute for our usual drum major. Mr. Angelus acted as if the absence of our usual drum major was no big deal, but he was obviously worried sick about it.

That announcement woke me up. Was Rothstein sick or something?

The band, 200 kids, marched up into the bleachers with our instruments and sat down in our reserved seats. We were not going to do the pre-game show. The East High pep band was going to do it. They were assigned to play both school songs and the national anthem. We were to sit silently and be polite while they led their side of the field in the East High fight song, but we should sing as loudly as we possibly could when they led us in the West High song. Of course, when they led us through the national anthem, we should stand proudly with our hands over our hearts.

The East High pep band was good. They were very good. I was not an aficionado of pep bands, but I felt any fool could see and hear how good they were. They were much better than us. That was the demoralizing thing.

The baritone player beside me, a junior named Barry, told me that I should not give the East High pep band too much credit. A pep band consists of only the most talented members of the school's full band. According to Barry, if we watched the entire East High marching band do its thing, we would soon realize they were not that great.

I had my doubts but kept them to myself.

The football game began, and it did not go well for our side. As Tommy White had predicted, his team kicked our asses, in no small part because of him. He was taller and stronger and faster than ever. He caught a pass in the end zone for one touchdown and then ran one in 15 yards for a second touchdown. Just before halftime, Tommy White intercepted a pass and ran it back the entire way for his third touchdown.

Barry said, "Holy cow, he's on offense AND defense, and he scores either way."

When halftime arrived, our side of the field was depressed. I am not sure if our fans were in the mood for our show or not. I like to think they were. I like to think the beginning of our show, the field maneuvers, the tunes from TV favorites, perked up the West High fans. I like to think for several minutes we helped them think of something besides the fact that the East football team was kicking our asses.

When it came time for the exciting climax of our halftime show, I ran off the field and picked up the fire extinguisher. I stood on the sidelines holding the extinguisher and waited for the rest of the band to create the giant Tape Recorder. Unfortunately, something went wrong.

The substitute drum major got confused. Barry told me later that the drum major lost his place and started blowing his whistle as if we were performing an earlier part of our show. It was as if he had totally forgotten the *Mission Impossible* part.

All the reeds mindlessly followed the drum major as he marched in the wrong direction. The entire brass section went where they were supposed to go. Clarinets collided with trumpets. The flutes grew disoriented. The huge rectangle failed to form properly. The two giant circles looked more like footballs, and when they attempted to revolve, they banged into one another.

Mr. Angelus experienced some sort of psychological breakdown and began screaming orders from the sidelines. Some band members attempted to obey his commands, but others failed to hear them, or misunderstood them.

I watched in dismay, as if I was witnessing the Apocalypse. At some point, I don't know why, I ran out into the chaos. I heard the announcer recite my cue. "This tape will self-destruct in five seconds."

I triggered the fire extinguisher. Foam sprayed into the air and fell back onto the field. If I do say so myself, it was a beautiful moment, and went exactly as we had rehearsed it. However, under the circumstances, it did not persuade the regional judges to give us any extra points.

In the second half, the band sat silent in the bleachers, while the East football team scored three more touchdowns. They brought in their second team, and our team managed to score one touchdown before the final whistle.

I am sorry to report that our band did not win regionals that year.

Over the weekend, I found out the thing about Rothstein. My friend

Calvin explained it to me. Rothstein was in the hospital, recovering from broken ribs and other injuries. "A couple guys beat the shit out of him. He's refusing to tell the cops who did it." Calvin's mom was best friends with a nurse, the source of this information.

I found this story impossible to believe. Why would anyone beat up Rothstein?

Calvin was not very happy with me. He felt I had been ignoring him, taking him for granted, and spending way too much time with my new friends.

"You are so clueless," Calvin said. He explained the thing about Epstein. "He's a queer. Everybody knows he's a queer. Guys beat him up. What do you expect? I can't believe you're friends with him."

The next time I saw Rothstein, he was wearing a neck brace. He acted as if nothing special had happened.

4

Miss Sweet

My mom's at-home behavior got worse that semester — the fits of rage and grief — though apparently at her school, teaching students, she was fine. When she would lose it at home, my dad would withdraw to the parental bedroom and work crossword puzzles. I got increasingly fed up with both of them. She was crazy, and he was useless.

One day Mom got so mad at my sister Ellen, she knocked her down and began kicking her. It wasn't hard to knock Ell down because of her shrunken leg. Dean and I stood there shocked, not knowing what to do. The little kids hid behind the sofa. My mom used to attack me like that before I got so tall, but never Ell.

The doctors tried many times to fix my sister Ell. She had three operations on her leg in hopes surgery could mollify the muscles that kept going into spasm for no good reason. None of these operations made a bit of difference. An eye surgeon attempted to fix Ell's crossed eyes and had some success, but afterward her eyes never seemed to work all that well. She wore thick glasses, but she always forgot to push them up when they slid to the end of her nose. For some reason that sight outraged our mother, my sister with her glasses balanced on the tip of her nose. "Push up your glasses, Ellen! How many times do I have to tell you to push up your glasses?!" Ell would obediently push her glasses back where they belonged but, ten seconds later, they would be perched on the end of her nose again.

Ell was terrified of big dogs because they would jump up on her and knock her flat and then they would sniff at her and retreat and bark loudly. She loved all human beings: children, teenagers, adults, old people. If anyone gave Ell a baby to hold, she was as enormously happy as if someone had given her a million dollars. Ell was by far the most extroverted and friendly member of our family, the kindest and most sentimental. She loved ice cream and cookies and candy. She hated snow and ice because she fell easily. She liked to draw pictures. If you gave her a newspaper, she could pick out a few familiar letters. "There's an E. Right there! E is in my name. My name's Ellen! Ellen starts with E!" She could write her signature, a large awkward scrawl, and would do so if asked. She knew her numbers up to ten. "That is a 1, and that is a 2, and that is a 3." She could never master arithmetic or sound out letters or remember our phone number. She was unsure how exactly a dollar bill is different in appearance and worth than a ten-dollar bill. She got angry and wept when she lost things; she jumped to the conclusion they were stolen. When her missing object was located and returned to her, she immediately brightened and smiled so contentedly it was as if the sun had come out from behind a cloud. She was like a child but not really. The older she got, the more obvious it was that she was not a child. She began to use the expression "like me." She would describe the students in her special school as "people like me." She believed she was in the tribe of kids and adults who were special — like her. There was not a cruel bone in her body.

When my dad heard Ell's screams, he dropped his crossword puzzle and came running. He dragged my mom off my sister and manhandled Mom back into the hallway and shoved her into the wall, not hurting her, just holding her tightly. "Pearl, you have to stop this, you have to stop this, you have to stop this." And then, gently, he herded my mom back into their bedroom and closed the door.

Ten minutes later, Mom emerged, her face red and wet with tears. She went to Ell and apologized and said, "I am a terrible mother!" Then she went to Ron and Lois and Dean. "I'm a bad mother. I'm sorry! I'm so so sorry!" Each kid said, "No, you're good, we're bad, it's our fault, we love you, Mom." Finally, she turned to me, but by then my disgust was so strong I wanted to start screaming at her, and at my dad too for letting her get like this. Dad was standing, silent and sheepish, in the background. I refused to tell her she was a great mom. Even my sister Ell told her she was a wonderful mom. A perfect mom. "We love you so much, Mom." My siblings clustered around her and hugged her. All of them were crying and then they were praying. I couldn't stand to watch another second of it, so I went back into my room and closed the door. I put a stack of records on my record player, turned up the sound, and lay on my side on my bed and read a book.

That night, before I went to sleep, my dad came into my room. He checked on my brothers to see if they were asleep and then came to my bed and sat on the side of it and told me my mom's cancer had come back. "She just found out today she's going to have to have another operation. They're going to do it over the Christmas break."

Things were not great at school either. I hated marching band, but I also hated gym and math class. Our gym teacher loved the game of Dodge Ball. This game has been banned in all civilized countries, but it was still popular at my high school in the 1960s.

The boys in the gym class are divided into two categories, Prey and Predators. If you are prey, you stand with your back against a wall of the gym. Other unfortunates are standing on both sides of you, and all of you are hopped up with fear and excitement. Each predator is given a ball. There is a special ball for this game. Dodge balls are slightly smaller than basket balls. They are said to be soft. The idea of the game is that the predators fling the rubber balls at the prey. The prey dodge or attempt to catch a flung ball. If a victim catches a ball without dropping it, the boy who flung the ball must drop out of the game. If a member of the prey team fails to dodge and is hit by a flung ball, he is out and has to exit the game. If he tries to catch a ball but drops it, he is out. The game continues until there is only one member of the prey team left. Always, there are several predators left. They concentrate their fire on the final victim until he is dead too. The predators always win this game.

In high school, some of the boys are tall, muscular athletes, and they can fling the ball so hard, it hurts like hell if it hits you. If it misses and slams into the wall beside your head, it makes a loud terrifying WHAP! If a ball flung that hard hits you, it leaves a bruise. Generally speaking, certain members of the prey team are disliked by a few of the predators. They are singled out for special abuse. Fortunately, I was not one of these pariahs. My goal when I was on the prey team was to try to catch a ball that was flung softly and purposefully drop it. "Dead! You're dead!" the kid who flung it would yell, and I would happily leave the floor. When I was a predator, I tossed my ball lazily at the prey until someone caught it.

The sole good thing about dodge ball was that it came to an end. We played the game for a couple weeks, and then the dodge balls were stored away for the next group of sadists and victims. For the next couple weeks, we played untraditional volleyball with a ball so huge that, to get it over the net, two or three boys had to get under it and heave. That game was called Super Blooper Ball.

I liked my English class even if it was taught by Miss Pross. She was stiff and proper, but she was smart. She really did love Shakespeare and Dickens and poetry. Any class taught by a teacher who loves her subject was in my opinion worth taking.

I didn't mind my other classes, all but one. Math class. It was taught by Miss Viola Sweet, and I soon came to hate it.

Behind her back we referred to Miss Sweet by her nickname Rhino. There was something rhinoceros- like about her. In the jungle, not even lions and tigers mess with a rhino. They are huge and have a low center of gravity and a great big horn in front and always appear to be in a bad mood. They have little piggy eyes that glare angrily out at the world. They fear nothing and no one. Except for the great big horn, all these attributes were also possessed by Miss Sweet.

Miss Sweet was the head of the math department, which besides her consisted of men, all of them younger than her. Two of them were coaches. You might not think a coach would fear a woman, but you would be so wrong. Even the football coach was terrified of her.

The men in her department acted as if she was their best friend. She would slap them on the back and tell them jokes and they would guffaw. For one thing she was smarter than them, much smarter. They were men of ordinary intelligence, coaches first and math teachers next. She probably had forgotten more math than they would know on their best day.

Miss Sweet loved to talk about football, especially her favorite team, The Green Bay Packers. The coach Vince Lombardi and the quarterback Bart Starr were in her opinion gods among men. It seemed to me if she dressed in a man's sport coat, got a haircut and a little hat with a feather, she would look so much like Coach Lombardi, she could pass as his older sister. I was not the only person in my school who believed if Miss Sweet was the coach of the football team, we would win a lot more games.

Miss Sweet taught the smart kid math classes. The rumor was that the coaches were so dumb, they could not even do the sort of math we had to learn in the advanced classes. One of the reasons they lived in fear and always tried to please her was they were terrified she might someday order them to teach one of her classes.

As a result, I could not escape Miss Sweet. For my entire high school career, I was doomed to take one of her classes every single semester. I began to brood about this fact. Her blue suit-like dresses smeared with chalk, inescapable! Her pepper and salt hair swept up to make her seem taller, inescapable! Her smeared bifocals and little piggy eyes, her two-inch heels, plump legs and arms, her vigor, the force of her gaze, inescapable!

But wait! I got an idea.

Many high school students, in fact most of them did not take math classes taught by Miss Sweet. They took one of the dumb kid math classes. Students in those classes did not have to learn advanced algebra or geometry or functions or calculus. They did not have to learn how to operate slide rules or fill up graph paper with carefully drawn curves. They did not have to stand at the blackboard in front of their entire class and demonstrate their ignorance by failing to solve equations so difficult they would have baffled Einstein. Never, not once did they have to endure the sarcasm of Miss Rhinoceros. Instead, those lucky students got to fill out easy-peasy worksheets and listen to a coach tell funny stories.

One day, when Michael and Calvin were complaining (again) about Miss Sweet and her class, I suggested we abandon it. Why take Advanced Math? Why take HER?

"Let's drop that class!"

Michael and Calvin were not sure how in the middle of a semester we could drop out of a math class. I didn't know either. We had never attempted anything like that. We discussed possible strategies. I began to fear my escape plan was going to fail before it even launched.

"We can't just give up! We have to at least TRY!"

Calvin suggested the solution. Who, he asked us, ran the school?

We looked at him in confusion, and then Michael said, "The principal?"

"Exactly!" If anyone could free us of Miss Sweet, it was the school principal, Mr. Giblet.

One afternoon, after the final class period was concluded and kids were streaming out of the school on their way home or to their practice or job, Mr. Giblet began to get a funny prickling feeling on the back of his neck. Was someone watching him? He was in the hallway near his office. He wheeled around and saw no one of any significance nearby, just three gangly boys, one of whom had an unfortunate acne problem.

The moment I saw Mr. Giblet stop and look back at us, I became terrified and froze. Never in my young life had I voluntarily spoken to a school principal. My hand reached out by itself, found the back of Calvin, and pushed him forward. To my surprise, the hand of Michael was doing exactly the same thing.

Finding himself suddenly propelled forward, Calvin nervously said, "Um, sir? Mr. Giblet, sir? Could we have a word with you, please?'

I admired how Calvin instinctively thought to call the principal "sir" and ended his request with the word "please."

Mr. Giblet smiled pleasantly and told us of course we could have a word with him. He said he always had time for students. "What's the problem, eh? How can I help you, boys?"

We clustered around him, all talking at once. Miss Sweet was the problem. Her class, it was too hard. Much too hard! We were lost. We hated math anyway. We didn't need to learn that stuff. Who needs that much math? We didn't want to be engineers or nuclear physicists. Arithmetic was fine for the likes of us. "Please, sir, Mr. Giblet, please, help us get out of that class!"

Mr. Giblet smiled blandly, touched his chin for a moment, as if the gesture assisted him as he solved our problem, told us to follow him, and briskly walked ahead of us to his office. His secretary looked up when she saw the three of us, students, following her boss.

Without even looking at her, Mr. Giblet said, "Get Miss Sweet on the phone for me, dear, will you please?"

Wait, what?

Mr. Giblet entered his office. We shuffled along behind him. What had he just said? What had he told the secretary to do?

"Please, sir, there's no need to—!"

"Don't you worry, fellas," Mr. Giblet said. He sat down in his big leather swivel chair behind his big shiny desk – nothing on it except framed photos and a telephone. "I bet you a nickel she's still in the building. She likes to sit up there after school and grade homework, you know?" He looked at us curiously. "Who are you boys, what are your names?"

We all told him our names.

I wanted to use a fake name. I wanted to declare that I had a sudden case of stomach flu and flee out of his office.

The phone on his desk rang, and he picked it up.

"Miss Sweet? Well, I am fine, how are you? I wonder, can we talk, have you got a minute? Well, um um, well I guess you could say we have a problem, a wee little fella of a problem. Right here in my office I've got some of your students, three of 'em. Three boys." And he said our names. Smiling at us, Mr. Giblet told Miss Sweet our names! "Well, they want to drop your class. I know, I know. Why don't you come down here, if you have a minute, and, um um. Well, I guess they're having just a little trouble understanding, um um, you bet, um um um. Exactly. Well, that's what I thought too, just a little extra help. Sure, all they need. Bye-bye, Miss Sweet. Always a pleasure."

He hung up and put his hands together, as if applauding himself for the dispatch with which he had solved our problem.

"Not to worry, boys. She's coming right down."

I don't know about Michael and Calvin, but I wanted to vomit into the principal's paper basket.

A minute later, Miss Sweet knocked on the door frame. I twisted around and there she was, chalk smeared on her blue dress, her little piggy eyes peering through her smeared glasses and taking it in, the sight of three of her students and her boss.

"Here she is, boys," Mr. Giblet said. "I will leave you in Miss Sweet's capable hands." He made a little fluttering gesture with his fingers which meant we were dismissed.

"Come with me, boys," said Miss Sweet.

We had no choice. We followed behind her all the way to her office.

5

Good Vibrations

Winter arrived as usual. As Miss Pross's favorite novelist Charles Dickens would say, snow fell on the rich and the poor, the good and the bad, the young and the old. I got a new parka and a pair of warm gloves for Christmas. Dean got a blue sweater and a board game.

My mom was not in good shape, but she was determined to finish out the semester before she went into the hospital. That was Mom. Tough as nails but trapped in a body that kept betraying her. Determined but also sickly. I stayed out of her way. We all stayed out of her way.

My favorite thing that happened that December: The Beach Boys' monster hit "Good Vibrations" climbed the charts until it occupied the #1 slot. The Beach Boys were a bit over-the-hill. Midwest kids like me lived a thousand miles from the nearest sandy beach. What did we care about surfing? They wore corny candy-striped shirts. The term "vibrations" was not what anyone would call science-based. Those facts did not stop me from loving the song.

The idea was people have supernatural vibrations. We are like tuning forks made of flesh and blood. We vibrate, baby! Supposedly, certain enlightened beings can see our vibrations. They spread out from us like waves of color, rainbow auras. Even unspiritual clods (me) who cannot see the vibrations can FEEL them.

If you bump into a person with BAD vibrations, your mood plunges. Their bad mood is infectious, and you start getting paranoid. Your self-esteem vanishes. Poof! When you encounter a person with GOOD vibrations, the sun comes out. Your entire body tingles with happiness. Everything seems possible. Dogs growl at people with bad vibrations, but they wag their tails and lick the hand of anyone with good vibrations. Cats purr when a person with good vibes appears; they wind themselves around the person's ankle. Probably even grizzly bears, even turtles love people with good vibes.

My friend Ray loved the song. It was not the sort of thing he usually loved. It was not hardcore and thumping. People said it was the most expensive single ever produced, made of thousands of little snippets of sound, taped together by Brian Wilson, the mad genius who composed all the best Beach Boy songs. It contained weird, hard-to-identify sounds.

Ray said, "An electro-theremin! What the hell is that?"

All I knew was that every time "Good Vibrations" played on the radio, I got happy.

Just before Christmas, the U.S. Air Force started dropping bombs on Hanoi. In the cities of the USA, massive anti-war protests took place.

On New Year's Day, my mom went into the hospital, and my Aunt Ruthie came all the way from California to stay with us.

Aunt Ruthie radiated Good Vibrations. So far as I could tell, my dad's sister did not have a negative bone in her entire body. She loved everything and everybody.

Dean and I got to accompany my dad when he drove to the airport to get Ruthie. Ellen and the little kids had to stay home because my dad said they were uncontrollable idiots and would jump all over her like crazy puppies the moment they saw her. Dean and I got to go because my dad had a faint hope that we were old enough to restrain ourselves and big and strong enough to help carry her bags. Dad said, if he knew his sister, she would have plenty of bags. He loaded a blanket into the car just in case she did not have enough sense to bring a winter coat. In California, Dad said, they do not even have winter. If you want to see snow, you have to drive up into the mountains.

When Aunt Ruthie got off the plane, she was wearing colorful, summery clothes and sunglasses, so the blanket proved to be a wise decision.

On the way home, our prettiest aunt kept stealing glances into the back seat and exclaiming about how tall and handsome Dean and I were. In fact, Dean was short for his age, and you would have to be blind to suppose I was handsome, but there was something about my aunt that made whatever crazy thing she said seem true. At least, sorta, kinda true.

The sight of snow everywhere delighted Aunt Ruthie. The white snow glistened in the sunlight. She declared it the most beautiful thing she had ever seen in her entire life, like a carpet of diamonds. My dad snorted skeptically, but Dean and I looked at the snow with new eyes. Maybe it really was beautiful if you could manage to ignore all the dirty slushy parts and forget about how exhausting it was to shovel a foot of it out of the driveway.

When we got our aunt into the house, Ellen and the kids jumped on her just as my dad had predicted. Aunt Ruthie wound up on the sofa with the three of them practically sitting in her lap, gazing up at her as if she was the Queen of California.

Aunt Ruthie handed out belated Christmas presents for all of us, tiny books probably purchased at the gift shop of an art museum. Ellen got a little book of pictures of Cezanne paintings. Ron and Lois got Chagall and Dali. Dean got Gauguin, and I got Van Gogh.

My dad rolled his eyes when these presents were distributed. Only his sister Ruthie could possibly imagine we kids gave a damn about art.

It will convey some of my aunt's power, the infectious and supernatural power of her vibrations, if I say that every kid thought his or her book of pictures was a tiny treasure.

My aunt was a bit plump; she was the mother of three sons, all of them older than me. Someone churlish might say she no longer possessed the girlish beauty that must have been hers when she was in her twenties, but we thought she was as breathtakingly gorgeous as a movie star. Her beauty was concentrated in her eyes and her mouth. There was something wonderful in her voice and the way her mind noted beauty everywhere she looked. She made us feel important, intelligent, funny.

That night after supper (prepared by my aunt out of the odds and ends she found in the refrigerator), my dad and Ruthie went to the hospital to visit my mother. The hospital did not allow children under the age of 12 to visit patients, so that ruled out Ron and Lois. We older kids did not get to go either because my mother had announced she did not want any of her kids to see her when she was in the hospital. We could see her when she got home.

When my dad and Ruthie backed out of the driveway and drove away that night, we pulled out our little art books and studied the pictures as if they contained important secrets. Soon, however, without the magic of Aunt Ruthie to make the pictures come alive, the books lost their charm for my siblings. In the long run, I inherited all five books. Eventually, I spent hours with each one. I never tired of looking at those pictures of famous paintings: Cezanne's apples, Dali's melted watches, Chagall's fiddler on the roof, Van Gogh's self-portraits, Gauguin's Tahitian girlfriend (naked). For me, each picture was a door that opened up an entire world.

When my dad and Ruthie got home, the little kids and Ellen were already asleep in their beds. They had wanted to stay up, but I had made them get into their pajamas and lied that I would wake them when Ruthie returned. They had attempted to stay awake but soon fell asleep.

Dean and I were still awake when Dad and Ruthie returned, both of them serious and sober because they had visited my mother and seen whatever the doctors had done to her.

Dad sent Dean and me to bed, but first Ruthie kissed our foreheads and told us, "Your mother is very brave and very strong. Never forget that!"

By the time I fell asleep in my bed that night, I was hopelessly in love with my California aunt.

The next day, Dad went to work leaving the car for Ruthie. After feeding us breakfast, she borrowed one of my mom's winter coats, loaded us into the car and took us to visit our grandparents.

Ruthie hugged her parents fiercely and told them they had not aged a day. My grandfather made us kneel and pray and thank God that Ruthie's plane had not crashed. My grandmother looked Ruthie up and down and told her that she had put on a few pounds. Also, the California sunshine had ruined her hair. "You had such beautiful hair!" It still looked OK to me. "And why are you so brown? You look like a brown Mexican!" Ruthie had a suntan. "You should always wear a hat in the sun. The sun out there is so bright, it will give you skin cancer!" Ruthie had great skin. "You should move back here. We have plenty of colleges and universities here. Why can't Rodney [Ruthie's husband, an art history professor] get a job out here? Why didn't you bring your boys?"

Ruthie got my grandmother out of her swivel chair and over to the sofa so she could sit beside her and show Grandma photos of my cousins playing golf and surfing, and Uncle Rodney posing in front of famous works of art. We kids sat beside them and peered at the photos of our lucky cousins.

After lunch, Ruthie led us upstairs into the attic. Usually, we were forbidden to set foot up there. Ruthie found lots of wonderful old things that she remembered, but the best one was my Uncle Whitey's flight jacket.

"Whitey was the best of us, you know, the handsomest and smartest of my brothers, the most athletic. He was on all the teams at school. And best of all, he was the funniest of us. Oh, my goodness gracious, he could make us laugh!"

"What happened to him, Aunt Ruthie?" asked my little brother Ron.

"Oh, it is so sad. It is the saddest and most tragic thing. Are you sure you want to hear the story?"

"Yes!" We all wanted to hear the story of my uncle's demise no matter how sad it was.

"He wanted to fly. Some boys want to fly like birds in the sky."

I felt sort of bad about myself because I had never wanted to fly.

"When the war came, he went right in, didn't wait to be drafted or anything, dropped out of college. He volunteered to be a pilot. Every week, he sent Mother a letter — beautiful, exciting letters. I bet they are still here somewhere in an old trunk or something." She looked around the attic as if she might find them.

I very much wanted to find and read my uncle's letters.

Lois asked, "Why do you call him Whitey? I thought his name was —."

"That's the funniest thing! Because of his hair! We called them Brownie, Blackie, and Whitey. Your dad was Brownie because of his brown hair, and Blackie – your uncle Milton – he had the blackest hair, jet black! But Whitey's hair, he was a towhead. Do you know that expression? Tow is like straw. Girls loved his hair! So, we called him Whitey."

By this time my brother Dean was holding the flight jacket in his hands and rubbing the fur collar against his chin while he listened.

"Whitey learned how to fly fighter planes off the deck of an aircraft carrier, can you imagine? It is terribly difficult to take off because the runway is so short, only as long as the flight deck, but what is truly difficult and almost impossible is LANDING on that little deck. You have to be just absolutely perfect, or you will go right over the side! The trainee pilots start out practicing on land. They have to land on a rectangle painted on the runway, and you better be able to do it, or you are washed right out of flight school. And then you have to do it at night! Land on that little bitty rectangle in the dark! Lots of the trainees failed that test, but Whitey didn't. He passed every test. Then they have to land the plane on an aircraft carrier that is anchored out in the harbor. First, they have to do it in daylight, and then at night. It is so much harder at night! And then, the aircraft carrier sails out into the ocean, and they have to do it again, take off and then land. First in the daylight, and then at night."

"Did he do it?" Ron asked. "Did Uncle Whitey do it in the dark and everything?"

"He passed every test with flying colors, of course. He won his wings. I bet we still have them somewhere. I believe Mother has them in a box with his medals."

I very much wished I could see that box of medals. Maybe Grandma would let Dean and me borrow it and take it home with us.

"What happened to him, Aunt Ruthie?" Lois asked.

"There is an island called Wake. Have you ever heard of it?"

None of us had ever heard of it.

"We were fighting the Japanese, taking back all the islands they had stolen. One day, Whitey took off from his carrier and flew to Wake Island."

"Are you all right, Aunt Ruthie?" Ron said.

"Don't cry, Aunt Ruthie!" Lois said.

"It is all right to cry, you know. When we cry for someone we have lost, you know what we are doing? We are saying *I love you* with every tear."

Dean and Ellen and the kids were wiping away their tears. I remained dry-eyed as usual, but at least my heart was thumping inside my chest and the palms of my hands were moist.

"Please, tell us what happened, Aunt Ruthie," Dean said. By then, he was wearing my uncle's flight jacket.

"We don't know, not for sure. One of Whitey's friends came to our house after the war, another pilot, and he said he believed Whitey got shot. Or perhaps it was a bit of shrapnel. Do you know what that is? The Japanese would fire their big anti-aircraft guns into the air, trying to hit the American planes. The shells would explode like fireworks and send bits of metal flying in every direction. The bits of metal were like bullets flying through the air. They called them shrapnel. Maybe something like that happened. Maybe a bit of shrapnel hit him. Whitey flew back to the carrier. He made it back, they could see him coming, but something was wrong. He wasn't responding to the radioman. On the deck was the signalman, and he was waving his flags to guide Whitey, but Whitey was not responding to the signals. His friend told us that would never have happened unless Whitey was wounded, terribly wounded. Because he was such a good pilot, the best of all the pilots, his friend said."

Ron and Lois said, "Oh no, Auntie Ruthie; oh no, oh no."

"His plane flew directly into the side of the carrier, and the wreckage slid down into the water, the dark cold water."

Dean said, "They never found him, Auntie Ruthie? They never ever recovered Uncle Whitey's body?"

"The friend told Mother nothing ever came up except grease."

Oh, how awful, how terrible! None of us kids could even speak.

In my mind's eye, I could see the grease floating in the waves.

My siblings crowded around Aunt Ruthie, and she managed to hug all four of them at once.

"That is why Whitey doesn't have a grave. But he has something even better. You'll see!"

The next day, after my dad went to work, Ruthie loaded us into the car again. She drove us to a flower shop where she bought a large ring of flowers and an assortment of long-stemmed red roses. When we got outside, she put the ring of flowers in the trunk and distributed the roses. Each of us got two. Then we got back into the car, and Aunt Ruthie drove us to the river that runs through the middle of our town. She parked the car as close as possible to a bridge and we all climbed out, clutching our flowers. She got the ring of flowers out of the trunk and carried it herself.

Aunt Ruthie had borrowed my grandmother's fur coat and she was wearing sunglasses. The brilliant sunshine and the icy cold air made her look so beautiful I could hardly stand to look at her.

Ruthie told us this is how we honor a hero like Whitey who has fallen into the ocean and does not have a grave. We honor them with flowers. Everywhere in the world is water, running water. Creeks and rivers run downhill until they find an ocean, and all of the oceans are connected. We throw our flowers into the water, and they drift downstream until they find our fallen loved one. It is sad and beautiful and appropriate that we do this.

We walked down the sidewalk that ran along the side of the bridge, clutching our flowers, until we got to the center of the bridge. Aunt Ruthie pointed out how the river below us was frozen over with ice and snow, but the middle was still clear. She said the icy water down there was flowing rapidly like a road of freedom.

Ruthie told us to shut our eyes. She prayed to the spirit of Uncle Whitey. She told Whitey she loved him very much and would never forget him and someday would join him in heaven. She said these children who were with her were his family, his nephews and nieces. "We have brought flowers to honor you, to show our love. Because love never ends. Amen."

She encouraged all of us to say, "Amen." Dean and Ellen and the kids said it, and I said it too.

Aunt Ruthie tossed down her ring of flowers. The ring fell into the icy water and floated away, and then we kids tossed down our roses. I tried to make mine land in the circle of flowers as if it was a target, as if I would get extra points if I hit it, but my flowers fell short. Ruthie's circle of flowers floated away, and our red roses followed after it like little ducklings following their mother, and it was the most beautiful and sad thing I ever saw or did up until that moment.

6

The Crow

That night after I fell asleep, Ruthie must have sneaked into the bedroom I shared with my brothers because when I woke up there was a pamphlet lying on top of our chest of drawers. The pamphlet was titled *Coping with Cancer (For the Family)*. Ruthie must have picked it up at the hospital and placed it there for me to read. The pamphlet said, when anyone in a family – especially one of the parents — gets cancer, it is as if the entire family also gets sick. Not really, but sort of. The children are affected. The spouse is affected.

At the end of the pamphlet, there was a part about what is likely to happen when the patient finishes treatment and comes home. The patient will be relieved she survived the operation — the cancer was removed, yay! — but the patient will almost certainly go on secretly worrying about the cancer coming back. Even when she gets home, the patient will be full of fear and not just about the cancer returning. "She will fear the return of pain; she will fear dying, and what happens after death. A mother will worry about what will become of her children."

On the back page of the pamphlet was a list titled Signs of Anxiety.

- Uncontrolled worry (anxiety)
- Muscle tension (the person may look tense or tight)
- Restlessness (the person may feel keyed up or on edge)
- Irritability or angry outbursts (grouchy)

That was my mom all right. She lived with the constant dread that her body still contained a few more cancer cells. No matter what the surgeons did to her, the bad cells were still in there, hiding, biding their time. Probably at night she often woke up with a sick feeling. "It's back!" Who knows what that would do to a person? I thought about all the times Mom lost her mind and started yelling at us like a nut. I vowed never again to yell at my mom, no matter what she said or did.

My pimples were bad in my opinion, but they were less horrible than cancer. Pimples stayed on the outside where they can be seen; it was not as if my insides were rotting away. Pimples are bad, but they won't kill you. Probably when I finished growing up, my pimples would go away. Cancer doesn't go away, not completely, not for sure. I needed to be nicer to my mom.

Aunt Ruthie told me I should eat only vegetables and fruit. She said vegetarians hardly ever have pimples. If I would become a vegetarian like her, my acne would probably vanish, not to mention my bad moods. I resolved that for the rest of my life I would eat nothing but lettuce and tomatoes and raw carrots. And apples.

It wasn't that hard to be a vegetarian while Aunt Ruthie was staying with us because she took over the cooking and fed us vegetarian dishes. "We never can eat too much fruit, can we?" Ruthie said she felt sorry for the poor cows. "We can't have hamburgers unless we murder cows, did you know that?" She said she felt so much better healthier and happier since she gave up meat.

Ruthie loved to sing. We could hear her pretty voice all over the house as she cooked and cleaned. It was as if for her cooking and cleaning were fun. She liked to dance, too. She did not share my mom's belief that dancing is immoral and leads straight to premarital sex.

Ruthie said that to be happy we need every single day to laugh and sing and dance. When she heard me playing my Beatles records, she would burst into my room and make me dance with her until we were laughing and singing along with the Beatles, crazy happy and sweaty. I didn't even know how to dance, didn't think I could do it, not until Ruthie inspired me. She told me we don't have to learn how to dance. All we have to do is feel the music and get happy. Just in case I was a bit dull in the feelings department, she taught me some cool dance moves that she had learned from her sons. "This is what they call The Jerk! This is The Swim! This is the Hitchhiker!"

Ruthie knew all about art. She would sit beside me on the sofa in the living room, and we would page through the little art books. She would point out interesting details and tell me stories about the lives of the artists, their wild parties and inner torments and intense friendships, their mistresses and poverty. She told me she thought I had an artistic temperament.

She told me her name Ruth means pity, sympathy for the aches and pains of others, which is why we say a cruel person is ruthless. "They have no ruth, poor things." It was amazing but Ruthie was able to find room in her heart even for dictators and murderers. She felt "poor Hitler" must have had a few good qualities. Perhaps he loved children and dogs. I felt I had more good qualities than poor Hitler and hoped I was not one of those ruthless people who are unable to pity anyone.

Ruthie loved my sister Ell. She would always make room on the sofa for Ell and hold her hand and kiss her on the cheek and make sure that Ell got to share in all our fun.

I resolved to be nicer to my sister Ell.

Ruthie loved the little kids. She got Ron to draw pictures and told him he had artistic talent. She got Lois to sing songs and told her she had perfect pitch. She looked at Dean's cartoons and said even the dirty ones were hilarious and very well drawn.

I wondered what our lives would be like if only we had had Aunt Ruthie and her art professor husband for parents instead of our real parents.

My Aunt Ruthie felt perhaps I did not admire her brother Brownie as much as I should. She told me how he guided and protected her all through her girlhood. "He wasn't just my big brother; he was my guardian angel!"

My aunt encouraged my dad to tell us stories. She told Dad his children did not realize he was a fantastic storyteller. "Tell them the Crow Story, Brownie! I love that one! Come here, you kids! Sit down and be quiet. Your dad is going to tell us a wonderful story. Go ahead, Brownie!"

I cannot recall exactly the words my dad used when he told us the Crow Story, so I will just summarize it and add a bit of commentary. Probably I will mess up the story and cheat it of its full wonderfulness.

When my dad was 12 years old, he was a cowboy. As soon as summer came, he left his home, the parsonage, temporarily abandoned his mom and dad, his siblings (including my aunt), and took up residence at a nearby ranch. The rancher attended my grandfather's church. Dad lived on the ranch all summer and earned money by doing chores.

"Tell them about the little girl, Brownie! All stories are much better when they include a little girl, isn't that right, Lois?"

My sister Lois nodded vigorously.

I forget the little girl's name, but my dad admitted to us that he was sweet on the girl, the rancher's daughter. She was 11 years old and had the prettiest eyes and the prettiest smile in the whole wide world.

"Tell them about the whip, Brownie!"

My siblings and I were still in shock caused by the fact that our dad had once been sweet on a girl who was not our mom. What if he had married her? We would not even exist.

My dad said, in those days, people spent lots of their spare time poring over the Mail Order Catalogue, the famous "wish book." Every product anyone could possibly want was in that catalogue. One evening Brownie found a section having to do with bullwhips. These weapons were long and dangerous. He would never dream of ordering one if he was living in his mom's house, but he was living on the ranch. Not only that; he was a goddamn cowboy.

My dad of course did not use the phrase "goddamn."

Every morning after milking the cows he got on a horse – I tried to imagine it, my dad on a horse! – and led the cows to a nearby pasture. In the evening, he led them back, but that return trip was no problem. By then, the cows had full udders again and were eager to get back to the barn to be milked.

When the bullwhip arrived in the mail, my dad began practicing with it out in the barnyard, and the little girl watched, thrilled. My dad said he got pretty darn good with the whip.

My dad of course did not use the phrase "pretty darn."

When he rode his horse every morning to the pasture with the cows following behind him, my dad practiced with the whip. He got so good he could snap the head off a daisy without even dismounting.

Sss-nap!

"Tell them about the crow, Brownie!"

Dad said there was a crow, a big black arrogant bird that liked to sit on a fence post as he and the cows approached. At first, the crow took off the moment Dad came into view, but as the days went by, the crow lost its fear. It waited for Dad to get closer. Each day, that smart-alecky crow sat there on the fencepost as if it owned the path and everything around it. That conceited crow would not take off until the very last moment. It would spread its wings and lazily flap away, demonstrating a complete lack of respect for my dad with every flap.

One morning, as Dad approached the fencepost where the crow was perched, he shook out his bullwhip. By then he had decided that what that crow needed was a good moral lesson.

That arrogant blackbird did not move. Maybe this time it would not bother to fly away at all.

When my dad got close enough —- sitting there on the sofa, he made the snapping motion with his wrist.

Ruthie and we kids yelled, "Ssss-NAP!"

The crow fell dead to the ground.

"Oh, no, Daddy," my sister Lois said. I could tell she felt sorry for the poor crow. "You killed it, Daddy? How could you?" Lois had a tender heart and loved all animals.

Dad said he too felt sorry for the crow. He had never meant to kill it. His intention was to snap the air close to the crow, not actually hit the bird. He had unintentionally murdered the creature. He felt horrible.

My dad led the cows the rest of the way to the pasture and then rode back to the fencepost. He hopped down from his horse, stood over the fallen crow, and then knelt to inspect it. Dead or alive, a crow is magnificent. Dad grabbed hold of the bird's talons and stood up with the huge blackbird. He thought of that little girl he admired, the rancher's daughter. He thought of her pretty eyes and her pretty smile. Maybe she would be thrilled to see a dead crow. Maybe she would turn its glossy black feathers into a dress for her doll or something. Probably she would love the story of how he'd taught that arrogant crow a good moral lesson, and the story would be lots better if he could show her the crow.

Holding onto the bird by its talons, my dad got back on his horse and urged it into a trot.

My dad said he figured we kids did not really know much about horses.

I thought of all the horse books I'd read when I was in elementary school but decided maybe this was not the time to pretend I was an expert on horses since I had never actually ridden one.

Dad said horses are huge and powerful but deep down they are cowards. Any little thing like a scrap of paper blowing by can panic a horse. In a split second, a horse can go from calm to crazy. My dad said, "I made a serious mistake that day." He looked at us for moment as if wondering if any of us could work out what his mistake was.

Ron said, "What happened, Daddy?"

Dad said, "That crow was not dead."

"Oh, wow," Ron said.

"He was just unconscious. I had knocked him cold. He seemed dead, but he wasn't."

I thought of my dad riding along, holding the crow by its talons, imagining it dead.

"I had that crow upside down," Dad reminded us. "The blood must have poured back into its head. Pretty soon, it came back to life! Now, a horse has eyes on the sides of its head. Know what I mean? Big enormous eyes. I was holding that formerly dead crow only one foot away from one of the horse's big eyeballs. That crow returned to life, spread its wings. The horse went crazy. Bolted!"

We did not need my dad to explain what it means when a horse "bolts."

"I lost my hold on the reins, but I was not going to let go of that damn crow!"

That time, my dad really did say the word "damn."

My dad stuck his arm straight up so we could imagine it: young Brownie DeWitt holding onto the galloping horse with nothing but his knees, his hand gripping the flapping crow.

"Oh, Daddy, did you scream?" Lois asked.

Approaching the barn at high speed, my dad noticed the little girl was out in the barnyard. She could see him coming. It must have been the most wonderful and exciting sight she had ever seen. The hired boy! The horse in a panic! The crow flapping its wings!

When Dad arrived in the barnyard, he performed the most amazing athletic maneuver of his entire life; he leapt off the horse and landed on his feet, still holding onto the crow. He kept his hold on the crow's feet with his right hand and gathered up the body of the crow with his left hand.

"You know what that crow did?"

Lois said, "What did it do, Daddy?"

"It bit me! It bit my thumb right down to the bone!"

"Oh, Daddy!"

"TO THE BONE! And you know what I did? You know what I did to that crow? I carried it over to the chopping block, picked up the hatchet, and CUT OFF ITS HEAD!"

Whack!

My dad stared at our shocked faces for a moment and then grinned. "And that, kiddos, is the Crow Story."

Late that night, in my bed, I couldn't stop thinking about my dad's story. I don't know why I liked it so much. My dad, the young hero. The little girl in the barnyard. The wonderful image of my dad on the back of the galloping horse, holding onto the crow as it tried to fly! The terrible bloody end of the story.

In a way, I related to the crow, the arrogant bird who needed to be taught a good moral lesson. And yet it returned to life. It attempted to fly free. It was brave. Brave all the way to the end!

That story made me think of my father in a new way. Once upon a time he had been a boy with a bullwhip, herding cattle and riding horses and falling in love with pretty girls. The killer of arrogant crows!

All of us kids got to come along when Dad drove our aunt back to the airport. Ruthie hugged us and kissed us and told us she loved us. After she climbed the stairs to the plane, she turned around and blew us one last big kiss.

On the way home, I got to ride shotgun in the front seat with my sister Lois between Dad and me. Lois wept silently all the way home.

7

Chicks Dig Knuckleheads

A month after she got home from the hospital, Mom was on the telephone talking to one of her friends, "She brings it with her to the store. I am NOT kidding! People have seen it. Betty Jane saw it with her own eyes. She pulled it out of her purse and laid it on the counter while paying her bill!"

The way my mom said the word "it" made me think "it" was something scary like maybe a gun.

When Mom hung up, I said, "Who were you talking about? What did she lay on the counter?"

Mom said, "None of your business, Mr. Nosy."

That January, I got invited to dinner at Naomi Kavanaugh's house again. It was a special occasion because Ray's favorite rock group The Rolling Stones was going to be on the Ed Sullivan Show.

The Nazi accompanied me. He had been banished from Naomi's house when he foolishly revealed he was an atheist, but he had been released from exile because he told Ray (who told Naomi) he believed in God after all.

"Really?" We were walking to Naomi's house.

He said, for him, atheism had been a temporary phase, and he had grown out of it. "I'm a Lutheran."

"Right." It was already dark and cold. "Let's walk faster. I'm freezing to death."

The Nazi said he was now going to church every Sunday with his parents. He said I should read a book about Luther because he was a pillar of Western Civilization, the man who freed Christianity from the corrupt cardinals in Rome.

"Right," I said.

The Nazi said I too would believe in God if I wasn't so arrogant. "You always think you're smarter than everyone else, but you're not." He said his German ancestors had been good Lutherans for the last 300 years.

"Great," I said.

When we got to Naomi's house, Ray must have seen us approaching because he threw open the door, not waiting for us to knock. He welcomed us to his mom's house and made us take off our shoes and coats.

The Nazi walked into the living room when I was still hanging up my coat. He backed up and told me, "Wait till you get a look at who's here!"

Little Grimm was sitting on the sofa with Ray's sister, Julie Ann. They were looking at a Stones album. Julie Ann looked up at me and said hi, but Little ignored me.

There were three Grimm sisters. They had normal names, but everyone called them Big, Middle, and Little. Little was my age and the nicest of the three.

In a whisper, the Nazi told me that Ray had completed the trifecta: first Middle, then Big, and now Little.

I whispered, "Who's next, the mom? I wonder if Little has a grandmother. Somebody better warn her."

The Nazi had to cover his mouth to keep from laughing.

Naomi came in from the kitchen to welcome me and the Nazi, and then demanded to see the Stones album that Julie Ann and Little were holding. She looked at the picture on the cover and said the Stones needed haircuts. "Such ugly boys! I don't know why you like them." She told Julie Ann to set the table and said dinner would be ready in half an hour.

Ed Sullivan had already started, so the Nazi and I found seats in the living room. Ray replaced Julie Ann on the sofa and put his arm around Little.

Little said, when she saw the Stones on TV, she would probably get so happy she would scream because she just loved Mick Jagger. She said she loved the Stones more than anything.

The Nazi said, "Even the Beatles?"

Little said she used to love the Beatles, especially Ringo, she just adored his big nose, but after John Lennon said the Beatles were better than Jesus, she hated them. When those freaks in Mississippi or Alabama or wherever burned their records, she didn't even care.

I rolled my eyes but didn't say anything. Lennon never said the Beatles were better than Jesus, just that they were more popular with kids than Jesus was. And probably they were, too. Those freaks in Alabama who burned up Beatles records would probably burn up people too if given half a chance. Also, the only reason she loved the Stones was because they were Ray's favorite group. In my opinion, the Beatles were twice as great as the Stones.

"You need any help, Julie Ann?" Little yelled, but she didn't move off the sofa. In fact, she and Ray started kissing.

"Get a room," the Nazi said.

Julie Ann had to clear stuff off the dining room table before she could set it. The stuff included Naomi's big black purse. Julie Ann made a big production out of it, attracting our attention by pretending the purse was so heavy she could hardly carry it, grunting and groaning as if it weighed a ton. Little and Ray quit kissing to see what she was up to. She carried it into the living room where the rest of us were and plumped it down on the little table beside the door. It made a startling CLUNK as if it contained something hard and heavy.

The Nazi said, "What's she got in there, rocks?"

I remembered the thing I had heard my mom say when she was on the phone, and I imagined Naomi pulling out a gun at the supermarket, laying it on the counter in front of the cashier while behind her the other customers freaked out.

Julie Ann looked toward the kitchen to make sure Naomi was nowhere in sight and then reached into the purse and pulled out the heavy thing. "It" was not a gun. "It" was a hammer.

"What the hell?" the Nazi said. "What's she need that for?"

"For the Other One!" Julie Ann said. Her eyes were bright, and she was grinning as if she thought the whole thing was hilarious.

And then Naomi was yelling at Julie Ann to come help with something, and we didn't have time to talk any more about the hammer because Ed Sullivan was introducing the Rolling Stones.

I didn't get a chance to see the Ed Sullivan Show that often and so the TV host's oddness really struck me. Ed was weird and stiff. He was weird in multiple ways: his lack of any neck and his huge head and his slicked back hair and his little dead eyes and thick lips. All this was contained in a tight suit. You sort of got the feeling that just before the show started someone broke off his head and then glued it back on.

The Nazi pointed at the TV and told me it was a present from Big Bill Ryan.

"He bought Naomi a color TV?!" I was shocked – and envious. I wished Bill Ryan would buy my family a TV, even a black and white one would be nice.

The Nazi said, "It pays to have rich friends. Big Bill's always doing stuff like that. My dad says he's the most generous man in town."

Ray looked down at his feet but didn't say anything.

For his TV appearance, the Stone's singer Mick Jagger was wearing white shoes and a white shirt with ruffles. His jacket was so dark and shiny I wondered if it was made of snakeskin. The Stones' first song was their new hit "Ruby Tuesday." Mick was having fun, but the rest of the band looked bored, especially Charlie Watts on drums. Bill Wyman was bowing a double bass. Brian Jones looked as if he hadn't gotten any sleep for weeks. He was playing the recorder, not one of your usual rock and roll instruments, and wearing a big white hat and a bright green shirt. Keith Richards was plunking away at a piano. In my opinion, the song was kind of a drag, but Ray said it was brilliant. He said Mick and Keith must have been on drugs when they wrote it. In his view, that was a good thing.

For their final songs, Bill Wyman switched to the electric bass, Charlie woke up a little, Brian took over the piano, and Keith switched to his guitar and appeared to be chewing gum. The Stones jumped into one of their best songs, "Let's Spend the Night Together," except after a minute we realized Mick was not singing the lyrics right. He was singing "Let's spend SOME TIME together."

Ray guessed Mick had been ordered by Ed Sullivan to sing the lyrics that way because the real version was too sexy for television. Probably FBI agents representing our government were standing in the wings, making sure Mick did not corrupt the morals of American teenagers. We noticed that Mick was singing the wrong words, but when he got to that part and sang SOME TIME, he rolled his eyes, and then toward the end of the song, when he arrived at the forbidden phrase, he looked up and sang THE NIGHT as if by accident.

We cheered. "Go, Mick!"

After the song, Ed Sullivan did not call the Stones over for a chat. In fact, Ed looked pissed off as if he'd heard Mick sing the forbidden phrase and wanted him to be arrested. Ray said he bet old Ed hated long-haired rock stars and only put them on his show because otherwise none of us kids would watch. The entire show would be nothing but jugglers and ancient comedians. Opera singers. Only the elderly would watch. Ray said Ed probably hadn't gotten laid since the 1950s.

Little gave him a poke in the ribs and whispered, "Shut up!"

Ray said, "You know you like it."

After the show was over, we went into the dining room for pork chops.

Naomi made the Nazi say grace. "Come, Lord Jesus, be our Guest, and let these gifts to us be blessed. Amen." Everyone except me said amen, and the Kavanaughs and Little crossed themselves.

I dived into my pork chop which was delicious. I am sorry to report that my resolution to be vegetarian had not lasted very long and my resolution to be nicer to everyone in my family was not going that well either, but at least I had avoided any outright fights with my mom.

Naomi said she wanted a full report on my mom's health. She said God had blessed my mother by giving her the ability to fight her way back from the edge of death again and again.

I told her my mom had been out of the hospital almost a month and was now fully recovered – which was only partially true. She was doing all the laundry and the ironing and most of the cooking. "We kids help out a lot, of course."

Naomi said she'd heard my mom was teaching again.

I said Mom wasn't teaching any more at the Catholic high school, but she had signed up to be a sub here in town. "She's supposed to take it easy, but you know her."

Little said, "Oh my god, what does she teach?"

"American history."

"I'm taking that. I'm taking that RIGHT NOW!"

"Well, maybe someday, you'll walk into the classroom and it will be my mom sitting there at the teacher's desk."

Naomi said she bet my mom was a tough grader.

I said, "You better believe it."

After dinner, Ray led me and the Nazi out to Naomi's garage and showed us his incomplete Harley Davidson motorcycle. When he had got it, a present from his uncle, the thing was held together by duct tape and bits of wire. Now, it was missing its front wheel and a couple other important parts, but Ray said it would be ready to go by spring. No problem.

Ray said he was a bit short of funds for parts because he had been laid off from his construction job due to the fact it was winter. He was working again at Big Bill's bowling alley, but he was going to get a better job soon. His uncle was going to get him a high-paying gig working for the railroad. "Those jobs are all union, you know." He said his uncle was already pulling strings to get him into the union. "By spring, I'll be rolling in dough." Ray said, when that happened, he was going to move out of the spare bedroom at the motel and get himself an apartment downtown.

"Good to know," I said.

The Nazi frowned and looked away, which I took to mean he wasn't thrilled to hear Ray was going to move out of his house.

Ray said staying in high school was slowing me and the Nazi down and keeping us from becoming independent adults like him. Ray was in our class at school, but he was two years older than us. He had been "held back."

Ray said Mama Grimm had a job at the country club as a cook, and Big and Middle had jobs there too as waitresses. "Great tips, and they don't even have to pay taxes on them." He said his girlfriend Little waitressed at the Spaghetti Ranch on weekends. "She hasn't dropped out yet, but she's thinking about it." He punched me on the shoulder, "She could get you a job there washing dishes if you want it. They always need dishwashers."

I said maybe next summer I would look into that possibility.

Ray said a crap job like washing dishes was OK for someone like me still in school and living at home with my parents, but he needed a full-time job like the great railroad job his uncle was going to get him.

I told him I loved his cool Harley. "It's gonna be far out when you get it all put together."

Ray said it was a knucklehead. He said the knuckleheads were way better, faster and more powerful than the flatheads.

"Of course," I said, having not the slightest idea what he was talking about.

He said the first knuckleheads had problems with oil leaks and the brakes and so on, but this model was perfect. Come summer, he would be flying down the highway with Little sitting behind him.

"Chicks dig knuckleheads," the Nazi said.

When we were walking home, the Nazi said, "He got into a fight. He punched his boss."

"Who did?" Snow was falling through the darkness, and I wanted to get home. It was just me and the Nazi. Ray was walking Little home.

"That's why he lost that construction job. That's what always happens. His uncle gets him a good job, and then he blows it by getting in a fight."

8

Are You Experienced?

That spring, Ray and the Nazi bawled me out (again) for neglecting them. By then, I was hanging out almost exclusively with Michael and Calvin, or Epstein and Cooper and Rothstein. I was also hanging out a bit with Eugene Masterson, the only black kid in my school. And pretty much every week, I was talking on the phone to Rose White. As a result, I did not have that much time for visits to the motel.

Ray and the Nazi did not like any of my other friends. Brains and bookworms were not high on their list of fun people. It probably didn't help that Epstein and Rothstein were Jews and Rose White was a black girl. Come to think of it, the real Nazis would have killed most of the people I liked.

Ray said there was going to be a big party at Mama Grimm's house Saturday night, and I should come.

I said I would think about it.

"Little wants you to come."

"Yeah, right."

"She likes your sorry ass."

"She won't even look at me. She hates me. Besides, isn't she your girlfriend?"

"She's ONE of my girlfriends. You should come. It's Big's birthday. There's gonna be plenty of beer. Marge is buying us a keg. Added attraction, me and Johnny are gonna play 'Purple Haze.' We're gonna rock the world."

Ray's band The Brain Damage had fallen apart, and he was trying to put together a new one. So far, the new band consisted of just Ray on drums and Johnny B Badd on guitar. The name Johnny B Badd was the guitarist's rock and roll name, not his real name. His real name was Kevin. In the opinion of the Marsh, Johnny was a guitar genius, a white Jimi Hendrix. He owned a bright red Fender Stratocaster electric guitar, not to mention an amp that could be dialed up until the sound hurt your ears. "Purple Haze" was a Hendrix song, not the sort of thing that could be played by an amateur. Ray and Johnny had been working on it in the motel basement for a month. The Nazi said if he had to hear it one more time, he was going to lose his mind.

"Micky will be there too." Ray had it in his head that I liked Micky because, on an earlier occasion, at another party in the Marsh, I spent half an hour trying to get Micky to tell me about his experiences in Vietnam. All I got out of him was, "She changes you, man. She rearranges the molecules in your head, man."

"She" was the country of South Vietnam.

I wanted to know if he killed anyone when he was over there, or if he got shot at, or if any of his friends got shot, that sort of stuff. Probably you should not ask a soldier those kinds of questions, but I didn't know any better.

Ray said Micky was now back for good. "You know what that means."

It meant Micky would be bringing goodies to the party. Goodies meant drugs. Pills and pot.

Micky had been in the Marines for a year or two, but then he got discharged —abruptly. I don't know for what, but it wasn't honorable. Now he had long greasy hair and dealt ounces. The rumor was he got kilo bricks of marijuana sent to him from military bases in Germany. People said the entire American military was a giant drug-dealing network, and Micky was connected.

"I'll probably come," I said.

That was the spring I got deeply into Bob Dylan. I owned *Another Side of Bob Dylan, Bringing It All Back Home,* and *Highway 61 Revisited.* I obtained Dylan's double album *Blonde on Blonde* (the first double album in the history of rock) from Eugene Masterson for one dollar. Eugene was not normally a rock fan, but he had heard Dylan was the thinking man's rock star, so he purchased *Blonde on Blonde.* He listened to it once and decided, never again. He told me. "It's hick music for hicks. The man can't even sing." He was going to charge me two bucks for the album, but I worked him down to one. I loved the album and played it or one of the other Dylan records almost every day.

On my recommendation, Eugene attempted to read *The Autobiography of Malcom X* but gave up before he got halfway through it. He questioned my taste in books and said Malcolm was a criminal. In his opinion, criminals are not good role models. The only part of the book he liked was the part making fun of hair straightener. Eugene did not approve of hair straightening. He had short fuzzy hair.

I told Eugene, "You should keep reading. He gives up crime after he goes to prison and meets this religious guy Elijah Muhammad and becomes a Black Muslim. After that, he's not a criminal anymore. He becomes a leader of his people. It's inspiring." Eugene said he never got that far and never would. There are way too many good books to read to waste your time reading junk like *The Autobiography of Malcolm X.* He said Malcolm X did not even write the book. Some guy named

Alex Haley wrote it. "It's not even a real autobiography!" He told me I should read more Shakespeare. Or Dickens. Eugene loved Dickens. "I just finished *Oliver Twist*. You would probably like it because it is about criminals." Eugene liked to predict that, because of my unfortunate fondness for "the literature of the gutter," I would wind up in prison.

I wondered if anyone had ever told Eugene that when he wore that stupid bowtie, he looked like a Black Muslim because they all wore bowties and had short fuzzy hair, just like him. I told myself I should start a rumor that Eugene was a Black Muslim.

But that would be wrong, Calvin's voice said inside my head.

Cooper, Rothstein, and Epstein shared my love for Bob Dylan. So did Four Point's brother, Jimmy Levine. They considered Dylan not just a rock star but a genius-level poet.

Every day that spring, I listened to Dylan's song "Desolation Row," all 11 minutes of it, trying to figure it out. There's this street called Desolation Row, but probably the street is a symbol, a metaphor for something else. Poverty? Wicked people? Our corrupt government? A ton of people live on the street, famous characters from literature like Cinderella and Casanova and the Hunchback of Notre Dame. Also, a few real people like Einstein. After you listen to the lyrics a few times, you realize the famous character names are just nicknames for the derelicts, junkies, thieves, and phonies who live on the Row. But the singer of the song also lives on the street. At the end of the song he says, unless you know about Desolation Row, he has no time for you. So, what does that mean? Is Desolation Row a good place or a bad place?

The song namedrops T. S. Eliot and Ezra Pound. I found out from Rothstein they were famous modern poets, difficult writers that give you a headache if you try to read them, but you should try to read them anyway. According to Rothstein, "Desolation Row" may be the greatest song written in a generation, so I kept listening to it. I never got to the bottom of it though. Rothstein said that is the way it is with great art. Great art is bottomless.

It seemed to me Ray's neighborhood the Marsh was pretty much the same thing as Desolation Row. It fit into the Desolation Row category even if it was not the exact street Dylan had in mind. Lots of weirdos and losers lived there — criminals, wife beaters, drunks, deadbeats, single moms.

When I was in my bedroom all by myself, listening to records, I often wished I could write songs. If I could, I'd write one about Ray and the Grimm girls and probably make a million dollars and people would say I was a great poet like Bob Dylan.

That would be nice.

I smoked my first joint at the party. I was in the Grimms' backyard with Ray and Johnny B Badd. Normally, I didn't even smoke cigarettes, so I took a drag and immediately started coughing. Ray said that was great. Coughing meant the smoke was getting deep down inside my lungs.

By the time we finished smoking the joint, dogs were barking at us. The fence at the back of the yard was six feet tall and made of vertical boards so you couldn't see through it. Ray said on the other side of the fence lived Mr. Rabbit, this old coot with a long white beard like Santa Claus. All the kids called him Mr. Rabbit because he raised rabbits in coops in his backyard. Also, he had three mean dogs chained up there. These dogs never were taken on walks. Every day of their lives, they got to look at those penned rabbits and the sky and that was it. Mr. Rabbit never even played with them. He would come out once a day with their food. You can imagine the kind of mood these mutts were in when they heard us on the other side of their fence. My coughing must have set them off because they started barking at us. They escalated all the way to howling and who knows what they would have done if old Mr. Rabbit hadn't heard the commotion, come out on his back porch, and ordered them to shut up.

Ray and Johnny smoked the joint down to nearly nothing, and then Ray dabbed out the embers with a spit-covered finger and ate the thing.

"Good to the last drop," Ray said.

Ray and Johnny went back inside, but I lingered a bit. I liked it out there in the backyard looking up at the dark night sky and the stars. When I was a kid my dad used to point up at the constellations, but I never could see whatever I was supposed to see, a scorpion or a ram or whatever. I wondered if the Ancient Greeks who named the constellations smoked pot. I pretended I was an Ancient Greek shepherd and tried to see shapes in the stars. All I could see was a random field of white dots. I remembered someone once told me that in the Dark Ages people thought the sky was covered with a huge dome, but the dome had little holes in it where the light of heaven shone though. That's what stars are really, thought the Dark Age people. Holes.

I decided pot was over-rated because I didn't feel a thing, I felt totally normal.

Back inside the house, I started enjoying the party but lost the ability to talk. I thought it kind of funny that people would attempt to engage me in conversation and all I could do was smile at them and wander away. They had no idea that words were whirling around inside my head like runaway stars.

I wandered from room to room smiling at everyone and digging the music, which was the Hendrix album *Are You Experienced?* The stereo was cranked up as loud as it could go, so it was hard to understand what people were saying. I realized something interesting: if you listen to what people say but ignore the words, just listen to the sounds, it is a weird kind of music – like listening to a foreign language. Probably a caveman listened to a couple foreign cavemen jabber at one another and invented music.

Or maybe it was dogs. You could probably invent choral music by listening to dogs bark.

As I meandered around the party, I wondered what Jimi Hendrix meant when he said the word "experienced." The song asks the musical question, '*Are you experienced?*' In the song, Jimi says, "Well, I am." Maybe he meant sex-experienced. No doubt Hendrix like all the rock stars had a ton of sex experience. But possibly he meant drug-experienced.

At some point in my wandering, I acquired food. I had a chocolate chip cookie in one hand and a potato chip in the other. I nibbled the cookie and experienced the chocolate taste and the crumbling texture, and then I bit off a corner of the chip, and experienced salt and crispness. The sweet and the salty mingled on my tongue.

Which taste is better, sweet or salty? Impossible to say.

I realized the cookie was the best cookie I ever tasted, and the chip was the best chip.

I felt too hot, so I pulled off my shirt. The next thing I knew, I was in the living room right in front of the stereo, dancing to "White Rabbit" by the Jefferson Airplane. I dug the way my body felt when it moved, my arms twisting and writhing to the music. People were pointing at me and laughing, and I didn't care a bit.

The doorbell started ringing over and over.

Mama Marge, the only grown up at the party, yelled, "Jesus Christ, will someone answer the fucking door?!"

Someone near me said, "It's the neighbor! Turn down the music!"

"Who?" I yelled.

I was pleasantly surprised to discover my voice worked again.

"It's Mr. Rabbit."

Someone turned down the music while Mama Grimm went to the door to deal with him.

Someone said, "Why doesn't he come in, join us, have a good time? She ought to offer him a beer."

Mrs. Grimm and Mr. Rabbit started yelling at one another. Everyone quieted down to listen. I dug how their voices overlapped.

Mr. Rabbit said she better get these kids out of her house. "There's underage kids here drinking." He threatened to call the cops.

Marge told him if he did, he would regret it. She told him his backyard rabbit herd was illegal. It was against the zoning code to raise animals for meat inside the city limits.

"For meat?" a girl said. "I didn't know he actually ATE the rabbits."

Another girl said she once saw him kill a rabbit by holding it by the ears and spinning it around until he broke its neck. "Then he carved on it with this big knife and peeled off the fur. It was disgusting and horrible! I hate him! I hate you, Mr. Rabbit!"

Mr. Rabbit exited the porch. Marge yelled after him, "I hope you have a heart attack, old man!" She slammed shut the door, turned around to face us, raised her fists in the air, and yelled, "Party on!"

We all cheered.

Ray got behind his drums. Johnny plugged in his Stratocaster, and they played their jam version of "Purple Haze" with Johnny's amp cranked up so loud my ears started ringing and I had to retreat to the kitchen. I experimented by putting my hands over my ears. I could dim the sound, and then make it loud again.

Before the song ended, I was back in the living room, dancing with Little, doing all the cool moves I learned from my aunt. Little handed me a plastic cup of beer, and I chugged the entire thing. Beer slopped down my naked chest, and Little told me I was SO cool.

When Ray and Johnny finished their rendition of "Purple Haze," Ray said they were going to play another Hendrix hit, "Hey Joe," but they needed a singer. "Who wants to sing? The lyrics are easy. Come on, we need a volunteer."

Little pushed me forward and said, "You do it! You can do it. Jack wants to do it!"

Kids started yelling at me, "Do it do it do it!"

And so that is how I stood up in front of a whole house full of kids with my shirt off and tried to sing "Hey Joe."

The lyrics to the song are simple. The singer asks Joe where he's going with that gun in his hand, and then Joe says he's going to kill his old lady because he caught her cheating with another man. If you can sing that, you can sing "Hey Joe."

Ray and Johnny kept playing the beginning of the song and telling me to start singing, but I kept missing my cue. It was as if I was standing beside a merry-go-round that was already spinning. I was supposed to jump on, but I kept not jumping, kept missing my opportunity.

Finally, after they played the intro for the fourth time, I just closed my eyes and yelled my line: *Hey Joe, where you goin' with that gun in your hand!*

I opened my eyes and discovered that my singing had reduced everyone at the party to helpless laughter. I stuck my hands up into the air and yelled, "I'm gonna shoot my old lady!"

Johnny and Ray fell off their stools laughing.

These idiots love me, I thought.

And then, before I could continue entertaining the crowd, someone yelled that Mr. Rabbit was back and he'd brought his shotgun with him.

Everyone cheered.

I thought: This party is so fucking GREAT!

9

Pity, Not Ridicule

That spring I got addicted to Motown singles and Van Gogh and Gauguin pictures. The pictures and the hits got mingled in my mind. Motown songs were on the radio all the time. Aretha Franklin had "R-E-S-P-E-C-T, find out what it means to me," not to mention "Chain of Fools" and "(You Make Me Feel Like) a Natural Woman." The Four Tops had "Bernadette." The Miracles had "I Second That Emotion." Martha and the Vandellas had "Jimmy Mack"; and Marvin Gaye and Tammi Terrell had "Ain't No Mountain High Enough."

Seven songs, seven masterpieces.

I had this idea that a great painting is like a great single. It gets stuck in your brain, inspires your soul, and you never grow tired of it. A great single comes on the radio and every atom in your entire body wants to dance. A painting can have that same effect on you. Even if you are not looking at the real painting, even if the actual masterpiece is hanging in a museum half-way around the world and all you are doing is looking at a little photo of the painting, it is expanding your mind. Every single time you turn the page of the book that contains the image, once again you have that feeling you love and need, that deep assurance that life is fascinating and full of wonder.

I never tired of looking at Van Gogh's sunflowers and irises and all those amazing self-portraits; or Gauguin's Tahitian pictures, those lush colors and beautiful half naked girls. They were as great in their way as Motown hits. Every time I was stuck in study hall, I would pull out the little art books Aunt Ruthie gave us, my two favorites, the one about Gauguin and the one about Van Gogh, and page through them.

Because I did this, I began to occupy a tiny corner of the heart of Cathy Ryan. It was as if Gauguin and Van Gogh became my wing-men. They whispered into Cathy's ear: *This boy is not as dopey as he looks.*

Cathy Ryan and I shared a study hall, but we didn't sit close together. She must have walked behind me and noticed me studying the little books. And then maybe she did it again, accidentally on purpose walked behind me and found me studying the pictures.

One day, she stopped me in the hall when I was on my way to my locker.

"Are you trying to impress me?"

I looked at her blankly. This was not a normal occurrence in my life. Cathy Ryan! Talking to me!

She said, "Which one do you like better, Gauguin or Van Gogh?"

I felt a stab of pure delight because I realized, if Cathy Ryan was asking me this question, it meant she was interested in me.

I said, "Is this one of those questions like: Who's my favorite Beatle? If I guess the wrong one, you won't like me?"

"I bet it's Gauguin."

"Why would you say that?"

"Because boys like you are all the same. You want to go to a tropical paradise and fall in love with topless native girls."

This was true. That was the thrilling thing about Gauguin. He abandoned his wife and kids in France and moved to Tahiti so he could get drunk on the beach and have sex with pretty girls who were half his age. If you were a teenage boy like me, Gauguin seemed a fantastic role model.

While I was trying to think up a cool response, something that would suggest I was not really a sex pervert, or that I was not JUST a pervert, Cathy Ryan turned on her heel and left me standing there beside my locker.

After that, I didn't exactly stalk Cathy Ryan but, when I was in study hall, I would accidentally on purpose wander past her chair and look over her shoulder to see what she was reading. Usually, it was poetry. She loved Emily Dickinson and Walt Whitman. If she wasn't reading them, she was reading poems by a guy named E. E. Cummings and another poet named Pablo Neruda.

One day, I dropped a folded-up note beside her elbow. "Which one do you like more, ee or Pablo? I bet it's ee." By then I had figured out that the poet Cummings had a gimmick; he spelled his name with only lower-case letters: e e cummings. I hoped to impress her by writing ee instead of EE and identifying the two poets just by their first names. It was like saying John and Paul instead of John Lennon and Paul McCartney.

Later that day, she left a note in my locker that said, "Pablo."

I called Rose White on Wednesday evenings when my siblings and parents were at church. As usual, we got right into our favorite thing: Book Chat. Rose was reading *The Naked Ape* by Desmond Morris, and I was reading *The Outsiders* by S. E. Hinton. S. E. Hinton was amazing, a teenager who wrote a novel. The whole idea of this writer thrilled me to my toes – a kid writing an entire book about teenagers, getting it published, selling a million copies!

"Stay gold, Ponyboy!"

Rose said she was sick to death of reading novels. Fictional characters – especially the white ones — were boring to her. "I prefer reality to make-believe." To me, this seemed outright blasphemy. Rose said I should start reading non-fiction books like *The Naked Ape* by Desmond Morris because that book would cure me of thinking human beings are special. As Mr. Morris explains in detail, we are merely one more species of mammal, a variety of the ape family like gorillas and chimps. We are "The Naked Ape." Once upon a time, we had beautiful bodies completely covered with glorious fur, but now we are (mostly) bald and have to wear clothes.

I was perfectly willing to believe I was a clothes-wearing animal but didn't see why I needed to read an entire book about the topic, especially a book that wasn't a novel. What I really wanted to do was change the subject. I wanted Rose to give me advice about how to make a move on a rich girl who has opinions about poetry. I didn't think Rose knew that much about e. e. cummings but at least she read Langston Hughes. I knew this fact about Rose because one time she told me her mom gave her an entire book of his poems and told her he was the Negro Poet Laureate. I remembered this fact because Rose had added she no longer approved of the word "negro." She said it was completely out of fashion, as was the word "colored." Rose said, "My mom is a cultural dinosaur. It's so embarrassing!" I thought if she thought her mom was a dinosaur, she ought to meet my mom.

Unfortunately, Rose did not have any good advice for me about how to make a move on Cathy Ryan. She said, "My recommendation to you is run from love, run as fast as you can!"

"So, I take it you still have the hots for your English teacher."

"I do not. I am over that fool."

"OK, I would love to hear how that happened."

Rose told me the sad and embarrassing story. When still insane, she rolled her chair into Mr. Kowalsky's office after school and confessed her love. She said this was an act of lunatic desperation akin to telling a cop you have murdered someone. Mr. Kowalsky was grading papers. He looked up at her for a moment, said not a word, stood up, rolled her out into the hall, closed his door, and went back to grading papers.

"So that's good. I guess. You're sane again. "

"I am not sane. I am far from sane." It turned out Rose was now in love with someone else, a tall boy named Evan, a black boy who was a star on the East High basketball team.

"At least he's your age. Have you told him yet?"

"What's the point? He has a girlfriend, a cheerleader!" She said the cheerleader had naturally straight hair and light skin. "Every single inch of her is beautiful."

Rose said because of love she hated herself. That is what hopeless stupid love does to girls, teaches them to hate their hair and skin and legs because they are not attractive enough to attract some stupid boy. Rose said, until she began to fall in love with men, she never before cared that much about her legs or her hair. Who obsesses about that kind of stuff? No one with a brain. Before love ruined her, she had ambitions. She wanted to write great science fiction stories and become a United States Senator or perhaps a Civil Rights lawyer like Thurgood Marshall. Before she was ruined by love, she cared about books and music and important stuff like political activism, but now she was secretly putting on lipstick in the girls' restroom at school.

"OK."

But it was impossible. No matter how much she changed her appearance, the basketball player could never love her because she was crippled and ugly. No man could ever love her. Even her hands were ugly; she had huge hands like a man.

I said, "OK, you know what? I can't take this anymore. You're not ugly. I mean if there's a distribution curve with ugly on one end and beautiful on the other, you would be in the middle. At least you don't have pimples. Count your blessings." I told her to get a grip.

She said, "Go on, bawl me out. I need this. Remind me again what I used to be before love got to me so bad."

I told her if she ever became a great scientist, she should work on a vaccine for love. "Ordinary-looking people like us should be immunized to love, especially when we are young and going to school. In a decent society, there would be a love repellent that you could buy for a dollar at the drugstore."

"That is so true."

"You need to get your mind off this love stuff. Tell me something good that is happening in your life."

She said because she was a senior with an excellent GPA, every week she was getting acceptance letters offering her scholarships from various colleges and universities. She was thinking about going to a famous all-black college in Atlanta where lots of black celebrities sent their kids.

"Do it!"

That night after my brothers fell asleep, I found myself wondering if Rose was right. Are average-looking people fated to fall in love with beautiful people, programmed by biology to lust after people who are completely out of our reach?

Then I started thinking about breasts. My careful inspection of Playboy foldouts suggested that human males prefer big breasts to little ones. There was probably a whole chapter about human male breast preferences in that book that Rose liked, *The Naked Ape.* I thought for a minute about the large breasts of Marilyn Monroe. And then I thought about Cathy Ryan's breasts, which were not as large as Marilyn's but seemed very beautiful. I thought about Cathy Ryan's long brown hair and her big blue eyes and then about what she would look like with her clothes off. I drifted into an elaborate fantasy about meeting Cathy Ryan on a beach in Tahiti, both of us naked. And then

I had to slip out of bed without waking my brothers and lock myself in the bathroom to do what needed to be done.

Two weeks before school dismissed for the summer, I wrote Cathy Ryan a note. "Because of powerful biological forces, our school is full of boys like me who are hopelessly in love with you. We can't help ourselves. We deserve pity, not ridicule. Signed, Anonymous."

10

The Spring Talent Show

I practiced a little speech designed to convince Eugene Masterson that I was right about the Beatles. I was right and he was wrong. My thesis was: The Beatles are the great musical geniuses of our time. I planned to focus on the two albums they made after they quit touring, *Revolver* and *Rubber Soul*.

Of course, they quit touring. They had to. Non-genius rock bands like (fill in the blank) would keep touring, keep raking in the money, but not the Beatles. Why did they quit? Why did they walk away from all that money and glory? Because everywhere they went, the venue filled with girls. The girls were in a state of insane excitement. The moment the Beatles walked onto the stage, the girls screamed. Screamed continuously. Screamed so loudly, the Beatles could not hear themselves. How nuts was that? The performances had nothing to do with music. So, what did the Beatles do? They did the noble thing, the artistic thing; they went back to England and made perfect rock and roll songs. They recorded the albums *Revolver* and *Rubber Soul*.

What was the idea of these albums? Every single song should be great!

That spring, the spring of 1967, while the entire world was waiting for them to bring out their next album, the Beatles released a single with "Penny Lane" on the A side and "Strawberry Fields Forever" on the B side.

My plan was to ask Eugene to consider how totally different and original those two songs are. Then, I would ask him to consider how wonderful and unique are the songs on *Revolver* and *Rubber Soul*, songs like "Here, There and Everywhere"; "Tomorrow Never Knows"; "Norwegian Wood"; "I've Just Seen a Face", and "Michelle My Belle." Who could create that much variety and wonderfulness except total badass geniuses?

I was going to clinch my argument and wow Eugene by concluding that we human beings should be like the songs on a Beatles album. We too should be wonderful and original. It is a lie that we have to be boring and predictable, dull, uninteresting, stuck in our ruts, doomed to follow the herd. Each one of us has the capacity to be GREAT. How can we locate our originality, our uniqueness, our inner greatness? By listening to Beatles records!

Eugene patiently waited for me to finish this speech. While I talked, a wrinkle formed at the base of his nose as if I was giving him a slight headache. When I finished, Eugene said, "You should listen to Mozart more often. That would help you with your over-rating the Beatles problem."

The Spring Talent Show was coming up, and I knew Eugene was going to be in it. I told him he should play a Beatles tune on his cello. The obvious choice was "Eleanor Rigby." "Kids will LOVE you if you play that song. I guarantee it. You'll get a standing ovation."

Eugene said he was going to play this other piece.

I told him no one likes music that is called a "piece." People like "songs." And they especially love Beatles songs. I asked him if someone like me would like this "piece."

Eugene said, "I doubt it. It's six minutes long and there are no words." Eugene said when I got done listening to Mozart, I should try Tchaikovsky. "He's overly emotional. You will probably like that."

While I was waiting for the new Beatles album to appear, I found out about "underground" music from Jimmy Levine. He talked me into buying a double album by the Mothers of Invention called *Freak Out*. The word "freak" had developed a new meaning. It used to be a bad thing. If you were a freak, your body was deformed, and your family locked you up in the attic or sold you to the circus. In our time, it was GOOD to be a freak. A freak was someone who loves special kinds of music, music too weird and wonderful and controversial and original and dark and funny for ordinary people, the squares, the norms. Who wants to be a square, a norm, if you can be a freak?

The Mothers of Invention were headed by a notorious freak named Frank Zappa, and all the other Mothers were flamboyantly weird and nerdy. Their album was full of amazing songs with excellent titles like "Hungry Freaks, Daddy" and "Who Are the Brain Police?" Side Four was titled "The Return of the Monster Magnet; Part 1: Ritual Dance of the Child-Killer" and "Part 2: No Commercial Potential."

That phrase "no commercial potential" captured the essence of underground music. Who cares about hits? Underground music was music made only for freaks! It was music so weird and wonderful that only dark and twisted nerds could even comprehend it.

Jimmy said the Beatles were rumored to be drifting toward creating their very own underground album. The single "Penny Lane" was happy music aimed at squares, but "Strawberry Fields Forever" was dark and strange freak music. According to Jimmy, John Lennon had created "Strawberry Fields Forever" after taking a dose of this scary and wonderful new illegal drug called acid. My friend Ray was desperate to get his hands on some.

The Talent Show was held in the school auditorium. Sixth and seventh periods were cancelled so we could all go see it. I filed in with my homeroom and sat beside a couple idiots that I will call Mope and Dope. The MC, the president of the junior class, an eager beaver who seemed likely to go through life selling life insurance, ran out and started telling corny jokes. He never stopped smiling and told us every single act was going to be awesome. "Hold onto your seats!"

We watched a two-hour parade of talent that included an amateur magician, a juggler, two unicyclists, a ventriloquist, three solo singers, an entire chorus, a jazz combo, and three kinds of dancers (modern and ballet and tap).

One hour into the show, the tone changed abruptly when the principal's son treated us to a display of patriotism. He solemnly read us the names of four former students who had enlisted in the service of our great country only to be killed in Vietnam. While he read the names, a drum pounded. Then he recited a poem that he said was written by a soldier who died in a military hospital during the first World War.

In Flanders fields the poppies blow
Between the crosses, row on row,
That mark our place; and in the sky
The larks, still bravely singing, fly
Scarce heard amid the guns below.

We are the Dead. Short days ago
We lived, felt dawn, saw sunset glow,
Loved and were loved, and now we lie,
In Flanders fields.

Take up our quarrel with the foe:
To you from failing hands we throw

The torch; be yours to hold it high.
If ye break faith with us who die
We shall not sleep, though poppies grow
In Flanders fields.

When the principal's son finished and took a deep bow, Mope poked Dope and said, "Soon as we graduate, I'm gonna enlist."

Dope said, "Don't be stupid."

I found out later that the patriotism was supposed to be followed by an intermission, but the director of the show, a teacher, said no way could students be allowed a twenty-minute break. We would leave the auditorium and never return. Or we would get into fights or start making out or who knows what. So instead of getting a break, we went directly into the rest of the show.

An accordion duo played a polka. We got another ventriloquist with another dummy. A guy walked across the stage on his hands. A quartet of girls sang a medley of Supremes songs. Rothstein accompanied them on piano.

Beside me, Dope said, "He the dick smoker?"

"That he is," said Mope.

Rothstein was the drum major for the marching band. He could play the piano like a pro, got an A in every course, had long conversations about jazz and philosophy and science fiction novels with Jimmy Levine. He could even tap dance. But what was his label?

Dick smoker.

Just before the end of the show, Eugene came out with his cello, took a seat in the middle of the stage, and played "Preludio-Fantasia" from the "Suite for Cello Solo" by Gaspar Cassado.

Eugene was talented. Even I could tell. Listening to him play, I felt bad about myself for being so ignorant. When it came to musical appreciation, I was stuck in Stupid Land, able to appreciate only pop songs. The Beatles. Motown. Obviously, there was a higher realm of musical appreciation inhabited by people like Eugene. While he made gorgeous and heart-rending sounds with his bow, I looked around at the audience. Students were falling asleep. Others were looking at their watches. But here and there, a few aficionados were vibrating with happiness. With his bow, Eugene was transporting them to Paradise. One girl was weeping. She had her hand over her mouth so no sounds of joy would escape, and tears were sliding down her cheeks.

When Eugene finished and took his bow, Mope nudged Dope and said, "Not bad for a nigger."

The big hit of the night was the finale. Every year, the talent show had the same conclusion. The audience never got tired of it. Someone cued up a record of up-tempo dance music. From the wings came a dozen football players in drag. They had their arms around one another's shoulders. They were high kicking. Every one of these dudes was wearing a grass skirt and absurdly big falsies. They pranced around the stage, and the audience went totally nuts. Kids and teachers fell out of their seats laughing. When the football team danced off the stage, they got a standing ovation that did not stop until they came back and took a bow. They danced offstage again, and then had to come back again. The audience simply could not get enough of them.

One week later, the Beatles released their new album, *Sgt. Pepper's Lonely Hearts Club Band*. Underground music. Freaky music that magically touched everyone. Irresistible weirdo music that conquered the universe. Every single kid in the world bought that album and listened to it until the grooves wore out. Jocks loved it. Brains and nerds loved it. Musicians and non-musicians. The popular kids and the hoods and the losers. The album cover was studied as if it contained the Secret Code to Happiness. The song lyrics on the back cover were memorized as if they were sacred poems.

We believed the album was drug-inspired. It had to be. The song

"Lucy in the Sky with Diamonds" was about LSD. Ringo sang that he got high with a little help from his friends. John Lennon sang, "I want to turn you on."

That album told us: A splendid time is guaranteed for all. But it also told us about the man who blew his mind out in his car. "He didn't notice that the lights had changed." We needed both, the dark and the light. We needed Paul to tell us Getting Better All the Time, and we needed John to tell us Can't Get No Worse. We needed Hello, and we also needed Goodbye.

Sgt. Pepper told us the world was delightful and terrifying. It told us the world was changing at the speed of light. And we were too.

11

Donald Simpson the Second

A t the end of the school year, mysterious gifts began to appear in my locker. First, *In His Own Write* a book by John Lennon. It's full of puns, funny stories, and drawings. Then I received *A Spaniard in the Works*, also by John Lennon – more cartoons, puns and stories. Then I got *The Curious Sofa* by Ogdred Weary. I found out from my favorite librarian that Ogdred Weary is an anagram for Edward Gorey, the cartoonist. According to its cover, the book is a "pornographic illustrated story about furniture." In fact, it's a collection of dark and hilarious cartoons that are not pornographic in the slightest. The fourth gift was a hand-drawn cartoon of me lying face-up on a bed with a thought bubble floating over my head. Inside the bubble was a realistic drawing of a rabbit. The caption was, "Confused Boy Dreams of Playboy Bunny."

I confronted Cathy Ryan in the hallway. "How are you doing it? How are you getting into my locker? How do you know the combination?"

Cathy Ryan looked at me blankly.

"I know it's you," I said.

Cathy Ryan said, "Who are you again?"

The last day of school, when I cleaned out my locker for the summer, I discovered it contained another gift, a Louis Prima album, *The Wildest*. (Dear Reader, I am not going to attempt to describe the wacky, boisterous, and hilarious excellence of Louis Prima. Discover it for yourself. You will thank me.)

That weekend when I was in my bedroom listening to the Louis Prima record for the tenth time, my dad knocked on my door and stuck in his head, "There's a boy on the porch wants to see you."

"Who? What?"

"Didn't say his name. Short fella."

I stood up and looked out my window. In our driveway was a blue MG convertible with the top down.

"He drives one of them little foreign cars," Dad said. "Says he needs to talk to you."

I opened the front door and found a kid my age that I had never seen before.

"We need to talk," he said. "Come outside. It's important." He abruptly turned around, walked off the porch, and into our front yard. He turned around and stared at me, waiting. He crossed his arms.

I went out into the yard and stood in front of this kid. I was at least three inches taller than him, maybe four. He did not look the least bit dangerous. My little brother Dean, who was practically a dwarf, could have beaten him up.

"Who are you?" I said.

It turned out he was Cathy Ryan's boyfriend. According to him, they had been going out since they were fourteen years old. Two entire years.

He told me he hoped he would not have to beat me up, but he would if he had to. He said, if necessary, he would knock me down and sit on me and punch me in the face until I was bloody. He didn't want to though. He was not normally violent. "It's your fault. You have driven me to this. She's my girlfriend, not yours."

The kid who lived next door, a ten-year-old, came out on his porch to look at us.

I said, "You OK? You all right? You look sort of —."

"I can't stand it," he said. "I won't allow it. I want your word. I demand your solemn oath."

The kid was so weird, so stiff and odd, I kept wondering if this was some kind of joke.

He put up his fists. "You want to fight. OK, let's fight."

My dad came out onto the porch. "Jack," he said, "who's your friend?"

The kid unclenched his fists and faced my dad, "Sir, my name is Donald Simpson the Second. My father knows you. I am glad to meet you, sir."

My dad walked out into the yard.

"You're Don Simpson's kid?"

"It's an honor to meet you, sir. My father speaks very highly of you." The kid shook hands with my dad.

"Well, I have to be going now," the kid said. He shot me a look. "Remember what we talked about. I hope I don't have to come back here." He walked over to his little car and jumped into it without opening the door. He had trouble starting it but finally backed out of our driveway into the street. He ground the gears putting it into first.

My dad and I and the neighbor kid watched him drive away.

"Don Simpson's a supervisor," my dad said. "Runs the whole purchasing department. Nice fella."

"Right," I said.

That night, my mom came into my bedroom where I was reading a book.

"You have a phone call. It's a girl."

When I got to the living room where the phone was, Dean and Ron and Lois were staring at me. I courteously suggested if they did not leave the room immediately, I would beat the crap out of them. They exited. Then I glared at my mom until she retreated to the kitchen.

"Hello?" I thought it might be Rose. Her mom's favorite poet Langston Hughes had just died, and I thought she probably wanted to talk about it.

"Is this Jack DeWitt?"

I recognized her voice. It wasn't Rose. "Cathy?"

"So... I guess you met Donald."

"You mean your boyfriend?"

"He is not my boyfriend. He says he is, but he is not."

"You might want to tell him that."

"He lives next door to me. I've known him since I was 3. OK, two years ago I made the mistake of kissing him."

"Wow. You kissed Donald Simpson the Second."

"He is not normally a bad person. He's just a bit intense and...odd. He was born without any sense of humor. It's not his fault."

"I figured out how you got into my locker."

"What? Oh."

"Are you going to tell me you don't know what I'm talking about?"

"If Donald comes to see you again – I have ORDERED him not to – but if he does..."

"Your friend Mary Ellen, she has a job in the main office. I've seen her in there. I bet somewhere in the office they have a list of all the lockers and all the combinations."

"I just don't want you to punch him or anything like that. He has asthma."

"You like me, don't you? That's why you gave me presents. You like me more than you like Donald Simpson the Second."

"Don't get carried away. I hate it when boys get carried away."

"It's because of those powerful biological forces. We can't help ourselves. People have written entire books about this topic."

"Please do not come see me uninvited. Or call me. I dislike phone calls."

"I can't call you?"

"You may write me."

"*Write* you?"

"I like to receive letters."

That summer, Cathy Ryan and I wrote each other letters. We did not write about important stuff like the Beatles or the shocking death (plane crash) of Otis Redding, even though both of us believed he was the greatest singer in the world. We did not write to one another about the fact the United States of America, the richest country in the world, was raining down bombs on Vietnam and Cambodia, two of the poorest countries in the world. Or the fact that every week, somewhere in the USA, white cops murdered another unarmed black man. We wrote about ordinary, unimportant, everyday stuff that happened to us.

Cathy's letters were beautifully written and often included whimsical drawings. My letters never contained any drawings and were not beautifully written. Cathy said in order to comprehend one of my letters, she had to look hard at a sentence, picking out what might be words. Then she had to guess at the meaning of several marks that seemed to be heavily disguised letters of the alphabet. Then she had to take a break, go for walk, listen to a record, eat something. Then, her energy renewed, she would take another hard look at the sentence and work out what it meant. Then, quite possibly, she would laugh.

I thought it was a good sign if I made Cathy Ryan laugh.

She said normally she was not the way she seemed when she was with me. I brought out her hidden side. She said ordinarily she was a timid person, but when she was around me, she became more assertive. She said she had only one good friend, Mary Ellen, the one who worked in the office and gave her the combination to my locker. She said she and Mary Ellen had been best friends since they met on the first day of fourth grade. Mary Ellen freed something inside her, so the way she was with Mary Ellen was different than the way she was with everyone else. With everyone else, she was shy. With Mary Ellen, only with Mary Ellen, she was smart and funny.

Until she met me.

She said she sometimes thought she was the princess in a story. The princess was under a spell and could not talk. She could talk but not easily. If she attempted to talk, the words that came out made little sense. So, her tendency was not to talk. Because of the spell. But Mary Ellen and I had a magical power to make the spell go away at least for a while. She said her mother had that same power. Some people have it, the power to make a shy princess brave.

She said she missed her mother every single day. Her father had never changed anything in her mother's bedroom. He would never enter that room, but sometimes he would open the door and stand there for five minutes looking into the room with tears in his eyes, and then he would go to his own room and close the door. She said she was the only one who ever entered her mother's room. Even the cleaning people were not allowed to go in there. She cleaned and dusted that room once a week. All her mother's things were in there, her mother's dresses and books. Her mother's wedding ring. Her mother's lipsticks, her little bottles of fingernail polish. She said she liked to go into her mother's room and sit in her mother's favorite chair and close her eyes and fall asleep, because when she awoke, she would think for a while that her mother was still alive and nearby. She said the room smelled like her mother, her mother's perfume. The scent of her mother's hair.

She always referred to her "mother," never her "mom." She always referred to Big Bill as "Father," never "Dad."

She said, when your mother dies, it is as if there is a huge hole following you around. Not a ghost. A huge empty hole that no one else can see. It is always there at the edge of your vision, and you can fall into it. She said sometimes you WANT to fall into the hole because, if you do, you do not have to feel anything, not for a long time. It is like being dead. It is like being a ghost.

She suspected ghosts have feelings, but they are not strong feelings; they have only the ghosts of feelings.

She said she liked to believe in ghosts because, if they exist, if they are real, then her mother might still be nearby. She said she suspected ghosts do not know they are dead, so you should never tell them. She said her mother sometimes visited her dreams.

12

Drivers Ed

My letters to Cathy were full of stories about the weird stuff that happened to me that summer. Like drivers training.

Cathy Ryan did not have to take the class. Her dad had taught her how to drive. When she successfully obtained her license, he bought her a car, a brand-new VW Beetle.

There was never any question of my dad buying me a car. That was never going to happen. But he did attempt to teach me how to drive. Unfortunately, our car had a stick shift. After several lessons, my father concluded that, if we continued, I was going to ruin his transmission. Transmissions are expensive. We figured I might have better luck with the cars the school used for drivers training class. They were automatics.

As soon as school got out, I started attending drivers ed summer school. My mom dropped me off at 9 AM and picked me up at 11 AM.

I was not a good student.

I started out well. Our instructor was the girls' basketball coach, Mr. Martini. The first few days, we studied the chapters of the official Drivers Manual issued by our state. We listened to the coach's summaries of the chapters and then took quizzes that consisted entirely of true/ false questions. I got a perfect score on all the quizzes and for those few days the coach imagined I was one of his best students. When he handed back my graded quizzes, Mr. Martini would point at the score – 100% — and say, "Good job, Jack!"

Then we began "driving" the simulators. Each simulator was a booth that contained something resembling a car seat. The novice driver sat inside the simulator and gripped its steering wheel with both hands, one in the ten o'clock position and one in the two o'clock position. On the floor of the simulator was a gas pedal and a brake pedal. The steering wheel was equipped with a turn signal. Every novice looked at the same thing, a rolling scroll that displayed a road. From time to time, we had to turn or come to a complete stop. Sometimes the cartoon of an obstacle appeared in the middle of the road. Yikes! A kitty-cat! Yikes! A little kid on a tricycle! There was no real need to press down on the gas pedal because the scroll unrolled at a set speed. The scroll came to a complete stop at stop signs so there wasn't any need for the brake either, but at appropriate moments you were supposed to press it with your foot. The simulator would notice if you didn't.

When we finished our driving adventure, we would sit in our simulators and wait for the coach to look at our score, which was a read-out on the backside of the simulator.

The first time, I felt great about my drive, but when Mr. Martini got to my simulator he pointed at my score and said, "You're over-steering, Jack. And one time you forgot your turn signal."

The second time, I tried to under-steer and made sure to operate my turn signal. That time, the coach said, "You ran over the cat."

The third time he said, "Looks like you sideswiped the school bus."

The fourth time, the coach backed up after reviewing my score and in a loud voice told the whole class, "I don't know why I try to teach you kids if you aren't gonna take this serious."

The second week, we started driving in real automobiles, brand-new sedans loaned to the school by the Ford dealer. More teachers arrived for that week, so that there were four students and one adult in each training vehicle. My adult driver turned out to be Miss Sweet, my math teacher.

It freaked me out to see Miss Sweet because, well, she was the most terrifying teacher at West High. But, also, because she was transformed. Ordinarily, she wore dresses that looked sort of like suits. Usually, a large brooch of some kind was attached to the jacket of the dress. She wore low heels and earrings. In the summer, she did not wear any part of her usual costume. She wore pants. Blue jeans with the cuffs rolled up! And tennis shoes. And a big colorful blouse with no sleeves. No sleeves! Not to mention sunglasses.

I wanted to say, "Miss Sweet, what did you do with the REAL Miss Sweet?"

There were three other kids in our car, two boys and a girl. One of the boys Johnny Abbas was a natural driver. Probably he had been driving cars like an expert since kindergarten. Miss Sweet decided after the first day there was nothing she could teach Johnny he did not already know, so she graduated him after one lesson. The other boy Bobby Foy needed instruction but learned at a reasonable pace. Then there was the girl, Patty Johnson. She was a good driver but had a phobia about left turns. Miss Sweet cured her by making her take twelve left turns in a row. Patty Johnson also had trouble in the parking ramp; she said it made her feel light-headed. With the help of Miss Sweet, Bobby and Patty improved at every task and, in due course, Miss Sweet graduated them.

For the last week, it was just me and Miss Sweet.

Over the course of our drives, Miss Sweet discovered several unfortunate facts about me. For example, I could not tell north from south or east from west. If Miss Sweet told me to turn and then turn again, I lost all sense of where we were or how to get back to the school parking lot. Also, I had very little grasp of spatial relationships. My hand-eye coordination was at best, haphazard. Miss Sweet felt this defect explained why I was no good at sports. For example, a car was approaching from the right. Did I have enough room to turn left in front of it? I had no idea. Sometimes I roared out into the street, causing the approaching driver to stand on his brake. For safety's sake, my tendency was to wait until the car passed. Unfortunately, it often happened that a whole stream of cars was passing, one after the other. Sometimes I waited so long for the road in front of us to clear that cars began to accumulate behind us. Eventually some of the drivers would become impatient and honk at me. I had a tendency in these situations to drift into a trance. "Go, Jack!" Miss Sweet would cry. "For God's sake, go!"

When Miss Sweet attempted to teach me how to pass cars on the highway, there were numerous occasions when she found it necessary to stomp on my gas pedal foot to prevent me from running head-on into an approaching vehicle. My side of the car had the only gas pedal, but the car was equipped with an extra brake on Miss Sweet's side. She used it frequently in every lesson. Sometimes she had to grab the wheel, wrench it into the proper direction, and stomp on my gas pedal foot simultaneously.

One time, after an incident of this sort, Miss Sweet told me, "Jack, I am not a young woman." She instructed me to pull over to the shoulder of the road. "I need a moment," she said.

I felt, in a weird way, Miss Sweet and I were becoming close.

I will not attempt to describe what happened when Miss Sweet tried to teach me how to parallel park. We both agreed in the end that some driving tasks were impossible for drivers of my type.

Eventually, we arrived at the final moments of the final day of drivers ed. Miss Sweet had to make a decision. I suspect she stayed awake the night before examining her conscience. Should she graduate Jack DeWitt? What if Jack DeWitt got into a head-on collision and killed innocent people, perhaps a family on its way to church? Would she, my driving instructor, have to carry the burden of that guilt for the rest of her life?

Miss Sweet told me. "Jack, with practice, we improve. We learn. Do you understand?"

"Practice makes perfect," I said.

Miss Sweet said once upon a time she had tried to learn how to cook. She had not learned quickly or easily. She had discovered she had no natural aptitude for cooking, but she had persevered and now she could make a cake from scratch. If necessary, she could put together an entire Thanksgiving meal for twelve. She said with patience and persistence we can learn anything.

"Sure, we can," I said.

Miss Sweet said she felt there was a chance I would not be able to pass my drivers exam with the police officer. She said, if that happened, I should not give up. Driving is an important life skill, one that every adult needs to master. She said, even if I failed my exam, I should try again. There is no shame in failure unless we give up.

I said, "If at first you don't succeed, try again."

Miss Sweet said we have strengths. Some things come easily for us. But we also have challenges, tasks that seem difficult or impossible. Challenges are good for us. Don't avoid them. Don't let despair win. Overcoming challenges is how we develop character.

"Overcome challenges," I said. "Develop character."

Miss Sweet graduated me.

A week later, when I took the licensing exam at the courthouse, I answered all the written questions successfully.

100%.

I showed my dad my score. He had come with me to the courthouse. "That's a darn good score, Jack," Dad said. "Now, all you have to do is drive with the cop."

"Stay positive," I said.

Dad asked if it would be OK if, while I was driving with the cop, he went to a nearby store and bought something he needed. He said fathers are not allowed to be in the car when the novice driver drives with the cop but, if it would make me feel better, he would be glad to wait here in the courthouse. He could do his errand afterward.

I said there was no need to wait. I would be fine.

The car we were using was not our family car. It was my grand-father's car, a two-year-old Buick with an automatic transmission. When my turn came, I got into Grandpa's Buick and drove it to the front of the courthouse, where a cop was waiting for me.

The cop knocked on my car window until I rolled it down. He demanded to know where my adult driver was. I said he was nearby buying something. If the cop wanted to wait, I could go find my dad and bring him back here. The cop didn't like that idea. He said in his experience some kids are know-it-alls who think the rules do not apply to them. Kids like that drive themselves to the courthouse without any adult in the car. He was sick of it.

I said I was extremely sorry to inconvenience him, but my father and I had not been told, and —

The cop told me to quit talking. He said we were now starting the official exam. He wrote my name on the piece of paper attached to his clipboard. Then he made me operate the lights and the turn signal and the horn. I performed these operations successfully. Then he began telling me where to go.

"Turn right at the stop light."

I noticed the cop had a gun in a holster on his hip.

Take deep breaths. Do your best. Any drive that does not involve a crash is a good drive.

On several occasions, the cop took off points. He would wait for me to make a minor mistake and then in a loud voice he would announce my mistake and make a mark on the piece of paper. Even though I was sitting right beside him, he referred to me as Driver.

"Driver waited too long to engage turn signal. Driver did not brake smoothly. Driver did not look both ways."

It was as if he was talking to an invisible person, or perhaps to the God of Driving.

For most of the drive, I had no idea where we were and just did whatever the cop told me to do. Nothing horrible happened. I did not run over any cats or sideswipe any school busses. It was a great relief to me when I saw, up ahead, the courthouse.

In a loud voice, the cop said, "Driver will now parallel park."

My heart sank. Never, not even once, had I succeeded in accomplishing that maneuver.

I told myself: *Challenges are good for us.*

This is when a miracle occurred. I parallel parked. Perfectly.

I was even more astonished than the cop.

"I am now adding up Driver's score," the cop said.

My heart sank.

"I may have made an arithmetic error," the cop said. He again added up my score. Then he did it a third time. "Damn it," the cop said. He signed my score sheet and handed it to me. "Take this back to the woman in the window."

Inside the courthouse, I gave my score sheet to the woman in the window. She looked at it twice and said, "Wow, you passed by one point. Lucky you."

I walked out of the courthouse. My dad was waiting beside Grandpa's Buick. "Did you pass?"

I told Dad I was still a bit nervous and would appreciate it if he drove us home. As we cruised down the highway, I gazed at my picture on my new driver's license and wished I did not have pimples.

After Cathy Ryan read my letter describing this adventure, she sent me a cartoon of cars on a highway streaming past a brand-new billboard: DRIVERS BEWARE! JACK RYAN PASSED HIS DRIVERS EXAM!

13

The Haircut

The fourth letter I received from Cathy Ryan told me she was now a free woman. Donald Simpson the Second had come to see her. He had stood on her front porch and rung her doorbell repeatedly until she went to see who it was. He told her he had given the matter a great deal of thought and he was going to have to terminate their love. Terminate was the word he used. He said he understood that she Cathy Ryan was not capable of loving him properly, the way he deserved to be loved. No matter how much he loved her, she refused to return his love. He said it was painfully obvious she was incapable of love. He pitied her because when a girl possesses a cold hard heart, she is doomed to go through life a lonely old maid. He said a clean break is the best break. He said goodbye forever and shook her hand. Cathy Ryan included a cartoon of herself as a lonely old maid. The caption was Cold-hearted Cathy Regrets Her Decision to Reject Love.

Just before I went on a vacation with my family, Rose White told me a weird story. Someone sent her mom a hammer in the mail, a big heavy carpenter's hammer. There was nothing else in the package, no note or anything. Just the hammer. Rose said her parents took it to the police, but the cops said it is not a crime to send someone a hammer in the mail. Rose said her entire family considered the hammer a threat. "It's like burning a cross on someone's lawn. What would you think if someone sent YOUR mom a hammer?"

I said I had no idea what to think.

The newspapers called that summer the Summer of Love. Thousands of penniless, drug-addled hippies went to San Francisco. More and more of them arrived every day. The mayor of San Francisco said the hippies were a health menace. Every night, hundreds of them were sleeping on the ground in the public parks. Moms and Dads were afraid to take their little kids to the parks for fear the hippies would be having sex or using drugs right out in the open. They mayor said the arrival of the hippies was caused by a song called "When You Come to San Francisco, Wear Flowers in Your Hair." This song was having a brainwashing effect on young people, causing them to leave their homes (in Kansas or Iowa or wherever) and hitchhike all the way to California.

That summer, most of the boys I knew started letting their hair grow longer. I did the same, but it caused trouble. My mother hated my long hair. She said it made me look like a bum. However, a pretty girl at our church who was two years younger than me liked my hair. She said it made me look cool.

Although I felt obliged to attend church on Sunday mornings, I refused any more to sit with my family. I sat in the back by myself. The girl who liked my hair started to sit beside me.

That summer, we took an unusual family vacation. Ordinarily, for his vacation, my dad took two weeks off work and we drove north or south and stayed for free with family members. This summer, we drove to a lake and rented a cabin. We could afford it because of all the money my mom made as a substitute teacher. Because of the extra money, we also could afford to build a garage for the family car.

My uncle Ted and his family (four kids) rented the cabin next door. Another uncle (three kids) rented the cabin on the other side of us.

The lake was cold and full of leeches. Uncle Ted and my dad loved the lake because they loved fishing. I hated fishing. Fishing meant that I was trapped in a motorboat with my father and my uncles. Also, there was the ever-present danger of jabbing a hook into my thumb.

What I liked was running around in the woods with my cousins. We played cool games like Capture the Flag. I also liked floating on the lake on an inner tube. I liked peering into the murky lake water and looking for fish. When we got out of the water, my cousins and I would sprinkle salt on the leeches that had attached themselves to us. The creepy things would squirm and twist and fall off, leaving behind a smear of blood.

Uncle Ted did not approve of my long hair. He was an assistant principal, which meant he was in charge of discipline at the school where he worked. No kid with long hair was allowed to attend that school. The school had a policy: no hair will touch a boy's collar. (We had the same policy at my high school.) My uncle said, in his school district, the worst offenders when it came to hair length were the Natives. The northern third of his school district was an Indian Reservation. My uncle had a low opinion of the Indians who lived there. He said most of the Indian men were unemployed drunks and their women were fat and promiscuous. According to my uncle, the Indian parents did not care if their kids went to school or not. Sometimes he had to assist the truant officer and drive around the reservation looking for underage boys who were not going to school. These Indian truants almost always had long hair. Since he was the vice principal, he had to enforce the hair policy. On more than one occasion, he personally had been forced to give one of these Indian kids a haircut because the kid was so poor, he could not afford to go to a barber. He had done that task out of the kindness of his heart because he felt sorry for the kids. He had not even charged them. One night, I told my cousins I thought our uncle might be a racist. My cousins told their mom, who told my uncle. My uncle went to my mom and told her he did not appreciate me undermining his authority. He said I was a bad influence on his kids. Long-haired boys like me become dropouts. They become alcoholics and drug users. My uncle asked my mom if she realized what became of drug users. They go to prison, that's what. You see a boy with long hair; you see a future jailbird. He asked my mom what did she think would happen if kids in his school district found out his own nephew had long hair.

My mom told me I had to get a haircut.

I said no way was I going to get a haircut.

She said, when we got home, I was going to look for a summer job. Who would hire me if I had long hair?

I said I would look for a job and I might have to get a haircut, but we were on vacation. I could get a haircut when we got home.

My mom had anticipated my objection. To my surprise, she made me an offer. If I agreed to go get a haircut in the nearby town, she would pay me $50. This was an unbelievably good offer. I had never in my entire life possessed that much money at one time. How many paperback books could I buy with $50? How many records?

My mother opened her purse and pulled out the cash. She laid five ten-dollar bills in my hand.

I said, "OK, I'll get a haircut."

That afternoon, we drove into town. We took two cars. My uncle Ted and his kids were in one car, and my mom and I and my brother Dean were in the other. The town was one of those blink-and-you-miss-it towns with a Main Street that consists of a few blocks lined with shops and bars. My uncle pointed out the barbershop. He said he and my mom would go shopping while I was in there getting a haircut.

I said, "You're not coming with me?"

"Of course not," my mom said.

I went by myself to the barbershop. There was only one barber, and when I entered the shop, he was working on the head of an old man. He told me to wait. I sat in a chair and looked around. The head of a moose was mounted on the wall at the back of the shop. The moose head had shiny black eyes made of plastic and a huge rack of horns. Beside it on a rectangle of plywood was an enormous fish that I was pretty sure was a Northern Pike. There was a little table beside my chair and on it was a pile of old magazines. All the magazines had to do with hunting and fishing. While I was paging through one of these magazines, looking at pictures of rifles, the door to the shop opened and in came one of my cousins. After him came more of my cousins and my brother Dean. Since none of them was going to get a haircut, I hoped the barber would order them to leave, but he just told them to find seats and keep quiet. My cousins sat down in the chairs on both sides of me and began whispering to one another. I ignored them.

The barber finished the old man's haircut, took his money, and motioned me to come sit in the chair.

I told him what I wanted, just a trim.

The barber said, "Get the hair over the collar but just a little bit; that the idea?" He tugged gently on the hair at the back of my head.

"Right," I said, "just a trim."

"No problem," the barber said.

None of my cousins was reading a magazine. They were staring at me and the barber as if we were characters in their favorite TV show.

The barber said, "Let me take your glasses." I took off my glasses. That summer, on an experimental basis, I was wearing my glasses out in public. The girl at church had told me they made me look intelligent.

I handed my glasses to the barber, and he set them on a little shelf. He draped a sheet around me and turned me away from the mirror.

The barber worked on my haircut. My cousins whispered to one another and giggled. I thought about asking the barber to make them leave.

I reminded the barber, "Just a trim."

"I heard you the first time," he said.

It seemed to me that quite a bit of hair was falling onto the sheet.

"Don't cut off too much," I said.

"Don't worry," the barber said.

By the time the barber finished, my cousins were giggling helplessly.

The barber handed me my glasses. He waited for me to put them on and then twisted me around so I could see my new haircut in the mirror. He had removed almost all my hair. I was practically bald.

I yelled. I jumped out of the chair. I swore. I told the barber I was not going to pay him.

My cousins doubled up, laughing hysterically. My brother Dean was laughing so hard, he fell out of his chair. I felt he did this on purpose, trying to get attention.

I swore at the barber again and then stomped out of the shop. My cousins trailed after me. I wanted to murder the barber. I also wanted to murder my cousins. They had watched the barber cut off all my hair and never once warned me. Traitors!

"I am not paying him," I yelled. "I will NEVER pay him."

I wanted to throw a big rock through the barber's front window. I wanted to yank his moose head off his back wall and set it on fire.

I rode back to our lake cabin with my mom. Dean rode with my cousins and my uncle.

I refused to speak to my mom.

I found out that night that Uncle Ted had visited the barber before we got there and told him no matter what I said, he should scalp me. My uncle paid the barber in advance for my haircut and included a generous tip. Also, he had given my mom the $50.

14

Fuzzy-Wuzzy

She called me on the phone and said she was coming over to look at my bald head. I awaited her arrival and got ever more nervous. I kept looking out the window.

My mom noticed my condition and got suspicious. "What is wrong with you?"

"Nothing, leave me alone."

The moment the yellow Beetle pulled into our driveway, I ran out into the front yard to greet Cathy Ryan. My idea was to tell her we should leave instantly. She should not even get out of the car. She got out despite me and made me stand there in the yard beside the driveway. She walked all the way around me as if I was a statue and she was a pigeon. Then, she touched my head and rubbed it with her fingers.

She said, "Fuzzy-Wuzzy had no hair. Fuzzy-Wuzzy wasn't fuzzy, was he?"

I said, "Let's get out of here. Please, can't we go somewhere?"

She drove us to a drive-in, the kind of place where a girl runs out and attaches a little tray to your partly rolled-down car window and asks you what you want.

We ordered root beer floats. I insisted on paying because I still had most of the fifty dollars I had received for getting a haircut.

The root beer float was delicious.

I was nervous but happy and kept stealing looks at her.

I thought we should talk. I should be talking. We should be having a conversation. But about what? I had already written her a long letter about my uncle and the haircut disaster, so she knew the entire story. I couldn't think of anything else to say.

I drank up my root beer float so fast I got an ice cream headache. I thought maybe we could discuss the irrational terror that long hair caused in grownup men. World War 2 was the coolest, bravest, most important thing in their entire lives, so they couldn't let go of it. During the war years, they wore uniforms and obeyed orders and had short hair, so now they felt that long hair was dangerous. Long hair was rebellious and against regulations. They wanted to do it again, have another war, except with the communists. World War Three! But they couldn't because the Russians had nukes. That was why all the men like my uncle Ted were war-crazy lunatics; that was why they were trying to make us young boys do it for them, go to Vietnam and kill people we didn't even know. And get haircuts! Because they wanted to be young again.

None of this speech managed to come out of my mouth.

It was very enjoyable to look at her. She did not mind not talking. She finished her float and dabbed her lips with a napkin.

She turned on her headlights, the signal that we were done. The waitress ran out and took away our empty glasses and the little trays.

I rubbed the center of my forehead because I still had a headache. Maybe I could tell her that I had a job. I was going to start working at the Spaghetti Ranch this weekend.

I was unable to say that either.

It was extremely lovely to look at her.

Cathy said, "Now, what shall we do?"

I amazed myself by telling her about a nearby make out spot, only three blocks away behind the discount store. One night I was with Ray and the Nazi. We had borrowed Mr. Broom's car. Ray drove us to the spot. Behind the store was a patch of woods. There was a path between the trees, not even a real road, just a path through the trees. Pretty soon, we came upon a car parked in the middle of the path. No one was inside it. At least it looked that way. We couldn't see anyone, but Ray honked and revved the engine until two heads popped up. We recognized them, this girl named Julie and this boy named Ronny, her boyfriend. I got scared because Ronny looked as if he wanted to murder someone, but Ray just kept honking. I feared Ronny was going to get out of his car and there would be a big fight, but instead he started his car, and they fled. I wanted to just wait there and let them drive away, but Ray was having too much fun to stop, so we chased them all over town. Ronny kept turning and turning, and we kept following but getting farther and farther behind, until they lost us at last. The next day the girl Julie told everyone about what happened. A car full of hoods chased her and her boyfriend all over town, and they were terrified for their lives.

Cathy listened to this entire story and, when I was done, she said, "Poor Julie."

I had imagined it was a funny story that would make her laugh, but now I felt stupid. Why had I told her such a dumb story? She probably thought I was a weirdo. She probably thought it super creepy to have a friend that everyone calls the Nazi and a friend like Ray who thought scaring people was funny.

I thought: *I am totally blowing this!* I thought: *Why is it so much easier to write her a letter than talk to her?*

Cathy said we could go there, to that make out spot I was talking about. Hopefully we would not have to chase out another couple, but wouldn't we be more comfortable at her house?

She started the car and drove out onto the highway.

"You are taking me to your house?"

"Father won't be there. He's working."

I experienced that feeling I had when something nice happened to me, the feeling that a miracle was occurring. The divine entity whose job it was to torment me had gone on a break and the substitute deity, not knowing any better, was making one of my most cherished dreams come true.

She drove us to her house. It was in the best part of town. Big wide boulevards with trees and flowers in the middle of the street. Fancy old-fashioned streetlights. Two-story houses and manicured lawns and huge old trees. Trimmed hedges, colorful flowerbeds. Even the birds seemed superior. In my neighborhood we had crows and sparrows. Here, they had cardinals and goldfinches.

She stopped in the middle of her street and pointed out two large bronze lions that were sitting in front of a large pink house. She said the lions were not hers; they belonged to her neighbor. She said she had grown up with the two lions and considered them to be good friends. She pointed to another house and said it was where Donald Simpson the Second lived.

"Wow," I said because I could not think of anything else to say.

Cathy Ryan's house was large and white, but it was hard for me to focus on it, because I was so nervous. We parked in the driveway and went into the house. I noticed the door had a brass knocker instead of a doorbell. It was one of those doors that is round at the top. The door was not locked. She just turned the knob and opened the door. We were met by a dog, an old fat beagle who barked at me as if I was a burglar.

"Be nice," she said. "You want a treat?" The dog quit barking at me and followed her into the kitchen to get a treat and soon fell asleep on the kitchen floor.

She gave me a tour of the house. Everything was so clean and brand-new and tidy that it felt to me as if no one actually lived in this house. The living room included a vase of fresh flowers and a fireplace and a large oil painting of Mrs. Ryan. The dining room included a long table surrounded by chairs.

"Father likes to have dinner parties."

There was a vase of red roses on the table.

"Are there fresh flowers in every room?"

"Father likes flowers."

She showed me the basement. It contained a rec room with a big TV and a Ping-Pong table. "I hate Ping-Pong, but Father loves it. He plays for money and always wins. If he asks you to play, tell him you don't know how. Just to be safe, tell him you have sprained your wrist. And definitely don't play for a dollar a point."

She took me upstairs where the bedrooms were. She said, "That's Father's room. That's Mother's old room. That's a guest room. And this is my room."

The first thing I saw in her room was an enormous bed.

On the wall above the bed was a poster of a Mexican woman with a little moustache. She said, "That's Frida Kahlo."

I had no idea who Frida Kahlo was.

She had bookshelves, not just one. One bookshelf contained nothing but art books. I recognized a few of the names, Gauguin and Van Gogh. Rembrandt. Michelangelo.

She said if I wanted, I could borrow any of her books.

The dog joined us. He kept sniffing at my heels and growling. She said, "Go to your bed, Carlo. Go lay down."

Carlo made a slow U-turn and left us alone.

Her bedroom was bigger than the room I shared with my two brothers. It was bigger than my parents' bedroom. It was bigger than our living room.

I realized I should quit staring at her bed, but I seemed unable to look for long at anything else.

I said, "No stuffed animals?"

She said, "I prefer real animals."

I noticed a framed portrait, a detailed drawing of George Harrison. "You drew that?"

She said, "I hope you will not say anything against George."

I remembered that George was her favorite Beatle and silently vowed that for the rest of my life I would never say a single bad word about him.

She showed me her books. She had hundreds. Many of them were hardbacks. She showed me her record collection. She removed a record from her stereo and put it back into its sleeve. She said, "I have a mad crush on Jerry Lee Lewis." She put the album back on the shelf.

I said, "Great balls of fire."

She said, "Whole lotta shakin' goin' on."

I became afraid to look at her.

"Do you like Peggy Lee?" she said. "I love her." She was removing another record from its sleeve.

She put the record on the turntable, and Peggy Lee began to sing.

She sat on the edge on her big bed and said, "Come here a second."

15

The Game of Breakage

Ray set it up with Little, but I still had to go see her. She said I was a snob and a stiff, a bad kisser, couldn't hold my liquor, and didn't even know how to fight. I used show-off words and talked too much about stuff no one else was interested in. Also, I was an atheist. No one cares about church and all that, but everyone believes in God. You can't go around being against God. That's just weird. On the plus side, I was a brain and probably in later life would become a lawyer or a professor or something like that. Being a brain isn't really a big plus because no one likes lawyers and professors, but it did explain why I was weird. Brains can't help being like that. Also, everyone in the neighborhood pitied me because of my cancer-riddled mother. Little said, all things considered, she would do me this favor. But I now owed her.

"Thanks," I said. "I appreciate it."

She took me to the Spaghetti Ranch in the afternoon before it opened for customers and introduced me to a short angry-looking man with Navy tattoos on his forearms, the cook. She said, "This is the kid I was telling you about. He wants to be a dishwasher."

The cook gave me the once-over and said, "Can he be here tonight at five?"

Little answered for me. "Of course."

She said the cook would yell at me, especially the first week, but I should not worry about it. She said if I never let the cook realize I was afraid of him, he might eventually respect me. Or at least not yell at me so frequently.

"OK," I said.

She showed me the dishwasher section of the restaurant, which was in a corner of the kitchen. At the heart of it was the big dishwashing machine. She said probably I would rarely be allowed to use the machine. Bub would run it, and all I would have to do was unload tubs. She said Bub would show me everything I needed to know. "Here are the clean aprons. Put one of these on tonight before you start your shift. These are the rubber gloves, but the other dishwashers never wear them. This is the break room. You get one fifteen-minute break which you can do back here. You can eat anything you like for free as long as it's spaghetti. Personally, I wouldn't touch the food we serve here."

She questioned me about Ray. Was he seeing other girls, who?

I said, "Don't know." (He was.)

The Spaghetti Ranch was the most successful restaurant in our town, and my dad said this was because the owner had a great business plan. The owner rented out a former discount store that went bankrupt when a cheaper discount store came to town. The owner remodeled the place, so it now seated nearly a thousand people when its every section was opened. The restaurant had a great many nooks and crannies, so diners did not feel as if they were eating in what used to be a discount store. On the wall of every booth was a photo of a celebrity. Young men liked to sit at the Sean Connery booth because it made them feel like James Bond. Older men liked the John Wayne booth. Women liked to sit in the Pat Nixon or Jackie Kennedy booths.

Little kids liked the Bugs Bunny booth. There was even a Lassie booth with the photo of a beautiful collie. The photo was autographed. I noticed Lassie had very good handwriting.

In the front by the cash register was a photo of the owner standing beside Richard Nixon. Nixon ate here once, when he was in town campaigning. Nixon was the only celebrity ever to eat here which is why his photo was right beside the cash register.

The menu was simple and short. Spaghetti and that's it. Well, you could order pork chops or spicy sausages but not that many people did. The spaghetti came with three kinds of sauce: red sauce with meat, red sauce without meat, or alfredo sauce. If you wanted any other kind of sauce, you were out of luck. Every meal came with a green salad that your waitress would prepare, a loaf of sourdough bread, and spumoni ice cream for dessert. Coffee or soda pop came with the meal. Beer and wine were extra. The Ranch make a big profit on alcohol. The overall price for a family of four was cheap for a sit-down restaurant. A bargain. My dad said you could take your entire family there and not wind up in bankruptcy court. If you were not married, you could take your date, and it would seem romantic because there were candles on the tables. On weekdays the place was half shut down, but on weekends every booth was open, and money poured into the cash register. An important aspect of the admirable business plan was that most of the money poured in the direction of the owner, not the staff.

The kitchen contained a serving line where the plates of spaghetti were doused with the appropriate sauce and then set on a shelf under a heat lamp for the waitresses to carry into the dining area. Behind the serving line was an enormous stove with a dozen burners. On top of the burners sat vats containing either sauce or boiling water full of spaghetti. There was a special stove so the cook could fry the pork chops and sausages whenever a customer decided he needed more protein in his diet. Above the vats was a huge hood that sucked up steam and odors and vented them to the sky outside, causing the air to reek of tomatoes for several blocks in every direction. The stove hood included enormous light bulbs.

One could describe the difference between the kitchen and the dining area as the difference between heaven and hell. The dining area, although busy, was ordered and friendly, dim and romantic. The waitresses were lovely creatures, kind-hearted angels who made the customers feel special. The kitchen on the other hand was hot and steamy. When the angels got back there and discovered one of their orders was incorrect or not yet ready, they transformed into demons. The waitresses yelled at the servers, and the servers roared back at them. When the waitresses finally got their orders, they carried the food into the dining area and in route transformed back into angels.

When I say the kitchen was hot, I mean rainforest hot. Sauna hot. At all times it was brightly lit and humid, and everyone was on the verge of anger. The anger was not deep, but it was necessary. The kitchen staff swore easily and frequently. Everyone in the kitchen hated the wait staff, and the wait staff felt the same way about the servers and the cook. But this hatred was not deep. The bursts of rage were short-lived and soon forgotten.

My dishwashing mentor was a middle-aged black man named Bub. No black person was allowed to work in the dining area, and Bub was the only black man who worked in the kitchen. Generally speaking, the white people who dined at the Ranch did not want to find out their food or plates had been touched by a black person, so Bub never appeared where he could be seen by a customer.

Bub ran the big dishwashing machine and occasionally helped unload bus tubs. My job and the job of my counterparts was to unload tubs as fast as we possibly could, so that Bub could pass the racks of plates and cups and so on through the machine. They would emerge from the machine sparkling clean, wet, and steaming. After they drained for a minute, Bub would carry the racks to a table at the end of the serving line, and the clean plates would soon be snatched up by the servers and sent out to the diners again.

The Circle of Life.

I soon found out why they always needed dishwashers at the Spaghetti Ranch. Dishwashers had to work in the hottest and most humid area of the kitchen. It really was like working in Hell. You did not get paid well. No one at the Ranch (except the owner) got paid well. Waitresses did OK because of tips. If they pleased their customers, they could earn much more from tips than they did from their wages. They shared their tips with their busboy, but it was not an even split. If a waitress wanted to be unpopular, she could take ninety percent of her tips for herself. If she wanted to be considered generous, she would give her busboy twenty-five percent. No one ever shared any tips with servers or dishwashers.

There was another reason so many dishwashers quit. They left the employ of the Ranch because of pain, cuts, and blood. It was impossible to unload tubs and not cut one's fingers.

When the restaurant was running at full blast, a busboy arrived with a tub every few seconds. The tubs contained whatever was left at a table after the no longer hungry diners left it. Spaghetti smeared with sauce, chunks of bread, half-eaten sausages and pork chops, empty wine decanters and beer pitchers. Silverware. Stemware. Plates. Coffee mugs. Drinking glasses.

My job was to unload tubs as fast as I could. When the restaurant was full and there was a line of people waiting to get tables, I could not keep up. Two of us could not keep up. Even if Bub paused the machine and helped us, we could not keep up. The assistant manager would have to help or else the tubs would mount to the ceiling.

Every night, at some point, maybe several times, the dishwasher would reach into a tub and his groping fingers would encounter a shard of glass. Busboys were supposed to tell us when they accidentally broke a wine glass or a beer pitcher, but they did not always do so. Or, the dishwasher might reach into the tub and stab himself on the tip of a knife or the tines of a fork. Just like that, the dishwasher would feel a jolt, a stab, pull back his hand, and find blood streaming down it.

There was no such thing as a medical break. If a dishwasher was bleeding, he wiped the blood off with a damp towel and slapped Band-Aids onto the wounded finger. Not just one. Four or five Band-Aids. Within a minute, the hand would be wet and slimy. The Band-Aids would slide off. The idea was to staunch the flow of blood with the Band-Aids long enough that the wound would close.

Silverware had to be flung into a tray of sterilizing chemicals; forks and knives and spoons had to sit in what looked like green soup for at least a few seconds before they could be run through the machine. It was nearly impossible not to get some of the chemicals into one's cuts. When that happened, the cuts stung like hell. One learned to ignore pain and blood in this job. I sometimes thought that a dishwasher could lose an entire finger. He could feel a jolt of pain, pull back his hand, and discover it was missing a finger. He could spy the severed finger lying at the bottom of the bus tub, and he would not care. He would toss the finger into the garbage disposal with all the other garbage, the hunks of soggy bread, the ropes of leftover spaghetti, and continue unloading tubs. He might pause for a moment to slap a dozen Band-Aids onto the stump of his former finger, but that is all. Who needs ten fingers?

All this — the low pay, the jolts of pain, the cuts, the heat and steam, the curses of the cook — had a tendency to spoil the mood of the dishwashers. At a certain point they would take off their filthy aprons, fling them to the floor, and tell the cook, "Fuck you, man! I quit!"

This is why the Spaghetti Ranch always needed dishwashers.

One night, after I had worked at the Ranch for an entire month, I invented the Game of Breakage. The night started out pretty normal, but then, when things got busy, I had an accident. The floor was wet and slippery. I had a rack of clean coffee mugs; I slipped and fell on my butt. It hurt but no one cared about that, including me. When I slipped, the rack left my hands, rose into the air, and then crashed onto the cement floor. The rack had contained 24 clean mugs; now 12 of them were broken. The cook came over, looked at the mess, and yelled at me for a minute. I did not pay much attention because I was on my knees, picking up pieces of the broken mugs and tossing them into a garbage can. The assistant manager also came over. He told me he could charge me for the breakage. The only reason he didn't was because he was a nice person. He told me to use a broom to finish cleaning up the mess and then get right back to my station because the tubs were piling up.

For the rest of the night, I did my job. My hands flew here and there pulling plates and glasses out of the tubs, tossing uneaten bread and gobs of spaghetti into the garbage, throwing silverware into the disinfectant soup, wedging dirty mugs into racks and so on, but my mind was busy working out the Official Rules of Breakage.

To play the game, you broke things on purpose. For everything you broke, you got at least one point. One point for a little water glass. Two points for a coffee mug or a wineglass. Two points for a plate. Three points for a decanter or a beer pitcher.

For breaking 12 mugs, I got 24 points. I added to my score by breaking a wine decanter, three points, and a beer pitcher, three more points. By the time I finished work for the night, I had a score of 30 points. Walking home, I thought of a cool new rule. If you got caught breaking something and then the cook or the assistant manager yelled at you, you got to double your score. That meant, for the inaugural game, I got 24 points for breaking the mugs, and then 24 more because

I got yelled at. That was 48 points right there. And then 6 more points for the decanter and the pitcher, for a grand total of 54 points.

A record that would be hard to beat.

The next night, I explained the Rules of Breakage to Dennis, my fellow dishwasher, a nineteen-year-old with even more pimples than me. I showed Dennis how to compete by tossing a handful of silverware into the garbage can and then covering the forks and knives with a handful of soppy napkins. "That's one point right there," I said. "If you don't break anything but just throw it away, it's worth one point."

Dennis said, "Jesus." He looked at me with new respect.

Some nights, Dennis competed with me, but I always won. He lacked my manic determination and complete lack of restraint. I added another rule. If you got caught and fired, you won the Grand Prize.

You never had to work for the Spaghetti Ranch ever again.

At first, only Dennis and I played Breakage, but pretty soon some of the bus boys found out about it, and then all of them found out. When they accidentally broke stuff, they would tell me about it and challenge me to a game. I thought about inventing a rule that said you got more points for breaking things on purpose than by accident, but I decided a rule like that might spoil the spirit of competition which was what made the game fun.

I accepted every challenge, and I always won.

I had an advantage. As a dishwasher, I was strategically placed. It was easy for me to break things or throw unbroken items into the garbage can and cover them up before anyone noticed. It was also easy for me to double my score. If I wanted to get caught and yelled at, all I had to do with toss a fork into the garbage disposal. The result would be an unearthly scream of metal as the disposal attempted to destroy the fork. If I was slow to switch off the disposal, the cook or the assistant manager came running, screaming at me as he came. Having doubled my score, I would calmly switch off the disposal and pull out the mangled fork. "Sorry," I would say, mentally adding up my score.

Only one time did I have serious competition. One weekend night, the cook ordered a spare busboy to pull out the filters that lined the inside of the big hood over the stoves. God knows why the cook thought this task had to be accomplished while the restaurant was operating at full blast. The stoves were occupied by vats of simmering sauce and boiling spaghetti. The kid was given a long pole with a hook on the end of it. He hooked a filter and carefully pulled it down, then reached up with the pole to capture the next filter. The idea was to collect all the filters, take them somewhere, and then hose them clean. The kid did fine with the first two filters, but he became over-confident when he was trying to take down the third. It got loose and swung to one side, striking two of the lightbulbs that lined the hood. The filter smashed the lightbulbs and shards of glass rained down into the vats. Probably glass fell into only one of the vats, but it was impossible to know for sure, so the cook said every single vat had to be removed from the stove and dumped. He and the assistant manager yelled at the kid for being so stupid and clumsy, so he got to double his score. But what was that worth? I had never said anything about breaking lightbulbs and ruining entire vats of sauce and spaghetti. The other busboys put their heads together and said the breakage was so wonderful it was worth 100 points.

Because the kid got yelled at, he got to double his score. 200 points.

"You can't beat that score," a busboy told me. "No one could. We close in ninety minutes."

That night, when I walked home, I was still the one and only World Champion of the Game of Breakage.

The manager figured out that the restaurant was losing a shocking number of decanters and pitchers and plates and drinking glasses and forks and knives. He consulted with the owner. They concluded that someone on the staff was stealing. One by one, everyone who worked in the kitchen was interviewed. "Did you steal anything? Do you know who is stealing?" No one in the kitchen including Bub squealed on me. Then they interviewed the entire wait staff and all the busboys. No one tattled. When anyone left for the night, they were stopped by the assistant manager. Girls had to open their purses. No one was ever discovered with stolen inventory. What was happening? It was a mystery. "Good thing we have insurance," the assistant manager said.

At the end of the summer, I gave notice that I was quitting my job. My mom had told me I couldn't continue working nights when school was in session. She didn't like me coming home after midnight and didn't want my grades to slip.

The assistant manager shook his head and said, "Dammit. You're the best dishwasher I've got."

16

Mr. Freeze

I arrived late at the last party of the summer, which was also my last night working for the Spaghetti Ranch. My fellow dishwasher Dennis and I were on the clean-up crew and did not get out of the restaurant until almost 11. The party was in a two-bedroom apartment shared by three of the waitresses. By the time we got there, the party was in full swing.

As usual Little Grimm was the queen of the party. Little wasn't the prettiest or the smartest waitress, but she always got the most tips. She was the most popular person in the entire restaurant. She had a way about her that male customers found irresistible, and she could do this thing that kept their wives and girlfriends happy too. If Little was in the mood, she could make anyone feel special. The customers liked her. The other waitresses liked her. All the busboys were in love with her. Even the cook liked her, and he didn't like anyone.

When Dennis and I walked into the party, Little was leading them in a game of In Bed. She had a bag of fortune cookies. The person playing the game would reach into the bag and pull out a cookie. The person would break apart the cookie, pull out the strip of paper, and read the fortune on it. Then everyone else yelled, "IN BED!"

"The current year will bring you much happiness... IN BED!"

"Nothing can keep you from reaching your goals... IN BED!"

"A stranger near you will soon become your best friend... IN BED!"

By the time this game started to get boring, the three fat girls saw me. Their leader Connie yelled, "Hey, look who's here. Hi, Mr. Freeze! Hi, Mr. Worst Kisser in the World." One of her friends yelled, "Hey, Pimple-Face, kissed anyone lately?"

The fat girls hated me. I know it is bad of me to call them the fat girls. No doubt each of them had her good points. Since I was skinny and pimply and awkward, who was I to mock someone else for not having an attractive body? Besides, it was my own fault they hated me. At a previous party, I had disgraced myself.

Connie was a waitress at the Ranch. The other two were her friends. The three of them showed up at every party and flirted with the busboys. One night at an after-work party I disgraced myself with Connie. Don't ask me why. I had never paid any attention to her except one time at the restaurant I made her laugh. After that, according to Little, I made Connie laugh a bunch more times. Little said this was my usual thing. If a girl was an easy laugh, then I kept talking to her. As a result, before long, Connie had a crush on me. Not that I noticed. Little said nerdy boys like me are too stupid to figure it out, but girls do not laugh at our jokes because they think we are funny. They laugh to signal they like us.

At that party, for no good reason, I wound up in a back bedroom making out with Connie. It just seemed to happen. But I came to my senses. At a certain point when we still had all our clothes on, I stopped kissing her. I couldn't figure out why it was so different to make out with Cathy Ryan than to kiss any other girl. Besides, if I was in love with Cathy Ryan, why was I kissing Connie? I felt weird and decided to stop. I didn't want to be rude to Connie, so I didn't push her away. I didn't even say anything. Instead I pretended I was too drunk to kiss.

I was in fact drunk. Not throwing-up-into-a-toilet drunk but drunk enough to wind up in a bedroom with Connie. I lay back on the bed and closed my eyes and pretended to pass out. Connie kept trying to kiss me, and I kept pretending I was unconscious, until finally she got disgusted and left me. *Oh good*, I thought, *I'll just stay here for a while*. Connie went out into the kitchen and told her friends I was frigid. For the rest of that week, at the restaurant, Connie told everyone the story. That was how I got the nickname Mr. Freeze.

The party paused in its tracks to watch Connie and her friends call me names. For a moment, I felt as if it could go either way. Either the whole party would swerve in a different direction and ignore us, or a whole bunch more people would start teasing me.

While I was awaiting my fate, Little decided to defend me. She said it was not proven that I was a terrible kisser who deserved to be called Mr. Freeze. She said she would be the judge.

Everyone settled down to watch.

"Come here, Jack DeWitt. Kiss me."

I was afraid to move. Did she want me to kiss her right in front of everyone?

Other people started pushing me toward Little.

"Kiss, kiss, kiss!"

I was forced to kiss Little on the lips with everyone watching. I did it (no tongue) and turned bright red. Everyone cheered and howled and laughed.

Connie said Little had to give me a grade.

People started shouting possible grades like F and F minus.

Little said she gave me a B minus. Then she said all I needed was a lesson. She said any boy could be an A+ kisser if he had enough lessons. "And no one is a better kissing teacher than me!"

Lots of laughter.

One of the busboys said he needed a lesson too. Then a whole bunch of busboys started yelling that they needed lessons.

Little said she might have to charge five dollars a lesson, and the busboys started pulling out their wallets.

"Come along, Jack DeWitt. It is time for your lesson."

With everyone watching, Little led me by the hand into an empty bedroom and closed the door. We were in the dark, and I was terrified. I was thinking about the horrible time we played Seven Minutes in Heaven. On that occasion I had disgraced myself by vomiting. I had drunk an entire tumbler of whiskey and Coke, but still! Little led me to the bed and pushed me. I sprawled back onto the bed. Little said, "Move over, dummy."

I scooted over.

Little got into the bed and lay down beside me. "Oh, calm down," she said. "You don't have to kiss me."

I felt a wave of relief and a wave of disappointment. Don't ask me how it is possible to feel extreme relief and extreme disappointment at the same time, but it is.

"I know about your little secret thing with Cathy Ryan," Little said. "I'm not stupid."

I was shocked because I didn't think anyone else knew about it.

She said Cathy Ryan was my Starter Girlfriend. She said boys tend to get carried away and imagine they are in love with their first girlfriend, and this is because boys are stupid. She told me not to be stupid.

"OK," I said.

She said she could call me names if she felt like it, but she did not like Connie and her friends doing it.

"Thanks," I said. "How long are we going to stay in here?"

She said, "Be quiet."

She asked me about Ray. Did he have another girlfriend? She said, "I know he runs around." She said, "He'd fuck a snake if someone would hold its head." She said she hated Ray's motorcycle – by then he had the Harley up and running. She told me a story about how one time she got on the back of the Harley, wrapped her arms around Ray. He took her on a ride and practically killed her. She said, while they were roaring down the highway, this old couple in a little Corvair switched lanes right in front of them. "They were going like 10 miles per hour SLOWER than us, so Ray has to SLAM on the brakes, and just like that we're going SIDEWAYS. We are leaning over, WAY OVER, and the highway is like… INCHES from my ankle, and I think I'm gonna DIE, and then we're like… SQUIRTING across the highway. Two lanes of traffic are like… SLAMMING on their brakes, and we wind up on the ACCESS ROAD before he can even get it stopped. And guess what, Jack? He's laughing. Ray wants to do it AGAIN! I will NEVER get on that thing with him again. NEVER!"

She said she knew he was seeing another girl.

She said she doubted Ray was even capable of love or of being faithful. In that regard, he was just like his father, Red. She said, "Unfortunately, I am only attracted to boys like that. My mom is the same way. My sisters are like that too. Love is like this disease that makes us stupid, can you explain that to me?"

I said I couldn't explain it.

She said, if girls had any sense, they would love a boy like me, a brainy nerd who wouldn't cheat, who would be GRATEFUL and never even DREAM of cheating. "But no, we go and fall for JERKS."

When we finally came out of the bedroom, everyone cheered and yelled, and Little told them, "Thanks to me, boys and girls, Jack DeWitt is now an A+ kisser."

17

The Doors

The darkness of the world was creeping into our pop music. Every day and every night in Vietnam, bombs were dropping from the sky and people were dying horrible deaths. In America, college kids fearing the draft were staging giant anti-war rallies. In the big cities, angry black people were marching, fighting back, demanding freedom. The government, the adults in charge, those old white men were refusing to listen.

The rock group everyone was talking about that fall was The Doors. Their debut album went off like a bomb. Everyone bought it. Everyone listened to it over and over. On the cover was a huge picture of the face of the singer, Jim Morrison, and then smaller photos of the three other guys in the band. The singer was dark and handsome and haunted and cool. Everyone I knew wanted to have hair that looked just like his hair — romantic poet hair, Rothstein called it. All their songs were rooted in the blues, the deep dark scary blues. Jim Morrison's voice (he was a baritone, not a tenor) sounded dangerous and slightly insane. Those long hypnotic swirling riffs Ray Manzarek the organist played were so weird and dark, they made us imagine Death was in the room with us.

The Doors' breakthrough single was "Light My Fire," which apparently was about sex — turn me on, girl, that sort of thing — but the organ break made us think it was about a different kind of fire, as if Jim Morrison was hoping someone or something would light the fires of hell inside him, as if he was asking a dark deity to make him insane, as if there is a special kind of inner fire that only geniuses have access to, but the only way to get there is to summon the demonic powers.

The album opened with the song "Break on Through (to the Other Side)." We thought "the other side" meant... like... you know, the afterlife, heaven... *or Hell, man.* We got scared listening to that song, as if Jim Morrison was recommending we jump off a cliff, off a tall building, off a bridge into... *The Other Side.* And that was just the *first* song on the album.

The most discussed song on the album was its last cut, a demented 11-minute monster of a song called "The End." Obviously, "the end" meant death. The lyrics were sung in the voice of a killer who murders his entire family, his brother, his sister. And then he walks on down the hall and enters the room of his parents. "Father, I want to kill you." Then, if your mind is not totally blown already, he says, "Mother, I want to..." He can't even say what he wants to do to his mother; instead he just lets out a blood-curdling scream.

Bad stuff is coming, and it is coming fast. The killers are loose, and no one is getting out alive. That is what we felt when we listened to the Doors. Evil, dark spirits were coming to visit. War. Insanity. Murder. Get ready, boys and girls.

That is what we felt.

And we were right.

But – a big but. I was just a 16-year-old kid living in relative comfort in a Midwest factory town with my family. Most of the time, the world's darkness seemed far away.

When I was not listening to The Doors album, I was experiencing a different thing, an unfamiliar thing. Happiness. No matter what Jim Morrison was singing, I had reason to think my junior year of high school was going to be fantastic.

Reasons my junior year was going to be great: Cathy Ryan. No more riding the bus to school. No more marching band. Did I mention Cathy Ryan? Plus, my dad traded in our old car and bought a Chevy Impala, an automatic, and told me I could borrow it occasionally, which meant on weekends I could go visit Cathy Ryan in style.

The reason I no longer had to ride the bus to school was Calvin's dad got a promotion at the factory and celebrated by buying his wife a 1964 Ford Falcon compact car with only 25K miles on it. It turned out Calvin's mom didn't much like to drive. Pretty soon, for all practical purposes, it was Calvin's car. He gave Michael and me a ride to and from school every day.

The reason my mom allowed me to drop out of marching band — who knows? She seemed less inclined to blow her stack after she recovered from her last trip to the hospital. Also, she now had a major distraction. She was teaching full-time again at the Catholic school out of town. Whoever the nuns hired to replace her got fired during the summer. Mom wouldn't say why. Her replacement was a young guy just out of college though, so my suspicion was he got caught nailing one of the cheerleaders. With my mom, that sort of thing was never going to be a problem.

The reason my dad was able to buy a new car with only 11 miles on the speedometer: Mom's job. It was amazing how much difference the extra income made. We also got a new davenport for the living room. Plus, my mom took my siblings and me to the discount store and let us pick out new clothes for school. Letting us choose our own clothes was nearly unheard of. Not "nearly." It was TOTALLY unheard of.

Did my mom have a brain transplant when she was in the hospital? Was it possible our real mom was replaced by a cyborg mom who was nice and generous, who never (hardly ever) lost her temper?

When Fortune smiles at you, just say, "Thank you!"

Ricky Fox was this guy I knew from church. We had a history. Ricky was two years older than me. When I was a little kid, I wrecked this cross he made out of matchsticks. Never mind why. I was in a bad mood at the time, and Ricky's cross was collateral damage. He got his revenge on me by throwing a handful of pepper in my face. After that, we retreated to our respective corners, but still saw each other once a week at church. We also had Little Grimm in common. She was a friend of mine, and he was one more guy she had gone out with and then dumped. He never really got over it. The year I was a junior in high school, he was taking classes at the junior college. I noticed he was letting his hair grow long. That was a surprise. Ricky was not really what I would call an aspiring hippie. He was the opposite of a hippie, an Eagle Scout who wanted to be a police officer. The classes he was taking at the junior college had to do with law enforcement.

One day after church, he complimented me on my sideburns. They were not that great, but I was proud of them. My hair was not as long as his, but it was getting there, growing back from my unfortunate summer experience at the barbershop up north.

Ricky pulled me back into a corner and said he was going to tell me a secret, but I had to promise to keep quiet. Could I do that?

"Sure," I said.

"Promise," he said.

"Cross my heart and hope to die."

He gave me a hard look to indicate the extreme seriousness of this moment. Was he going to reveal the secrets of the atom bomb? He said he was not just taking how-to-be-a-cop courses at the junior college.

He was already working for the police force. Undercover. That was why his hair was long. On a regular basis, at night, he was visiting the hippie park downtown, striking up conversations, buying dope, taking names, finding out who the dealers were. Maybe I did not know it, a brain like me would never hear, but our town was being invaded by dealers from the big cities, from Cincinnati and Cleveland, places like that. They were bringing in dangerous drugs, not just marijuana, and selling them to school kids. He said a lot of these dealers would not talk to anyone over the age of 25, so the regular police officers were no good at going undercover, but he was the perfect age. He said pretty soon there was going to be a major bust. He wouldn't be surprised if there was a picture of him on the front page of the newspaper standing proudly behind a table piled high with dope. After the bust, he would graduate from the junior college and become a normal police officer.

"Cool."

He said lots of girls are attracted to cops. Unfortunately, he could not yet wear a uniform. He said lots of girls cannot resist a man in uniform, especially if he has a loaded gun on his hip.

"Naturally," I said.

He said probably I wanted to be a cop, but I should give up all hope because I was not the type the police force was looking for.

I said, "They're looking for guys like you?"

He said he was going to the police gym almost every night. He asked me to feel his bicep.

I said, "No thanks." But I could see his biceps were bigger than they were a year ago.

"Much bigger," he said. "I can handle myself."

"Right."

He wondered if I had seen Little lately.

I lied and said I hadn't seen her in a while.

"She still going out with that Ray Kavanaugh?"

I said, "Don't know." (She was.)

He advised me to stay away from Ray Kavanaugh. He said the cops had their eye on him.

"Really?"

He said the cops had their eyes on Ray and his friend Micky. They knew drugs were being sold under the stands at the football game. He said the cops also had their eye on the motel. The cops knew the motel was a notorious love nest, but now they were suspicious it was also the center for a drug-dealing network.

"I hardly ever go up there anymore."

"Well, avoid it."

"I will."

He said if I saw Little, I could tell her he would soon be a full-fledged police officer.

"In a uniform?" I said. "With a loaded gun and everything?"

He looked up at the ceiling of the Sunday School Wing and said, "Pretty soon."

18

Micky's Parrot

On the way there, Ray told me not to talk too much. "And don't start asking a bunch of stupid questions the way you do."

"OK," I said.

"Don't ask him about ... "

"You don't have to tell me three times."

"Nothing about what happened to him in 'Nam. Nothing about the Marines period," Ray said. "I mean it."

"I don't see why we couldn't just call him. I don't see why we have to go all the way out here."

"He's not answering the phone."

"Maybe he's not even home. Did you think of that? We drive all the way out to the boondocks. He's not even there."

"He'll be there. He hardly ever goes anywhere."

We were in the Nazi's mom's car. Ray was driving. The Nazi had to stay home and watch the motel. It was square dance night for his parents. The Nazi said we better not get a scratch on his mom's car. Ray told him to quit being an old woman.

We were on our way to see Micky to warn him the cops were

watching him. That was the gossip, but it was probably reliable because it was something I heard from this guy in my church, this guy who was a part-time narc.

"Micky's a little weird," Ray said. "He doesn't have a TV. He'll offer us a beer. Just drink your beer and don't say anything and then we'll leave. I'll do the talking."

"Right," I said.

Micky's house had belonged to his grandparents. Both of them had died the previous year. They were one of those old couples who got married right after high school, lived together fifty years, and then died within 24 hours of one another. The family sold their farmland and divided up the money but gave their old house out in the boondocks to Micky. Right out of high school, Micky had joined the Marines. At the time, Big Grimm was his girlfriend. He had everything Big liked in a guy: tattoos, muscles, and a big car. He was only in the Marines for 18 months. They trained him and sent him to Vietnam. He came home after his year was up and never went back to the Marines. Ray said Micky got some kind of discharge, but it was not an honorable one. He said it was for something psychological. Since then, Micky had become a drug dealer.

"What he has in there," Ray said, "is a bunch of animals. So, when we get inside, don't make any sudden moves."

"What kind of animals?"

"Watch out for the monkey, it bites."

As we drove through the darkness, out into the country, Ray told me about Micky's monkey. Ray spent the night at Micky's house one time. He passed out on Micky's sofa and woke up at 3 AM to find the monkey on his chest. It had opened his eye lid with its fingers and was staring at him. "I'm telling you, man, for a second I thought it wanted to yank out my eyeball and eat it."

"What'd you do?"

"What do you think? I yelled at it. The thing jumped off me and ran away. Plus, his dog was there, this big German shepherd. It was about three feet away from me, just looking at me."

"Wow," I said.

"I couldn't get a wink of sleep the rest of the night. I just lay there worrying the monkey was gonna come back."

"Maybe it thought you were dead," I suggested. "It was just checking to see, maybe. I'm pretty sure they're vegetarians, monkeys are."

Ray told me no pet on earth is more disgusting than a monkey. He said he took a girl there one time and at a certain point in the evening she screamed. The monkey was on top of the curtains, balanced on the curtain rod, playing with its wiener and grinning at her and making this chattering noise. He said if the monkey didn't like you, it would poop into its hand and fling the poop at your head. "That's when it's feeling friendly. If it hates you bad, it will bite you."

"Maybe I'll just wait in the car," I said.

We parked beside Micky's house, a little dark house at the end of a long gravel driveway. No lights were on. "He's not home," I said.

"He's in there. Don't worry."

"In the dark?"

We got out of our car and I said, "Hear that barking? There's a dog in there." We heard a voice telling the dog to shut up.

"That's the German shepherd," Ray said. The dog quit barking. "Come on. He knows we're here."

I followed Ray up on the porch, and Ray knocked on the door.

The door opened a crack and a voice, Micky's, said, "What you want?"

"It's me," Ray said. "It's Ray. What you gonna do, shoot me with that?"

I noticed a telephone at my feet on the porch. It looked as if someone had yanked it off the wall and thrown it out the door. It was still attached to its cord.

The door opened all the way, and there was Micky with his German shepherd right beside him. The dog was showing its teeth and growling. Micky was holding a shot gun.

"Ray? That you?"

Ray said, "This is Jack DeWitt. You know him. Invite us in, you paranoid bastard."

Inside, I was introduced to Champ, Micky's German shepherd. Champ sniffed the palm of my hand and then backed up. Ray said Micky also had a tarantula in a ten-gallon fish tank and a monkey and a parrot. I couldn't see the monkey or the parrot. I didn't want to get anywhere near the tarantula.

Ray didn't waste any time. He told Micky what I had heard from Ricky Fox, that the cops suspected Micky was selling drugs to high school kids.

"It's not just the cops," Micky said, "it's the feds, man, it's the government. All of 'em. Watching, watching, watching."

"We thought you should know," I said. It occurred to me that maybe Micky believed his phone was tapped. Maybe that was why he tore it off the wall and tossed it out onto the porch.

The German shepherd was one foot from me, staring at me.

"You guys want a beer?" Micky said. "Come out in the kitchen."

By then, I had drifted over to a bookshelf. It surprised me to find out Micky had a bookshelf full of paperbacks. Ray said Micky didn't have a TV. Was it possible that Micky was a reader? I noticed there was only one light in the room, a lamp on a little table beside an overstuffed armchair. There was a paperback book on the armchair. Maybe, when Ray and I arrived, Micky had been sitting there reading. It made me feel better about Micky.

Micky noticed what I was doing and came over. "You like crime stories?" he said.

"You've got a lot of Micky Spillane." I pointed at the shelf.

Micky said, "I like him." Micky Spillane was a popular writer who wrote about hardboiled detectives and dames with large breasts. I pulled a book out of his shelf. "I like this writer," I said.

The book was *Red Harvest* by Dashiell Hammett, the guy who wrote *The Maltese Falcon*, which I considered to be the best hard-boiled detective novel ever written.

"It's pretty good," Micky said. "I read it twice."

I felt we were bonding.

Ray was already in the kitchen, getting himself a beer.

"Wanna meet my parrot?" Micky said.

It turned out Micky's monkey loathed the parrot. Or maybe it just loved the parrot's tail feathers. The bird was emerald green and had long tail feathers. The bird lived in a tall wire cage that was sitting on the counter beside the kitchen sink. Micky opened the door so the parrot could get out and perch on the outside of the cage. Ray and I admired the bird. Ray said the bird cost $200. Micky said, when he did the dishes, he tried to teach the parrot swear words.

"How's that going?" I said.

Micky said so far the only words the parrot said were FAR OUT! And NO WAY!

As if to demonstrate its vocabulary, the parrot turned its head and said NO WAY!

"What's wrong with it?" Ray said. "It looks funny."

The parrot said, "FAR OUT!"

Micky said sometimes the monkey would sneak up on the parrot, rip out one of its long tail feathers, and then run around the house screeching in triumph, waving the tail feather. That is why the bird now looked weird. It had only one tail feather left.

Ray gave me a nudge which I think meant: Didn't I tell you the monkey was weird?

I still had not seen the simian. Micky said it was probably "sleeping it off" somewhere. Ray nudged me again which I think meant that he believed the monkey was an alcoholic.

I didn't like the idea the monkey might be lurking in the shadows watching us, so I kept looking around.

Ray said, "Watch your glasses, man."

I touched my glasses. "Why?"

"The monkey likes to steal 'em. You remember, Micky? When Four Eyes was here? That party?"

"Let's go out in the living room," Micky said.

We carried our beers out to the living room. The place was Micky's now, but it still looked like a house belonging to old people. There were photos in frames hanging on the wall. Family members. There were doilies on the armchairs. There was a coffee table with a little pot of plastic flowers on it. I sat in one of the armchairs and set my can of beer on an end table.

Ray said, "Use the coaster, man!"

I moved my beer to the coaster.

"Have some manners, man," Ray said.

This was the year when everyone started using the word "man."

We hardly got settled down before there was a blood-curdling shriek from the kitchen. While we were talking, the monkey had snuck up on the parrot and ripped out its last tail feather. The bird must have spread its wings and attempted to escape because it flew out of the kitchen, aimed at one of the floor lamps. The dog jumped to its feet and started barking. The monkey appeared in the kitchen doorway with the tail feather. It had its lips pulled back so you could see all its teeth. It was jumping up and down and shrieking and waving the tail feather.

The parrot attempted to land on top of the floor lamp, but its weight was too much to be supported by the lamp. The lamp toppled over. As the lamp fell, the parrot spread its wings and took off again, aimed at another floor lamp. The dog was outraged at this destruction and lunged at the parrot, knocking over a footstool and the coffee table. In a few moments, the parrot knocked over three lamps. Two of them broke when they hit the floor. The loss of its final tail feather, the monkey, and the lunging dog had driven it insane. I don't think it could fly right. Aerodynamically, it was no longer stable.

This is what I think happened. At the end of the living room was a little bathroom. The door was open. There was a sink in there. Above the sink was a mirror. The light from the reading lamp beside Micky's chair was reflected in the mirror. I think the parrot saw that reflected light, and it seemed the light of salvation. In that split second of panic and destruction and noise, the parrot believed what it saw was an open window. It forgot it was the nighttime. It saw daylight, freedom, the great outdoors, and attempted to fly there.

The parrot sailed into the bathroom. We heard a thud. The dog quit barking and began whining. It lay down on the floor and laid its chin on its paws as if it did not want to be blamed for the fact that the living room was now a crime scene with fallen lamps and broken glass. The monkey kept hold of the feather but quit jumping up and down. It had a thoughtful, almost serene expression on its face.

Micky was the first of us to enter the bathroom. There was not enough room in there for all three of us, so Ray and I stood outside the door. The parrot was on its back in the sink. It must have broken its neck when it collided with the mirror.

On the way back to the Nazi's motel, Ray said Micky was probably burying the parrot. "He's already out in the back yard digging its little grave. He'll make a coffin for it out of a shoebox or something. Think I'm lying? The dude loves animals more than people. At dawn, he'll be out there, standing at attention, playing Taps on his bugle."

"He plays the bugle?"

"I'm talking about a funeral with full military honors. He'll even fire off his rifle a bunch of times and save the cartridges. Think I'm lying? He will!"

When we got back to the motel, Ray said I better tell the Nazi the cops were suspicious about the motel too. "The maids will have to give this place a good scrub. They use drug-sniffing dogs, man."

19

Slim O'Malley

That fall, my brother Dean started staying at my grandparents' house on Friday nights. His excuse was he and his pals were going to football games. My grandparents' house was within walking distance of the stadium. Their front door was never locked so he could go to the game and then walk over to their house and spend the night sleeping in their guest room. The reason he did this was because we were supposed to be home by midnight. My mom would wait up to be sure we obeyed this rule. By staying at our grandparents, he could get in at 2 AM and no one would be the wiser. Grandpa went to bed early and slept like a log. Grandma went to bed as soon as Johnny Carson was over. She would haul herself upstairs without help. She slept like a log too, so Dean could come in when he pleased.

By then, Dean knew plenty of kids who did not have to be home by midnight. He could run around with them until the wee hours. I have no idea what all they got up to. We were not on close terms. In the neighborhood, he was well known for being a pint-sized shoplifter who smoked cigarettes. I figured he was over-compensating for his height problem. Dean was a sophomore in high school by then but still looked like a seventh grader, one who has yet to experience puberty.

Dad and Mom got so worried about his failure to grow they took him to the doc, but the doc said not to worry. It would happen eventually. Some boys are just slow to develop. At school, other kids pointed him out as proof positive that smoking stunts your growth. Probably because he was so short, Dean developed the personality of the class clown. He knew an unbelievable number of dirty jokes and people said he was so wild and funny he should be on TV.

After my grandma broke her hip, my grandfather got pretty good at cooking and canning and cleaning. He did all the shopping too. My grandmother mostly stayed in the house; it was a major expedition to take her anywhere. In his spare time, when he wasn't cooking or canning or cleaning or shopping, Grandpa went upstairs and read the Gospel of John in the original Greek. He spent an hour a day on his knees praying.

One time, when I was visiting my grandparents on a Sunday afternoon, I asked Grandpa about the War in Heaven. This was a story our pastor told in church.

Lucifer was God's favorite archangel, but he got uppity and conceited, and decided he was just as good as or even better than God. He wanted to be "the god of God." Big mistake. Lucifer recruited thousands of other angels and started the War in Heaven, which was similar to our Civil War. The rebel angels were on the verge of defeating the loyal angels but, guess what, Jesus got pissed off. Normally speaking, Jesus is a sweet dude with sad eyes, gentle as a lamb, but you definitely don't want to anger him. Jesus snapped his fingers or something, and that was it for Lucifer and his troops. Jesus flung them out of heaven. The bad angels and their commander (now called Satan) fell for days and days and finally splashed into a fiery lake which turned out to be Hell. Even then, broken and defeated, soppy wet and paradoxically on fire, did any of those rebels learn their lesson, give up their uppity ways, ask forgiveness, and worship God?

Nope.

I thought this was a pretty good story. I admired Lucifer and his rebels, and I wanted to read the bible story for myself. I asked Grandpa, "Where is it?" He thought maybe it was in the Old Testament, but he couldn't find it. He looked all through his well-thumbed bible and seemed confounded, as if it was there the last time he looked, but now he couldn't find the darn story anywhere.

I asked him did he think most of the crazy stories in the bible are just made up lies? Like Noah and the ark. Who can believe that one? Grandpa got so upset by my question that he had to go upstairs to pray. I experienced a feeling of triumph, but I could see my brother Dean did not approve of what had happened.

Dean adored our grandfather and did not appreciate me making Grandpa feel bad. Dean said I was disrespectful and mean to old people. He said I was disrespectful to lots of people, not just Grandpa. I was disrespectful to our parents, to my teachers, to our pastor, and even to other kids, especially older ones. I seemed to enjoy contradicting them and attacking their beliefs. It was no wonder I had hardly any friends. He said Grandpa was a lot smarter than I thought. He pointed out that Grandpa kept up with lots of current events. He watched the TV news every night; he watched a soap opera called The Edge of Night, and he read *TV Guide* and *Life* magazine. He even subscribed to the *Readers Digest*.

All this was true. I seemed to have a compulsion to show off intellectually, to make others squirm (especially adults) by challenging their deepest beliefs. It was no accident that everyone at church considered me a teenage version of Lucifer. Sooner or later, Dean predicted, I was going to experience a fall.

When I was over there at my grandparents' house, I spent a lot of time leafing through Grandpas *Life* magazines looking at pictures. *Life* was a large-format magazine and had a lot of wonderful photographs.

I especially liked the photo-essays having to do with rock stars and war protestors, hippies, drug culture, anything like that. The times they were a-changing, and *Life* was doing its best to document those changes with great photographs.

Sometimes I would try to strike up a conversation with my Grandpa about something I found in his magazines, but he was not a fan of rock stars or hippies or war protestors. He never read those articles, so he had no clue what I was talking about. He preferred the articles that were about medical advances or astronauts. He was a nice old man, and I could see in his eyes that he was attempting to understand me. I got the feeling he did not listen to my words; he was looking into my eyes and seeing his idea of my soul (shriveled, sick, tattered, bruised, twisted, undernourished), and trying to figure out a way to help it.

I preferred the company of my grandmother. All she wanted to do with me was play board games. She loved to win, cackled when she did, and was not above cheating.

I spent my Saturdays with Cathy Ryan, but on Friday nights I went to football games with Calvin. Who knew where Michael the Man of Mystery was on Friday night? Calvin said Michael had a secret girlfriend, probably a girl who went to his church. Cathy Ryan spent her Friday nights with her best friend Mary Ellen. Girls Night. This was their long-standing custom. They listened to records and watched TV shows and talked and laughed and danced and drew pictures of George Harrison and stuff like that. I was not allowed to visit her until Saturday.

Epstein (and Four Point Levine, now his girlfriend) and Cooper (accompanied by various blondes) also attended the football games, but Calvin and I did not sit with them. Cooper and Epstein sat in the section where the seniors sat. Calvin and I sat with the juniors. Rothstein was still doing his drum major thing and sat with the marching band when he was not out on the field. Thanks to my mom coming to her senses, I could sit in the stands with Calvin and watch my former bandmates, still doomed to march around the field in their dorky uniforms. My brother Dean could be found with his hoodlum friends in the sophomore section, or else under the stands.

Ray and the Nazi did not attend games. God knows what they got up to. I did not see them that much. I wondered if Ricky Fox was right. Were they selling dope at the motel? I had my doubts. The Nazi didn't like pot. He said it made him paranoid. He didn't even like beer. Ray on the other hand wanted to be high or drunk all the time. Beer for breakfast, beer for lunch, beer all day long. He liked pot too, and anything else he could get his hands on.

By then, it was easy for kids in our town to buy drugs. If you didn't mind the presence of undercover cops, you could buy anything you wanted at the hippie park downtown. At the games, you could buy loose joints under the stands, a dollar a joint. Lots of kids sneaked cans of beer into the stadium. Even the parents arrived with coolers. They tailgated with their friends in the parking lot. By game time, half the crowd was drunk or high. This is why non-drinkers like my parents and grandparents did not come to games. They didn't enjoy the company of drunks.

East and West High shared the same football field, which was located on the west side of town, not far from where my grandparents lived. One Friday, West would be at home, and East would be on the road. The next Friday, West was away, and East was home. Calvin and I sometimes went to East games even when our team was out of town because it was thrilling to watch Tommy White zigzag past defenders and score touchdowns.

At East games, the hometown crowd divided into the black people section and the white people section. Calvin and I sat with the whites and made sure never to wear or say anything that revealed we were from West. Calvin said it was possible, if East fans found out we were students from West, we might get jumped in the parking lot. People might imagine we were spies. I thought this was unlikely, but who knows?

By then, I had learned to enjoy football games. I didn't tell Calvin, but I liked the East games more than the West games. Besides Tommy White, East had amazingly athletic cheerleaders (half of them were black girls, half were whites). Their bodies seemed made of rubber. They radiated a sexy vibe and in my opinion were almost as hot as Motown backup singers. The West cheerleaders were a little too wholesome for my taste. The Eastside black fans had so much fun at games it was impossible to sit anywhere near them and not get happy. Even the Eastside white fans seemed freer and happier than the West fans. At the West games, the entire crowd consisted of white people. They would cheer grimly when instructed to and sit there sick with anxiety when the West team fell behind. They exploded with happiness only when our team scored a touchdown and could not relax unless we were at least two touchdowns ahead. They were not as used to winning as the East fans were. The East fans expected to win every single game. The West fans were full of fear that each game was going to be the one when they finally lost.

The East star was Tommy White. He played various positions, halfback, fullback, and wide receiver. Sometimes the East coach used him to catch kickoffs. The West star was Slim O'Malley, our new quarterback. He was a tall white boy with a southern accent and colorful expressions that all the girls found hilarious.

Examples of Slim's expressions.

- All y'all
- Get r done
- Oh, my goodness gracious

- Fixin tuh
- Right quick
- Sho nuff
- Bless your heart, darlin'
- Hotter than a Houston parkin' lot

Slim's mom was a local girl. She moved to Texas when she was fresh out of high school, married a Texas guy, and had one kid, Slim. She and her husband raised Slim who soon proved himself a great athlete and became a high school star. Then, after 16 years of marriage, Slim's mom evicted her husband after she caught him cheating with some other guy's wife. This was the story anyway. She got revenge on her faithless husband not only by divorcing him but by moving back here to her hometown in the Midwest, bringing Slim with her. According to the stories that swirled around our high school, when they lost their star quarterback, the people down there in that Texas town just about went crazy. Slim's dad sued for custody but lost the case because of provable adultery and too many drunk driving offenses. I heard that the high school principal down there in Texas actually attempted to adopt Slim just so he could play his senior year for their school.

That Texas town's loss was our gain. Not only did West High finally acquire a great quarterback, its front line improved. Two brothers (twins) named Jerry and Barry spent their entire summer lifting weights, drinking protein drinks, and eating steaks — by the fall they were the size of bulls. The Hulk was our center. Jerry and Barry and the Hulk were like a wall protecting Slim. The first game of the season, Slim threw three touchdown passes. We won the game. Game two, he threw four. Game three, same story. Was it possible? Could West High go undefeated – all season?

At the pre-game pep assemblies, the best part was when the coach

155

handed the microphone to Slim. "How all y'all doin'?" Huge cheer. "All kiddin' aside, it's a pure honor to play fer the West High Warriors. Amiright?" Wild cheers. "Can I get a hoot and a hollar for my buddies here?" More cheers. "Know why I love these boys? Know why? Cuz there aint no I in team, amirite?" Cheers of agreement. "The good Lord willin', me and my boys are gonna do y'all proud tonight. Ain't that right, boys?" Huge cheer. "I ain't gonna lie. It was a shock to my delicate system to hear I was gonna have to spend my senior year up here with you Yankees. But know what? Y'all have took me into your hearts. I sure do 'preciate it!" Cries of *Slim, we love you!* "It was hard as heck to leave behind all my boys down there in Texas, but – I hope I don't choke up here." Shouts of encouragement. "Today, I got a whole bunch of new friends. Good uns!" Deafening cheer. "WE LOVE YOU, SLIM!" "Well, guess what, boys and girls? I love yuh back!" Screams. "Fact is, I'm developin' a downright fondness for you Yankees." Huge cheer. "Far as I can tell, y'all up here are pretty near perfect, 'cept maybe y'all need a few more pickup trucks. And what say y'all tone down the winters — just a little bit?" Big laugh. "I got a promise. Y'all ready fer my promise?" Deafening cheer. "Tonight, y'all come see us, cuz we're gonna *get 'r done!*" Standing ovation. Five straight minutes of applause and cheers and foot stomping.

After the third game and the third victory, Slim O'Malley was adored by every single West fan. After the fourth victory, he was worshipped like a god.

20

Big Bill's Party

East High was also experiencing a run of victories. The two football teams were scheduled to meet the final game of the regular season. Every Friday night, each team won another game. People were getting excited. What if both teams were still undefeated all the way to the end?

That game's gonna be HISTORIC!

"Slim won't stay in the pocket," said Calvin. "He scrambles too much. This is dangerous." Calvin had to explain to me that the pocket is the space behind the front line, the space where the quarterback is protected at least for a few seconds from the onrushing defenders who want to smash his ass to the turf. When Slim scrambled, when he trotted out of the pocket scanning for receivers, he was vulnerable, unprotected. Calvin said the scramble was a radical and reckless innovation, probably the kind of thing Slim learned down there in Texas. It exposed the QB to too much danger. Plus, Slim threw the ball too often, usually waiting till the last minute. As a result, several times a game, he got knocked flat the moment he released. "What we gonna do if he gets hurt – is what I'm sayin'."

I pointed out that Slim seemed indestructible. Every time he got knocked down, he jumped right up like nothing happened. "Isn't that why he wears all those pads, to protect him?"

Calvin said, "He needs to trust his front line and his running backs." Calvin said a sophomore player told him Slim often ignored the coach's commands and did what he felt like on the field. "He passes more than the coach wants him to."

"Hey, since they win every game…. What's not to like?"

Calvin said I simply did not understand football.

The local paper, radio and TV pumped up the conflict. Every few days we heard about what Tommy White said about the upcoming East-West game and what Slim said in response. Inspired by the heavyweight champion of the world Muhammad Ali (aka The Mouth, now stripped of his title for refusing to be drafted), Tommy White indulged in trash talk and predicted East would crush West by three, maybe four TDs. He said he figured the shock would be so great that, by the fourth quarter, Slim O'Malley would be on the sidelines, bawling like a baby. Tommy said he was gonna bring a clean handkerchief to the game just in case Slim needed one to dry his tears. This comment and other similar ones were considered wicked and outrageous by everyone at my school. People said Tommy should be thrown off the team for saying things like that. He should be expelled. Even my dad said Tommy's comments were unsportsmanlike. The paper said Tommy White was the brother of the well-known political agitator Rose White who last year led a "racially-charged" prom protest at East. My mom said she had heard that Tommy's entire family was uppity and disrespectful. She had seen Tommy's mom shopping at the grocery store one time and in her cart was a bottle of wine. In my mom's book, a woman who drinks wine has fallen about as far as it is possible to fall.

When the press interviewed Slim O'Malley, he said, "I tell you what. That Tommy White's a good un, ain't he?" Slim said he looked forward to the game. "May the best team win." West fans said our team captain was a true sportsman, but the East captain was mouthy and prideful and deserved a good swift kick in the pants.

Rumors circulated that Slim O'Malley was a red-white-and-blue patriot. He loved our country and was even thinking about enlisting in the Marines the moment he graduated from high school. But Tommy White, again like his role model Muhammad Ali, was against the war and would not support our brave boys fighting the communists over there in Vietnam. Tommy White was practically a traitor.

Calvin said if there was one thing he admired about Tommy besides his open field running, it was that he was darn good at marketing. "If we get to that game, both teams still undefeated, wowie-zowie, it's gonna be standing room only. Amirite? It's gonna be World War 3. Y'all come see us!"

Tommy's sister Rose White never did go to one of the black private colleges down south. She ended up staying home, enrolled at the local university. She attended every East game with her parents, sitting right behind the team. By then, Rose and I had drifted apart again and were no longer talking on the phone, so I was not sure why she decided to stay home, maybe because of money or because she was worried about the health of her grandmother who'd had a stroke and now lived with them. Or maybe the reason she stayed home was because she relied on her family to be her support system. Rose hated to talk about the fact she often had to use a wheelchair, but it must have made a huge difference in what she could do and not do. A big university consists of lots of old buildings without elevators, lots of steps. I wondered if her mom was chauffeuring her to her classes and pushing her to where she needed to go, maybe sitting in the back reading a book until class was over.

Big Bill Ryan, Cathy Ryan's father, attended every West High football game, including the away games. He sat in a lawn chair reserved for him that was parked at the end of the West bench. He travelled to and from games in the team bus. Cathy Ryan never attended the games. She was not a sports fan.

That fall, on Saturday nights in her bedroom or sometimes in her car or my dad's Impala, Cathy Ryan and I were discovering love. We did not go All The Way, but we got close. We kept at it until we got that Glorious Release. We explored First Base and Second Base. We investigated Heavy Petting. I was convinced Cathy and I invented Dry Humping until Ray told me he and Norma May Schmitt invented it when he was 11 years old.

So far as I was concerned, every single inch of Cathy Ryan's body was worthy of my full attention. Even when we were not together, I thought obsessively about various parts of her body. I could be in school, for example, in a class. My mind would wander, my blood pressure would rise, and all of a sudden, I would have to inform the teacher I needed to go the rest room. Really bad!

I believed Cathy Ryan was improving me. Every Saturday night, love sweet love was making me a better human being. I was becoming nicer to people, less inclined to mock and complain and ridicule and disagree. The Beatles were right: *All We Need is Love*. Who needs food? Marvin Gaye was correct: *How sweet it is to be loved by you!* When Dionne Warwick sang *What the world needs now is love sweet love, it's the only thing that there's just too little of,* I sang along with her. Loudly!

If I did this sort of thing when I was all alone in my bedroom, my brother Dean would come in, stare at me until I stopped, and then threaten to hire someone to kill me if he ever heard me sing again.

Cathy Ryan loved movies, so we went to lots of them. She loved British movie stars like Julie Christie (*Dr. Zhivago*). She had a crush on Lawrence Harvey and David Hemmings almost equal to her crush on George Harrison. We went to see *Bonnie and Clyde* the first night it opened at the Strand Movie Theater (Warren Beatty and Faye

Dunaway; a woman gets shot in the eye; and that horrifying and unforgettable final shot: their beautiful movie star bodies jerking as the bullets rain into them). We went to see *The Valley of the Dolls* ("dolls" are diet pills). Cathy said it was a stupid soap opera, but I thought Patty Duke deserved an Oscar. We saw *The Graduate*. I said Dustin Hoffman was not cool, but Mrs. Robinson was hot. Cathy said Mrs. Robinson would eat me alive. Two nuns in habits sat together in the row in front of us and kept cracking up. It turned out Cathy knew them, so we had to relocate to the back row because she didn't want them to see us. (When a movie got boring, we liked to make out.) We saw *Cool Hand Luke*. Paul Newman was our candidate for Coolest Movie Star on Earth. We saw Sidney Poitier's great anti-racism movie, *In the Heat of the Night*. The best part was when this white racist creep slaps Sidney in the face, and Sidney slaps him right back. Cathy said Sidney was the definition of dreamy.

I decided it was impossible for me to be even half as cool as Paul Newman or even one quarter as dreamy as Sidney Poitier, but maybe if Cathy Ryan would just give me enough love lessons, I might drift up into the higher levels of nerdiness. Love might even heal me of acne.

A boy can dream.

Our habit that fall was to go to a movie on Saturday night (I paid). We would go in my dad's Impala if I could get it, or in Cathy's VW Beetle if I could not get it. After the movie we would go to her house for love's sweet release, and then out to eat. I paid for our food, or I did until I used up all my Spaghetti Ranch money. My mom had made me put it all into the bank in a savings account that was supposed to be my college fund.

My mom knew about my thing with Cathy Ryan, and to my surprise she did not disapprove. I am pretty sure Mom got into my drawer in the dresser I shared with my two brothers. The Cathy letters were hidden under my underwear. I had no doubt my mom read every one of those letters, so I was glad they did not contain anything too steamy.

When I ran out of money, Cathy Ryan paid for both of us. She got a fat allowance every week from her dad. She was the only teenager I knew who had her own American Express card.

One Saturday night, I arrived in my dad's car at Cathy's house. I rang the doorbell, and Big Bill opened it. This was a surprise to me because normally Bill was not home on a Saturday night. Cathy said he was a frequent guest at the two country clubs. There was also a Supervisors Club which was supposed to be exclusively for the use of the supervisors at the factory, but Big Bill was a welcome guest there too. It turned out that, on this particular Saturday night, Bill was throwing a party.

Bill was a large man with a wide body, broad shoulders, big hands, big smile, lots of hair. He was the sort of man who likes to hug people. He had a big, booming voice and reminded me of a game show host. Everyone said he was the Most Popular Man in Town. Cathy said she and her dad were opposites. He loved people. She did not. He hated to be alone. She craved solitude.

When I got upstairs, Cathy said she had forgotten about this party. She called it "this STUPID party."

I said, "Why don't we just leave? Wanna go to a movie?"

She said she promised her dad she would make an appearance. Besides, she had already stolen two bottles of wine. She handed me the bottle of red and the corkscrew. I noticed she had already started on the bottle of white. She said I was going to have to be with her while she mingled. She said she hated mingling. To do it at all, she was going to need moral support (me) and plenty of wine. By then, people were arriving, and Bill had Frank Sinatra playing on the living room stereo.

By the time we went downstairs, every room of the first floor was crowded with people. I got introduced to the wife of the mayor and the wife of the fire chief and Mrs. Brown the wife of Brown's Department Store. Cathy referred to her as Mrs. Department Store. People kept asking Cathy where she was going to go to college. She kept saying she had no idea. Perhaps she would not go to college at all, or maybe she would go to art school in Paris. People pointed at me and asked, "And who is your friend?" She identified me as George Harrison, the musician. "I like to call him Georgie, but you shouldn't."

At a certain point, I began to enjoy myself. The bar in the basement was manned by a rented bartender wearing a bowtie. His name was Tony. He made me a rum and Coke. There was a stereo down there too, playing Ella Fitzgerald, and people were dancing beside the ping pong table. I seemed to have lost Cathy and wondered if she had gone back upstairs. Tony made me another rum and Coke.

"Go easy on these, kid."

I noticed the basement walls (paneling) were lined with framed photos of Big Bill and teams – football, basketball, swimming. Some of the photos were of Bill with his arm around an athlete. One was our new star quarterback, Slim O'Malley. All of the athletes, at least the ones I recognized (except for one), were West High jocks. The one exception was a photo of Bill and Tommy White – not the current Superman-sized Tommy, but the Tommy of a few years ago. Cathy touched the photo with her fingertip and said, "The one who got away."

"There you are," I said.

She glanced at my drink. "I see you've met Bowtie Tony."

At some point, I was sitting on a leather sofa and Big Bill was beside me, talking about ducks. I think it was ducks. Or else hockey pucks.

I kept saying, "That is so true."

The stereo was playing Peggy Lee, that song about *Why don't you do right?*

Then Mrs. Department Store and I played a game of ping pong

163

against Big Bill and Mrs. Police Chief.

Then I danced real slow with Cathy Ryan.

Bowtie Tony made me another rum and Coke.

At some point, I fell asleep on the leather sofa. When I awoke, everyone had gone home, and most of the lights had been turned off. I looked at my watch. It was 2:30 AM. My mom was going to go insane when I finally got home – and I had my dad's car. Someone had draped a blanket over me. A radio somewhere was playing soft jazz. I found a note with my name on it on the coffee table beside the sofa.

The note said: "You fell asleep. I went upstairs. Come up and see me if you want."

21

West is Best, East is Least

In our town, white kids went to West. Black people were not allowed to buy houses on our side of town. They lived in crappy rented houses on the east side of the river. Their kids went to East, not West. There were white kids in that school too, white kids who belonged to families that did not have enough money to buy a house on the West side of town. As a result, the East High student body was half-white, half-black. West High, where I went, was 100% white (except for Eugene Masterson).

That was not the only result. Because of segregation, East had all the black athletes. What do I know about sports and athletes? Nothing. Practically nothing. Is it possible that in the 1960s, black jocks were on average simply stronger and faster and more coordinated than white jocks? Is it sort of racist even to ask that question? Beats me. I do know this. Every year, when East and West met to play a football game, the East fans arrived jubilant. The West fans arrived drunk and grim. The West fans expected to watch their team take a beating. The East team expected to see Divine Justice. God knew what white folks did to black folks. God did not approve. God was up there in the sky looking down, seeing the racism and the injustice, the segregation, the cruelty and snobbery and greed. He looked down and gave the full measure of his blessing to the East team. He assisted them as they beat the West team. He withheld his entire blessing from the West High School. He smiled as the East football team trampled the white boys who played for the West team, ran over them and through them, broke them and bruised them, outplayed, and humiliated them, and in the end (again) defeated them.

The East-West Game was always the last game of the season. The East fans anticipated it every year. They could hardly wait for the game to arrive. Even if they were not having a good season, that game was waiting for them just a few weeks away. The West fans tried not to think about that game. They never spoke about it. Only extreme loyalty to the West team kept them from finding something else to do that night. For them, the game was an Annual Penance, a painful ordeal that God in his Awful Wisdom forced them to endure once a year.

When the tradition of East High beating West High began, most of the black people of our town did not own automobiles. There were buses ready to carry them to the game, which was always held on the West side of town because that is where the white town fathers saw fit to place the Municipal Football Stadium. If the weather was bad, if it was cold or raining, if there was snow a foot deep on the ground, then lots of East fans rode the buses. If the weather was dry and mild, only whites and black people who were not in good health rode to the game on the buses. The black fans who were healthy and vigorous walked from their side of town, across the bridge to the west side of town, and all the rest of the way to the stadium. After the game, victorious, happy, blessed once again by God Himself, the East fans walked home. Some of them danced the entire way. The East fans paraded through our downtown, marched back across the bridge past the police station, past the John the Revelator Temple of the Lord, to the parking lots of

East High School, where they had a huge outdoor celebration of God and Football that lasted until dawn.

The West fans had a different experience. Before the game even began, they fell into despair. They dutifully attended the game but did not arrive in a festive or hopeful mood. They watched the carnage of the first half. By halftime, broken in spirit, many of them abandoned the game. They did not talk to each other. They got in their cars and drove home. By the end of each East-West game, the bleachers on the West side of the field were half-deserted, while the stands on the East side of the field were full of happy people jumping up and down and yelling themselves hoarse.

This year, the West side of town wondered if things might be different. Was it crazy to think so? Was it possible that God in His infinite wisdom had changed His mind about the white boys on our football team and decided to extend His blessing?

We had Slim O'Malley the greatest high school quarterback in the entire state, brought to us by his divorced mother all the way from Texas, bless her heart. We were undefeated going into the game. Undefeated! The state's most popular newspaper ranked us Number 1. The oddsmakers gave us a three-point edge. We were favored to win. This could be Our Year!

Led by Slim O'Malley our star QB, West scored the first TD. Our side of the stadium got happy. The hell with that Loser Attitude! We had been losing to East year after year. No one could even remember the last time we scored first. God was on our side!

Then, that goddamn Tommy White scored for East. At the end of the first quarter, it was 7-7. Calvin noted that our defenders were doing a good job containing Tommy. Unfortunately, their defenders were doing an equally good job frustrating Slim. Neither team seemed able to make much progress. The fans on both sides of the field were anxious, muttering.

At halftime, the teams were still tied. 7-7.

At the start of the second half, East ran the ball all the way to our 30-yard line. And then, something wonderful happened. Their QB fumbled the snap from the center, and we recovered. Slim started moving the ball down the field, doing the sort of thing our coach loved best, little buttonhook passes that got us five yards, four yards every time.

Pretty soon, our boys were in the middle of the field. We were starting to feel good. We were up on our feet, yelling, cheering. *Go, team, go!* After another successful play, we were on their 40. And then something terrible happened. The Hulk hiked the ball. There was a lot of confusion, a running play for no gain. When the ref blew his whistle, the Hulk did not get up. He just lay there on the field like a beached whale.

"Get up, goddamn you," Calvin said.

The Hulk attempted to get back on his feet. Other players attempted to haul him up, but each time he yelled and fell back. Finally, the trainer and our coach ran out onto the field. It was unbelievable. Everyone on our side of the field stood up and watched. The Hulk had to be helped off the field. He couldn't put any weight on his right ankle. "This is bad," Calvin said.

Without the Hulk snapping the ball, Slim no longer seemed as confident. The coach was calling the plays from the sidelines. Slim was taking the ball from the second-string center. Everything seemed OK, but something seemed to be bothering Slim. He started releasing the ball quicker than he needed to, throwing it over the heads of the receivers. The coach started sending in more running plays. The fans were getting jittery.

In terms of scoring, all that happened in the third quarter was that both teams kicked a field goal, so now it was 10-10. In the fourth quarter, Slim ran out onto the field and he seemed happy again. Calvin watched him for a while and said Slim was blowing off the coach's commands every time a running play was called. Slim was calling his own plays. He was passing all the time, quick little passes that gained us five yards, four yards. He was marching the team down the field. We started to feel good. We started to feel great! And when we looked across the field to where the East fans were sitting, they were looking scared.

Can we win? *We are going to win.* Are we for sure? *Yes!* Can we beat East? For years, they have kicked our asses. *Not this time!* Usually by halftime, East is so far ahead fans from our side are already leaving. *Not tonight! This is our year! God is on our side! Their star, Tommy White is struggling. A halfback is not as impactful as a star QB. All they have is Tommy, and we are containing Tommy. And we have Slim! The arm on that kid! That kid could turn pro today! Slim has solved their pass defense. We're gonna MURDER 'em!*

Know what, baby? When this game is over, we're gonna be State Champions!

State champions!

I could see Rose White sitting across the field, and I thought about going over there to say hi. I didn't though. She was going to the university now. I figured she no longer wanted to talk to someone like me, a mere high school kid. Besides, it could be dangerous for me, a West student, to approach the East side of the stadium.

Slim had us on the fifteen-yard line. He got the ball, moved backwards, left the pocket, moved to his left, dancing, having fun. He found a receiver in the endzone, released the ball, oh it was a beautiful thing to see! Our guy reached up, a defender hanging on him, caught the ball with one hand, brought it down.

Touchdown! We were up 16-10. God was on our side!

Slim was still lying on the field. *What happened? Did anyone see what happened?*

Calvin said, right when Slim released the ball, two East defenders got to him at the same time. One hit him high; the other hit him low. From opposite sides.

Slim just kept lying there. Everyone on our side stood up.

The West coach came running. "Get up, Slim," Calvin said.

"Late hit," someone behind us said.

"It wasn't a late hit," Calvin said.

People on our side started chanting: *Late hit late hit late hit!*

The coach motioned at the sidelines and the team doctor ran out with his bag. Slim just kept lying there. Screaming.

The doctor must have given Slim an injection because he quit screaming. A stretcher was brought out. Slim was carried off the field.

It was as if we had all been kicked in the stomach.

"He'll come back," someone said.

"No, he won't," Calvin said under his breath.

"He's not hurt that bad," someone said.

"This can't be happening," someone said.

We kicked the extra point. 17-10.

Slim never returned.

We kicked off to them. Tommy White was waiting for the ball and ran it all the way back, the sort of thing I had seen him do in other games, zigzagging past our defenders until finally he was free, sprinting like a deer down the sideline.

Now it was tied, 17-17. Bad things in a row like that do something to a crowd. It was as if we got punched in the stomach when the Hulk left the game and never returned, and then we got kicked in the nuts when Slim got hurt, and then when Tommy ran past all our defenders as if they were standing still, I don't even know what that was like. I think it is possible for an entire crowd of people to go into shock.

They kicked off, and our guy caught the ball in the endzone and stayed there. Our second string QB ran out onto the field. He handed the ball off twice for no gain and threw it on the third down right into the hands of one of their pass defenders, who ran it back all the way to our ten-yard line. They scored on the next play. Kicked the extra point. Now they were ahead, 17-24.

It was sickening. Everyone on our side sat down. It was happening again. God hated us. The Almighty let us almost win. The Lord let us glimpse victory, and then he poured His blessings out not upon us but upon the East High Football team. They were his beloved sons, not our boys. Our boys were cursed.

At the end of the game, the score was 17-38.

After the game, the East fans walked home. They were state champions, not us. The newspaper said they sang the whole way. They sang their school fight song, they sang "We Shall Overcome," they sang "God Bless America." They were partying in earnest by the time they got downtown. A few of them got so exuberant they started throwing rocks through store windows. The cops came out in force. The paper said the crowd wouldn't disperse until the cops fired off some tear gas. The crowd proceeded across the bridge, past the cop station to the high school. The victory party at the high school lasted till dawn. The paper said the East crowd consumed an estimated one hundred and fifty-two kegs of beer that night, all of it provided for free by the generous folks at the Eastside beer distributor.

22

Mace for Christmas

That year at Christmastime two things happened. Cathy Ryan and I got in a fight, our first fight, and Ray got maced by Ricky Fox, Mall Cop.

Big Bill threw a Christmas party and invited his entire neighborhood. When I got there, the whole house was full of people. Christmas music was playing on the stereo, Nat King Cole. I went up to Cathy's room. She was sitting on her bed when I came in and did not say anything or make eye contact with me.

"It's me," I said. Cathy did not say anything. "You're not dressed up. Aren't you going to the party?"

Cathy looked down at her hands, "I would rather die." She glared at me. "You can go down there if you want. Go ahead. You're all dressed up. Go on, go down there, go to the party."

I sat beside her on the bed and took her hand and kissed it and pretty soon we were making out. After a while, I stopped and said, "What's wrong?"

She said, "Nothing's wrong. Does something seem wrong?"

I said, "You're not into this."

She said, "So what? Does that even matter?"

"Yes, of course. Are you kidding?"

"I'm fine. I am in every way excellent and fine and as I should be. The trouble is you are making me talk." She kissed me again. It was like kissing a stranger, and I could smell wine on her breath. "Do you hate me now? You should hate me. Because I am obviously bad at kissing and I may be drunk."

"Why are you acting like this?" Now, I felt weird. "Come here."

More kissing.

But it felt wrong. I pulled away from her just a little.

She didn't look at me. It was as if she was thinking to herself and not realizing she was speaking out loud. "I don't kiss right. And also I am drunk. What else can I do wrong? Oh yes, I forgot, I am not even dressed up."

I stood up. "What is it? Why are you being like this? What's going on?"

"I told you nothing is going on, but perhaps that is a lie. It may be something is wrong with me. There may in fact be many things wrong with me. I should make a list."

I looked down at her. She looked down at her hands. It was as if she was someone I didn't know. I felt I should apologize but I hadn't done anything wrong.

"It may be that I'm not fit for human consumption."

"Yes, you are. Quit talking like that."

"I may intermittently resemble a person someone else would wish to know, but at other times I may be... there may be... it is possible I am not... at those times, I am not what anyone else would in fact wish to know. Please listen, Jack. Would you mind terribly just leaving me alone up here?"

"What? No, I mean. Are you OK? Are you sick or something?"

I noticed she had been drawing a picture of her mother.

JACK DEWITT IS AN IDIOT

"Yes, that's it — she is ill — but do not worry." She was talking about herself in the third person. "It's all in her head. Because she is drunk and doesn't know how to kiss and failed to dress up and is anti-social. There are many things wrong with Cathy Ryan. But do not worry, do not think, do not contemplate. I will make a list and then when people ask what is wrong with me, I will not have to talk, I will just hand them the list."

I should have stayed with her. I should have apologized even though I hadn't done anything bad. I don't know how it happened exactly, but ten minutes later I went downstairs to the party. There were so many people downstairs that it was hard to believe Cathy was upstairs, alone in her room, acting like a drunk crazy person. All of them were talking and holding drinks. Now, it was Bing Crosby on the stereo singing "Here Comes Santa Claus."

My plan was to get my coat and leave, but I wound up wandering around the party. There were people my age there, teenagers, but I didn't know them. I figured they were the sons and daughters of the adult guests. Probably they attended Cathy's old school, the high school where the rich Catholic kids went.

I saw Big Bill. He was in the kitchen telling a funny story to a bunch of people. Mrs. Department Store was right beside him. I wondered if maybe that was why Cathy was acting crazy; she figured something was going on between her dad and Mrs. Department Store.

I went downstairs to the basement and watched two skinny men playing ping pong. There was a hired bartender down there serving drinks. I didn't want anything with alcohol in it. I would just drink a glass of Coca-Cola and go home.

I sipped my soft drink and watched the ping-pong game. One of the skinny guys was pretty good; he was killing the other guy. Every time he won a point, he yelled, "Bingo!" I thought maybe I should go back upstairs and see how Cathy was doing.

"Jack DeWitt, let me introduce you to my mother."

I turned around and found Donald Simpson the Second and a middle-aged woman wearing pearls. "Mother, this is Jack DeWitt. Father knows Mr. DeWitt; they are co-workers."

"Nice to meet you, Jack," the woman said. "Well, I'll leave you with your friend, Donald. Have fun.

Donald and I watched the ping pong game for a while. "Do you play ping pong?" I asked.

"I do not play games."

"OK."

Donald elevated his chin so he could stare me in the eye. "She's not alone."

"What?"

"When you came down, he went up."

"Who did? What are you talking about?"

"They're speaking French, I imagine. They enjoy conversing in the French language."

I should have gotten my coat and left, got in my dad's car, driven home, but instead I went upstairs to Cathy's bedroom. The door was closed, but I didn't knock. She was in there with some guy I didn't know. They were not touching or anything. He was in a chair and she was in the middle of the room holding a glass of something.

"Jack!" she said.

The moment I saw the other guy, I was mad. Crazy mad. It was my first experience with insane jealousy. I didn't even talk. I just left. I could hear Cathy calling my name, but I didn't turn around. I ran downstairs, taking the steps two at a time. Partiers looked up at me startled as if they were thinking maybe the house was on fire, or maybe I was being chased by a bear. I found my coat. The closet by the front door was overflowing with coats. I was so mad I just about stole someone else's coat, and then I found my coat and went out the door. I had the idea she might be following me. I hoped she was. I expected at any second, she might grab my arm and beg me to stay, but that didn't happen. I went out into the cold still holding my coat. No one was following me. She was probably still up there with that guy. I hated her. I put on my coat and found the car keys in my pocket. I wanted to make her cry. I wanted to kill that guy she was with. Wayne.

Donald Simpson the Second had told me Wayne was an old friend of Cathy's, someone she had known since she was in elementary school.

I hated Wayne. I hated his handsome pimple-free face and his cool clothes and the fact that, according to Donald Simpson the Second, he and Cathy Ryan spoke French to one another. I hated both of them, and I hated love. Rose White was right about love. It is a disease worse than the flu. It makes everyone stupid. I wanted to do something reckless and dangerous.

I drove home the long way. It was snowing and the streets were slippery. I wanted to get into an accident. I wanted to slam into something. I had a moment of sanity and turned into a big empty parking lot and made my dad's Chevy Impala do doughnuts in the snow. I didn't go home until I calmed down.

But I still wanted to kill Wayne.

Cathy Ryan and I made up two days later. She cried and said she was sorry. She said nothing happened with Wayne. I said it was my fault. Jealousy made me stupid. We kissed. I wiped away her tears with my fingertips. She said I shouldn't be jealous of Wayne. She hardly saw him anymore. He was at her dad's party with his parents and came upstairs to say hi. That's all it was. He went to her old school. He was dating this other girl. "I drank too much that night and got into a bad mood, that's all it was."

I told Cathy Ryan I was in love with her. I apologized for being so jealous. She said she was so in love with me it hurt. She couldn't bear it if we broke up. I said I couldn't bear it either. More kissing. I decided I didn't hate love after all.

* * *

This is what happened with Ray a few nights later. I went to the mall with my little brother Dean. It was a week before Christmas. We were on a mission to buy presents. Neither of us had much money, so whatever we bought had to be cheap.

I hated Christmas shopping. I wasn't even crazy about Christmas. Christmas is great when you're a little kid because you get toys and stuff. But it is boring and disappointing when you're older. Maybe not for rich kids; they probably get everything they want, but I wasn't rich. If I really wanted something, that meant I wouldn't get it.

Christmas shopping is its own kind of hell. First, you have no idea what to buy your siblings. That means you have to wander into a toy store and look at stuff, shelf after shelf of crap. There will be some cool stuff, but it will be too expensive. Pretty soon all the toys you can afford will look equally stupid. And you will be hot. It is wintertime, so you enter the mall wearing a big heavy coat, but the mall isn't cold, it's heated, so you take off the coat, but there is no place to put it, so you have to carry it with you wherever you go. Pretty soon, you have bought some presents, so you carry them too. You go to six more stores and the whole time you have to carry your coat and your packages and try not to drop anything.

Dean and I were not the only people who put off Christmas shopping till the last minute. There were thousands of shoppers, desperate to buy crap. All of them were over-heated, carrying their coats and their packages. No one was happy. Those stupid Christmas songs that everyone has heard a zillion times were playing. The songs were ordering us to be happy, be merry, Christmas is wonderful, Christmas is love and family and happiness, but really Christmas is a mob of over-heated last-minute shoppers who are in a bad mood.

Dean and I were in the middle of the mall, looking around at all the stores, trying to decide which one we should go to first, and then we heard someone yelling our names. We looked up. Ray was above us, hanging over a balcony, waving his arms, happy to see us, yelling down at us, attracting attention. We were beside the up escalator, which was full of shoppers ascending to the second floor, but that did not matter to Ray. He came bounding down the up escalator, pushing startled shoppers out of his way, yelling at us. His face was bright red the way it got when he was drunk. He was wearing big fluffy bedroom slippers — like something an old lady might wear. I was stupefied by the fact he was wearing slippers. We were in the middle of a mall and it was wintertime!

"Pinky! Pinky! Pinky!" Ray was acting as if Dean was the long-lost relative that he had not seen in twenty years. Pinky was my brother's nickname because, one time at a party, a drunk guy held up his pinky finger and in a loud voice told Dean, "Why, you're no bigger than my little pinky."

I felt slighted because I was standing there too, but no, as usual my little brother was more popular than me, even with Ray, a person who had been my friend since we were in elementary school.

Ray grabbed Dean in a bear hug and lifted him up and swung him around – more attention-grabbing activity. Even when sober, Ray loved attention, and when he was drunk that tendency got worse. Dean was doing his best to pretend he enjoyed being bear-hugged by a guy twice his size in the middle of a mall.

Hundreds of shoppers were watching all this. It probably looked to them as if an insane, dangerous, red-faced, bedroom-slipper-wearing maniac was attacking a little kid.

Mall security showed up.

"Put him down! Sir, put that child DOWN!"

I realized I knew the mall cop. It was Ricky Fox; a guy I had known forever because he went to our church. It was Ricky's big ambition in life to become a police officer, so he was taking law enforcement courses at the community college. For the holiday season, Ricky had gotten himself a job at the mall as Mall Security. He was wearing a uniform. No gun was holstered on his hip, but he did have a can of Mace attached to his belt.

Ricky knew darn well what was happening. He knew Dean, just like he knew me. He also knew Ray. He knew Ray and Dean were friends. He knew Dean was in no danger whatever. Obviously, Ray was drunk and he was wearing bedroom slippers, OK, no argument, but he was not hurting anyone, certainly not Dean.

Ray set Dean down on the floor of the mall and turned to confront Ricky. He was grinning, not a good sign. Ray liked fights. Something in him burned bright and hot when he got into a fight, and to get into a fight with a Mall Security Guard? That was in the area that Ray considered Fun.

I am not sure that Ray really knew who Ricky was.

Ricky knew Ray because for a long time Ricky was in love with Little Grimm. She dumped him, broke his heart, and he never got over it. Some guys are like that. They can't let go. On a regular basis, Ricky would pull me aside at our church and want to know if I had seen her lately, was she OK, was she going out with anyone. He knew the answer, so I hated this question. I would say, "Don't know. I hardly ever see her." Little Grimm was Ray's girlfriend. One of Ray's girlfriends. Why girls – so many of them – were crazy about Ray Kavanaugh was one of the mysteries of the universe. He was not faithful. He was often drunk or high on something. He was frequently unemployed. He was a liar and a thief. None of that seemed to matter.

Ricky hated Ray because of Little. It drove him insane that she preferred Ray to a guy like him, a guy who graduated from high school (Ray was a dropout), a guy who was taking classes at the junior college, a guy who would soon be a police officer. Ricky hated Ray with a passion, but Ray was hardly aware that Ricky Fox even existed. So far as Ray was concerned, he was being confronted in the middle of the mall by a mere security cop, one who looked high-strung and inexperienced and nervous.

I noticed Micky. He was standing in the crowd that now surrounded us; he had his eyes fixed on Ricky. If Ray was barely aware of who Ricky was, Micky had zero idea who he was.

Ray was living with Micky now. He had moved out of the Nazi's house after he and the Nazi got in a fight over Ray's drinking and smoking. The Nazi was worried about Ray's health. According to him, Ray needed to go to the doctor. Ray didn't have insurance or much money, so he wouldn't go. Even when the Nazi's parents, Mr. and Mrs. Broom, offered to pay for the doctor, Ray said he couldn't be bothered. The Nazi said Ray kept getting colds. He had a cough that wouldn't go away. His hands and feet kept swelling up. I looked again at the slippers on Ray's bare feet and realized why he didn't have regular shoes on. His feet had swollen up until he couldn't fit them into his shoes. Ray must have come here to the mall with Micky. Probably, in the car, they got drunk and/ or high.

I was a little worried about Micky. Micky had been to Vietnam. He was a weird guy, unpredictable. According to Ray, the United States Marine Corps had trained Micky how to kill people. The way Ray put it was that Micky knew six ways to kill a guy with his bare hands, and five more ways to kill a guy using his elbows.

Ray kept grinning and took a step toward Ricky.

Ricky pulled his canister of Mace off of his belt and aimed it directly at Ray's face.

Dean started begging Ricky to calm down, this was no problem, he was fine, but Ray just pushed Dean aside and took another step toward Ricky and his can of Mace.

Ricky said, "Sir, you are creating a disturbance and will leave this mall NOW!" He took a step toward Ray.

Dean said, "Ray, don't do it!"

Ray did not take another step toward Ricky. I think it was finally occurring to him that the aerosol canister in the mall cop's hand contained Mace. Mace was this horrible stuff like pepper spray.

Years ago, angry at me, Ricky Fox had flung an entire handful of pepper into my face. That was one of the most painful and horrible things that had ever happened to me, and now Ricky was getting ready to do it again, to Ray, in a mall with a hundred people watching.

I said, "Ray, that's a can of MACE!"

Dean said, "We can go, Ray. Let's just go." He turned to Ricky. "You don't need to do this, Ricky."

Micky was now only a few feet behind Ricky. We were completely surrounded by people, excited, thrilled to see this commotion, hoping it would escalate to a fight.

I wished that Dean had not revealed to Micky that we knew the mall security guard.

"Squirt him!" someone said. People in mobs are like that; they want to see someone get hurt.

Ray kept grinning, but he backed up a step. Ricky immediately took a step forward.

I think an internal war was going on in Ray's brain. On one hand, he wanted to leap on the mall cop and beat the shit out of him. To give a mall cop a smack-down with a crowd watching, what could be sweeter? On the other hand, he did not see how he could do it and not get squirted in the face with Mace. Ray retreated another step.

It was as if they were locked in a weird dance. Ray kept slowly retreating and Ricky kept slowly advancing with this big doughnut of people around them. We crossed the entire floor of the mall that way and wound up by the front doors. The whole way, Ricky and Ray had been locked in a stare-down.

Still glaring at Ricky, Ray retreated out one of the glass doors. Ricky, with his can of Mace, followed Ray out onto the sidewalk. It was as if the doors were some kind of important barrier. The mob of people that had surrounded us dispersed; apparently none of those people wanted to follow Ray and Ricky out into the cold night.

Now, Ray and Ricky were outside the mall. No one was with them except Dean and me. And Micky.

"OK," I said. "It's over." I told Ricky, "Go back in the mall, man."

I noticed Micky had his fists clenched.

Dean said, "Please, Ricky, don't squirt him."

Ray swore at Ricky, and Ricky squirted him right in the face. Ray screamed, put up his hands. The horrible burning stuff was splashing off his fingers and running down his cheeks.

I thought for a moment that Micky might kill Ricky using one of the techniques he had learned in the Marines, but instead, he just pushed Ricky out of the way and went to help Ray, who by that time was down on his knees, screaming and pawing at his eyes.

Dean and I went over to help Ray too, and the next time I looked Ricky was gone. He must have run back into the mall.

Micky said we better get out of here before real cops showed up.

Dean went with Micky and Ray in Micky's car. They got Ray into the back seat and Dean used a wadded-up Kleenex to mop up the mace that was still on Ray's face. I said I would follow them in my dad's car.

They decided Micky's place out in the sticks was too far away, so we went to Ray's mom's house. By the time I got there, they had Ray inside. He was sitting at the kitchen table with his shirt off. The skin around his eyes was bright red, and Ray's mom Naomi was dabbing his cheeks with a washcloth.

23

Brocklehurst

I forgot about the fact I signed up for dumb kid chemistry until school started up again in January and I walked into my Chem class and discovered it did not contain a single one of my friends. Epstein, Cooper, and Calvin were all taking chemistry that semester, but they were in the smart kid class. I found a seat in the back with two guys I knew from my neighborhood, Larry and Barry.

Our Chemistry class was a lunch hour class. The school cafeteria was not big enough to hold all the hungry kids at the same time, so the lunch hour classes had to be staggered. Teachers released their students in waves. Lots of classes ran for a while, then got interrupted so the kids could go eat lunch. We got 25 minutes to eat, then had to return for the rest of the class. The first wave of lunchers went straight to the cafeteria from their previous class. Our class was in the second wave. We went to class for ten minutes and then got released. There wasn't enough time to do much so, during that ten minutes, our teacher Mr. Gold took attendance, collected our new homework, returned our graded homework, and then sent us to lunch.

After one week of class, it dawned on me I did not need to return to class at all. In that first ten minutes, Mr. Gold took attendance.

He attached the attendance slip to the clip on the classroom door and went to lunch in his office. He didn't take attendance when we came back. I could spend the entire ninety minutes of lunch period in the student lounge hanging out with my friends. Mr. Gold never noticed.

I found out our homework assignments from Larry and Barry. Homework was easy. All you had to do was read a chapter in the textbook and fill out a worksheet. If we had a unit test, I returned from lunch to take it. Except for me, the class did not include a single smart kid, so there was no competition.

One day, Mr. Gold returned the first big unit test before we broke for lunch. When he handed me my test, he told me I got the highest score in his class, 100%.

"Thanks, Mr. Gold," I said.

"Well, you earned it." He said the funny thing was he had never noticed me in his class before. I told him I was a quiet person. Mr. Gold said lots of the best students are like that, shy. He was like that when he was a kid too.

After handing back the tests, he sent us out for lunch. I didn't return that day either.

When kids would come back after lunch, they would cluster around the classroom door, waiting for Mr. Gold to return and unlock the door. One day, Larry and Barry noticed the attendance slip clipped to the door. Larry snatched it and pretended to tear it up. Barry found this amusing. Then Larry got an idea. "Give me a pencil, stupid." Barry gave him a pencil, and Larry added a name to the attendance slip.

Mickey Mouse.

When class resumed, a kid came, plucked the altered slip off our classroom door and took it back to the main office, along with all the other attendance slips. When the principal's secretary looked at the slip for our class, she noticed the added name. She sighed – this sort of prank was not unusual – and sent the attendance kid back to our class. She told him he was going to have to show Mr. Gold the slip and tell him attendance would have to be retaken.

Mr. Gold got mad at the class, but no one fessed up. He took attendance again, crossed out the name of Mickey Mouse, and added the name of Jack DeWitt. He was a little surprised that he had somehow missed the fact I was absent the first time he took attendance that day.

All that commotion was so much fun that Barry and Larry played the same trick the next day. This time they added two names to the slip: Donald Duck and Goofy.

Sure enough, the same thing happened again. The attendance kid returned, and Mr. Gold got mad and had to take attendance a second time. Once again, he was startled to discover he had failed to notice earlier that Jack DeWitt was absent. He asked the class, did anyone know, was Jack sick?

"Sick in the head," someone said.

That afternoon, a girl in the class told me what had happened.

"Shit," I said.

"I thought you should know."

The next morning when I was in homeroom, the intercom whistled, and the vice principal's voice boomed out. The vice principal was a huge man named Mr. Brocklehurst. Kids said, during the war, he had killed Germans with a machine gun. Some people claimed he was still at it, killing people, except now he was killing students. This was ridiculous, of course, but it was sorta, kinda believable. Brocklehurst was good at being scary. He could just look at you, and your heart started thumping and your mouth got dry.

Brocklehurst's voice asked my homeroom teacher if the student Jack DeWitt was in the room. Everyone looked at me. My heart started thumping erratically. My homeroom teacher said I was there all right. Brocklehurst said, "Send him to my office."

Five minutes later, I was in Brocklehurst's office. We had met one time before – the tee-shirt incident.

My friend Michael liked to talk me into doing stupid things. One time he had talked me into buying a tee-shirt with the number 69 on it. The tee-shirt was bright yellow and the number on the front of it was bright green. I knew 69 meant something dirty, but I didn't know what exactly and did not want to reveal my ignorance by asking. Michael said I would never have the guts to wear that shirt to school, so the next Monday, I wore it. As soon as I walked into homeroom, I was like a movie star. Everyone, even the girls, said my shirt was cool. Even my homeroom teacher thought it was cool, but he said he could not allow it. He sent me to Brocklehurst. When Brocklehurst was looking at my shirt, I pretended I had no idea the number was considered dirty. I pointed out I was going to graduate in 1969. I said a lot of the jocks wore class rings and, right beside the gemstone, it said 1969.

Brocklehurst listened to me telling this story and growled to indicate his disgust. I couldn't tell if he was disgusted that I was bullshitting him or that I was wearing the stupid tee-shirt. He said I could not go to classes wearing the shirt. Didn't I have any more shirts? I said maybe I could wear my gym tee-shirt over my 69 shirt, but it was dirty. "Go get it," he said. The rest of the day I wore my smelly gym tee-shirt over my new tee shirt, but the number 69 was still visible. You could see it hiding, not very well, beneath the gym shirt. I got compliments and sympathy from other students all day long.

On this occasion, when I walked into his office, Brocklehurst said, "Well, if it isn't Mr. DeWitt."

"Yes, sir. It's me."

He asked me if I liked my chemistry class.

"Sure. I mean, it's OK. It's not very challenging though." My hands were sweating.

"Tell me something, DeWitt. You ever skip your chemistry class?"

"Um, yeah. Yes, sir. Sorry, sir. I skipped it one time."

He looked right at me. "How many times?"

I felt I was at a crossroads. Should I lie? How much did he know? I had skipped class dozens of times, but I was pretty sure Brocklehurst did not know it, at least not for sure. I said, "I skipped it two times."

"Only twice?"

"Right. Twice, sir. I know I should never have done it. I'm very sorry, sir."

For a moment, I believed that, if Brocklehurst knew for sure I was lying to him, he would kill me with his bare hands.

"Skipped chemistry class twice," Brocklehurst said. He wrote something on a piece of paper. "You know what I do to students who skip class, DeWitt?"

I shook my head.

"I give 'em indefinite detention."

"Yes, sir."

"You know where the detention room is?"

"I think so. I mean, yes sir. I know where it is."

"You planning to skip any more classes, DeWitt?"

"No, sir. I won't, sir. I promise."

So, that was how I got indefinite detention.

It turned out indefinite detention lasted for only two weeks. Since Calvin was not going to wait around for me after school, I had to get rides home from my mom. I thought she was going to go nuts but in fact she seemed to think the whole skipping-class thing was kind of funny. She told me Brocklehurst called her at her school and told her what had happened. She said Brocklehurst lightened up as soon as he found out she was a teacher. He said a kid like me was too smart for Mr. Gold's chemistry class – he called it Chemistry for Dummies – so, with her permission, he was going to switch me to the advanced class. I wound up in the same chemistry class as my friends after all.

The only thing bad about the switch was I no longer got 100% on all the tests.

In March of that year, a kid came to my third period class. He told my teacher I needed to go see Brocklehurst.

"What is it this time?" I said as soon as we were out in the hall.

"How would I know? Like they ever tell me anything."

He was a senior, so I followed a step behind him all the way to Brocklehurst's office.

The moment I appeared in his doorway, Brocklehurst stood up. He did not seem angry. "Jack, your mother called." He handed me a piece of paper. "You need to call this number."

I got scared, but not of Brocklehurst. It was a number I recognized, my grandparents' number.

"You can use my phone," Brocklehurst said. "This phone here. Just dial 9 first for an outside line. I'll give you some privacy." It made me nervous that he was being so nice. Brocklehurst went out the door, leaving me all alone in his office.

I called the number, and my mom answered the phone. For a moment, I couldn't understand what she was saying. Why wasn't she at work? It was a school day; she was supposed to be at her school. What was she doing at my grandparents' house?

She told me what happened and said I would have to get my brother Dean out of school and bring him to my grandparents' house. "It's just down the street," she said. "You boys can walk."

I found out from the office secretary what classroom Dean was in. I went there, rapped on the door. The teacher came. She didn't look thrilled to see me. "What is it?" I told her Dean had to come with me. She gave me a suspicious look, so I told her what had happened.

When Dean got out in the hall, he was happy and excited. How did I get him out of class?

It was raining outside, just a light rain. The sky was dark. Wind was blowing. My glasses got wet and useless, so I took them off and put them in my pocket. Dean was crying. He and my grandfather had always been close. I didn't feel anything, and I couldn't think of anything to say. Dean cried all the way to our grandparents' house.

When we got there, my grandfather's body had already been removed. My dad was on the phone talking long distance to his brother Milton. My grandmother was in her swivel chair, talking to her pastor. The pastor's wife was there too. My mom told Dean and me to sit on the sofa.

24

Blood and Peaches

Maybe some stories we need to tell over and over. I don't know what it is that makes the telling necessary. Are we trying to get the story right, trying to get the right response? And until we do, we have to keep telling it?

My grandmother found herself compelled to tell the story of how she learned her husband of more than fifty years was dead. She could not resist her need to tell it over and over. By the time my dad, Dean, and I were at the airport waiting for Uncle Milton's plane to land, I had already heard Grandma tell the story four times. She told it three times to others when I was nearby, and then she told it just to me. I am not sure if she failed to realize I had already heard the story, or if she knew but it didn't matter.

Everyone around my grandmother had moved on in the usual way along the stream of time. They were in the Now, where they were supposed to be. Grandma was still stuck in the Then. Maybe she thought if she kept telling the story, the past would eventually let her go. The death of her husband would quit being Real – more Real than everything else. It would finally turn into a mere Story. And then she would be allowed to go on with her life. Oh, who knows? For whatever reason, Grandma DeWitt told it to anyone who would listen.

That morning, she woke up at the usual time, but Grandpa was not there. That was weird. They had their morning routine. She always woke up at 9 AM exactly. Grandpa would have been up and moving about downstairs since 7 AM. Just before she woke up, he would be in the kitchen fixing her breakfast: a poached egg, a slice of unbuttered toast, a half of a grapefruit, and a cup of black coffee. This time, when she awoke at 9 AM, Grandpa did not come into the room with her breakfast on a tray. She had a handbell on a stand beside her bed for exactly this situation. She called my grandfather's name and rang the handbell. She listened. Was he coming up the steps? Not a sound. Where was he? She called again, rang the bell again. Nothing. She got a Feeling. For twenty minutes she rang her bell and shouted.

Finally, Grandma got herself out of bed. Since she broke her hip, she needed help with pretty much everything. Ordinarily, Grandpa helped her out of bed and then helped her into the bathroom to take care of her lady needs. When she was finished, he helped her back to the bedroom, helped her get dressed, helped her to the steps. Grandma did not like to talk about her manner of descent because it was unladylike. It was impossible to use a walker to go down the steps. Canes were hopeless. The only way to accomplish the descent involved Grandma getting down on her butt and scooting herself down the steps. Grandpa would be waiting at the bottom with her walker. He would help her get to her feet and help her use the walker to get out into the living room to her swivel chair. Her pleasant day of watching television, reading the paper, working the daily crossword puzzle, eating cookies, making phone calls, and so on could get going.

This time, without any help, she had to get down the steps. She had to scoot herself out into the living room and haul herself into the swivel chair. She could see her walker in the place where Grandpa left it, but where was Grandpa?

My grandmother referred to her husband as Father. *Where was Father? Where was the Rev. Virgil DeWitt?*

Grandma used the phone to call up one of her neighbors, a nice young man who mowed their yard for them. She told him what had happened. Could he come over? The neighbor came in through the backdoor and found her in her swivel chair. He investigated every room on the first floor. He went upstairs and did not come down for ten minutes. He came downstairs and told Grandma he was going to look in the basement.

He came back after a few minutes.

"Is he there? Did you find him?"

"He's gone, Mrs. DeWitt."

It turned out my grandfather had been canning peaches that morning. He had filled a wooden box with glass jars full of fruit and carried it down the basement steps. The steps were narrow and uneven. At the bottom of the steps was a freezer. My grandfather must have tripped and tossed the lug of glass jars out in front of him. He must have pitched forward, fallen down the steps, and smacked his head hard against the side of the freezer. The neighbor found him at the foot of the steps in a pool of blood and peaches.

My dad, Dean, and I were going to pick up Uncle Milton at the airport. In the morning, we were going to pick up Aunt Ruthie. A dozen businessmen got off the plane and filed past us, on their way to the luggage carousel. My uncle appeared. He looked great: handsome, nicely dressed. I always thought he looked a bit like Cary Grant. He lit up when he saw us, waved as he approached, big smile on his face. My dad was the older brother in the family, but he was not as good looking or extroverted as his siblings, Ruthie and Milton. Milton looked like what he was, a highly successful pastor. He was naturally gregarious, energetic, helpful. He expected people to like him, and sure enough they did.

I had imagined he might be sad, thinking about the death of his father. I was pretty sure my grandmother must have told him the story on the phone, his dad dead down there in the basement, but you would never know it. He shook hands with my dad, his brother, using both his hands, and then he took a good long look at me and Dean, and told us it was amazing how tall and grown up we were getting.

"I guess you heard what happened?" he said to my dad.

We stared at him, confused. Was he talking about Grandpa's death?

"They shot Martin Luther King. We heard the announcement on the plane."

To this day, my grandfather's death is all mixed up in my head with the murder of Martin Luther King, Jr. For a while, the whole country went crazy.

MARTIN LUTHER KING SLAIN

A WHITE IS SUSPECTED

SNIPER FELLS MLK AT MEMPHIS MOTEL

DC ON FIRE

PRES. JOHNSON DELAYS TRIP TO HONOLULU

IN INDIANAPOLIS, RFK CALMS CROWD WITH WORDS

MLK HIT IN NECK BY BULLET

CHICAGO EXPLODES

GOVERNOR CALLS UP NATIONAL GUARD

POLICE SEEK SHOOTER

GOVERNOR CALLS OUT STATE POLICE

4 DAYS OF RAGE IN BALTIMORE

GOVERNOR CALLS UP PARATROOPERS, COMBAT ENGI-NEERS, ARTILLERYMEN

JAMES EARL RAY CAPTURED

LBJ APPEALS FOR CALM AND NONVIOLENCE

110 CITIES IN FLAMES

Meanwhile, we ran around town setting up the funeral arrangements. At least, my dad did. Uncle Milton did. They picked up their sister Ruthie at the airport. Dean and I usually got left at home. All sorts of people, relatives and family friends arrived in town for my grandfather's funeral.

There were numerous discussions about what to do with my grandmother. Ruthie stayed at Grandma's house to nursemaid her, but the day after the funeral, Ruthie was going to have to go back home to her own family. After the funeral, Grandma was going to have to be moved to a care facility. Her house would have to be sold; all the contents auctioned. At the best of times, Grandma was a difficult personality, a packrat. She had been collecting what she considered valuable stuff for eighty years. She wasn't going to be happy about losing any of that stuff.

For a while it looked as if my dad was going to have to handle most of the job by himself, but then Uncle Milton said he was going to clear his calendar. He was going to do nothing but help out for one week beyond the funeral. He said in that one week, we were going to find Grandma a new home and get her moved. We were going to contact a real estate person and get her house listed. Every single thing that could be done in that week was going to be done. When Milton left, my dad would still have a lot to do. A great deal. But at least Grandma would be moved. She could yell, Milton said; she could scream and cry and beg, but one way or another, she was going to be moved.

Uncle Milton never seemed sad about the death of his father. He said Grandpa was in heaven, sitting at the right hand of God, so why be sad? When we took him to Grandma's house, he went down in the basement and looked at the dent on the side of the freezer where Grandpa's head hit. "I doubt he felt anything," Milton said. "Disorientation when he lost his balance, and then BANG, lights out." When we took him to the funeral home, the undertaker had my grandfather dressed up in a suit and tie, made up for viewing, lying in a wooden coffin. Milton peered carefully at the body as if he was a critic checking out the undertaker's work. He was a pastor and had presided over hundreds of funerals. He reached out and turned his father's head to see if there was a visible dent anywhere. "Good work," he told my dad. "Looks natural. Very professional."

The morning before the funeral, Aunt Ruthie and Uncle Milton were in our living room with my dad, telling funny stories about how peculiar and superstitious and narrow-minded Grandma was. My dad made them stop it. He said, "She was a wonderful mother, and she gave us a good Christian home." Ruthie and Milton ducked their heads and looked contrite. "Yes, she was," Milton said.

"She loved us very much," Ruthie said.

My dad made them kneel right there in our living room and thank God for their high-quality parents.

Grandpa's funeral was held in a big, new Methodist church. I thought since Grandpa had been a retired Methodist pastor himself, he would have been a person of consequence at the church, but the pastor who delivered the eulogy that day did not seem to know him very well. He had spent an hour with my grandmother, taking notes about things he could say, and during his eulogy he kept pausing to check his notes. He told us where my grandfather was born, where he went to school, his college, his seminary, the little towns where he preached for decades. He said Grandpa was a loving father and a faithful husband. He said everyone testified to Grandpa's calmness and decency. He said by all accounts the Rev. Virgil DeWitt had led hundreds of souls to the Lord. He had not met my grandfather until the very last part of his life, but he had learned that the Rev. DeWitt was a man of many talents, not just a retired pastor. The Rev. DeWitt was a gardener and a cook and a canner of peaches. In his old age, the Rev. DeWitt had never stopped growing; he had developed an artistic talent and turned himself into a talented painter.

I looked at my mom in confusion. "Is he talking about those paint-by-number things?"

Mom shushed me.

In the last year of his life, Grandpa had developed a fondness for paint-by-number pictures. These things were popular in those days. The results were horrible. The Last Supper turned into a bunch of blobs. We had Grandpa's version of Jesus Knocking on a Door hanging on a wall in our house. The day before his accident, he had been working on a paint-by-numbers Last Supper.

I don't remember much about the grave-site service at the Methodist cemetery. It was cold. The sky was overcast, and a light rain was falling. My dad held an umbrella over Grandma. Afterward, my mom said we had to hurry home because a lot of people were coming to our house and she had to get the food ready.

25

The Memorial Service

Uncle Milton said he wanted to attend a Martin Luther King memorial service. He looked all through the paper until he finally found an announcement for one. "It's this afternoon," he told my dad. "Hey, let's go."

My dad was surprised any church in our town was conducting a memorial service for MLK, so he took the paper and examined the announcement. "Milton," he said, "this is a BLACK church."

I think it bothered my dad that his brother seemed to care more about MLK than their father. It made sense in a way, but only if you took the civil rights movement seriously. MLK was a truly great man, perhaps the greatest and most important man of our time, a national hero, and my grandfather was just an ordinary man who had spent his life preaching to congregations of farmers.

My dad agreed that my grandfather was in heaven at the right hand of God so maybe there was no need for weeping but still, a father is a father. The death of a father should strike a son, wound a son much more deeply than the death of a famous person.

Milton admired my dad and had no desire to upset him, but he still wanted to attend the service.

"For Pete's sake, Milton! Didn't you hear what I said? It's a *black* church!"

Milton said if my dad did not want to go, could he borrow our car? My dad said he could. Then Milton looked at me. Maybe I would like to go with him? I said sure. "I'll go."

Dean said, "Hey, what about me? Can I go? I wanna go too!"

"What do you say, Verle, can I take your boys with me?"

The church was a huge place downtown. It had once housed Presbyterians but over the decades their congregation must have dwindled because it went out of business. The church stood empty for years and then was purchased by a black congregation and renamed the New Pentecostal Freedom Church. The church was on the east side of town right on the edge of the black neighborhood. Generally speaking, white people avoided that part of town.

My uncle drove around for a while trying to find a place to park. I noticed all the cars that passed us were driven by black people. There was not a white person in sight. I got a little nervous but didn't want to let my brother Dean know it. "There's a space," I said.

We parked two blocks from the church and walked there. It was one of those grand old churches with a steeple and tall white pillars and lots of marble steps. One had the feeling that the entire church was trying to reach up all the way to heaven. Dressed-up black people were on the sidewalk in front of us and behind us, heading for the church.

At the top of the steps in front of two tall wooden doors stood four black men in suits. They were wearing black armbands and purple sashes that said USHER. When we arrived at the bottom of the steps, they took a step down to get closer to us and blocked our way to the doors.

One of them said, "What you folks want?"

The usher had a stern expression, a low rumbly voice, and reminded me of Mr. Brocklehurst. The other three ushers were looking at us as if they wanted to pull out guns and shoot us. I wanted to make a U-turn and run straight back to our car. Already, right behind us were a half dozen more black people. They were standing there watching to see what was going to happen.

My uncle ran up the steps with his hand out. "I'm the Reverend Milton DeWitt. These boys here are my nephews. We're hoping to attend the memorial service for Martin Luther King, Jr. We sure would love to worship with you folks today if that's all right."

My uncle had a magical power to do things like that. Resistance evaporated. No one could look at my uncle's smile or his outstretched hand or the friendliness in his eyes and believe he was trouble. The four men eased up, stepped back, and told us we were welcome to come inside.

The church was much bigger than the one my folks took me to. When our church was full to the rafters, it could hold 200 people. This one must have held at least 600. It had a high ceiling and stained-glass windows. By the time we got inside, the sanctuary was two-thirds full. An usher, another guy in a black suit with an armband and a sash, guided us to our seats. He put us in the middle of a pew five rows from the back. Pretty soon, we had black people on both sides of us. Every person in front of us was black. More black people were seated behind us. An old black man sitting in front of us turned around and stared at us. My uncle stuck out his hand and said, "God bless you, sir. These boys here are my nephews."

Everything about the service was a revelation to me. Until that day I had always wondered how anyone with sense could enjoy a church service: the boring old-fashioned music, the tedious bible readings, the loud pompous prayers, and the sleep-inducing sermons.

The people who attended this church believed in the holy spirit.

What is the holy spirit? Don't ask me. It is this thing, this invisible force that works its way right into people, drives them out of their minds, makes them sing and dance, makes them fearless, indifferent to how they look. In the grip of the holy spirit, people speak in tongues. They jerk as if they are having grand mal seizures. They stand up, bow their heads and spin. They whirl and twirl and jerk until every bit of sense leaves their heads. Other people have to care for them, prop them up, keep them from falling on their faces and breaking their noses.

Did the holy spirit descend upon the congregation of the New Pentecostal Freedom Church that day? Is the holy spirit real? Is it imaginary? Is it a form of crowd psychosis? Don't ask me.

The memorial service started with an enormous, crowd-silencing chord played on the pipe organ. The doors in the rear burst open and the pastor skipped in, clapping his hands. Right behind him came the men and women of the choir. They came in singing and dancing, wearing colorful robes. The entire congregation rose to its feet and joined them. I don't mean the congregation just stood up and looked at the choir. The energy of the choir flew right out of them and infected the congregation. People around me started swaying and clapping and dancing and smiling and calling out as the choir sang and danced its way down the aisle to the front of the church and filled up the choir section behind the pulpit. I had been in a marching band so I was familiar with how a bunch of people can be trained to move together as if they are One Being, but these people were better at it than my high school band, much better.

So many things happened during the course of that memorial service that were unfamiliar to me that I was soon lost in confusion. It was as if the components of a church service, the ones I was familiar with, were jumbled together by the holy spirit, merged into a brand-new thing. A living thing. The pastor was not merely the pastor; he was a cheerleader and a dancer and a singer and a conductor. The congregation was not a mere collection of people; it was an extension of the choir, an extension of the pastor. When the pastor stood, we stood. When he raised up his hands, our hands shot straight up too. When the choir sang, when the people around me sang, I found myself attempting to join my adolescent croak of a voice to all the other voices. The same thing happened to my brother Dean and my uncle.

The preacher said he was here today to deliver a message that was not taken from the bible. He said, "Do not fear; the bible is here with us, do you FEEL the bible?" Apparently, everyone did feel the bible. We felt the gospels all around us, above us, below us, within us. The pastor said over there in England when the king dies, people say: The King is Dead. Long live the King! That was his theme today. "Say it with me. The King is Dead!"

And we all said it: The King is Dead.

Long live the King!

We shouted: Long Live the King!

Martin Luther King is dead. He was our King. Our King is dead and gone. Shot dead. Murdered by a white man. But is he dead? He is NOT dead! Like the bible, Martin Luther King is inside us, over us, under us, in the air we breathe.

The King is Dead! Long Live the King!

The pastor could say something like that, something crazy and yet true, something impossible to take seriously but impossible not to believe, and then he would motion to the organist, and suddenly the whole church would be full of the huge vibrating sound of a pipe organ, and then the choir would join in. People around me would feel the holy spirit surging inside them and leap up and sing or shout or dance. None of these interruptions seemed to bother the pastor one bit.

At times, we felt that Martin Luther King had deserted his place in heaven at the right hand of God to be here with us.

202

I have a DREAM TODAY! Do we still have a dream? *Do we?*
WE HAVE A DREAM!

We ain't gonna turn back! Are we gonna turn back? Give up? Lay down and die? Is that what we're gonna do?

WE WILL NOT TURN BACK!

When our King is killed, how do we feel? When evil is triumphant, what do we want? Right now! Do we feel love and forgiveness? We want revenge! Do you feel it? Do you feel that anger? You want that revenge? Don't lie to me. Because I feel it! Bitterness and hatred! Rage! Have you too been drinkin' from that cup? Our king is dead! Shot down like a dog! How 'bout you? You been drinkin' from the cup of bitterness and hatred? Don't lie. Right now, this minute, do you have that bitter taste in your mouth, that taste of hatred? We can't go on, not without our King. How can we? We gotta kill someone, or else we gotta lay down and die, because this is too much, this here is TOO DAMN MUCH!

Let's taste it together. Evil triumphant. Everyone taste it. Bitterness and hatred. Oh yes, we taste it.

What did our king tell us? He said: "Right, temporarily defeated, is stronger than evil triumphant." Did you hear me? I will say it again. "Right, temporarily defeated, is stronger than evil triumphant."

Choirmaster, my heart is too full. I can't go on; can you help us?

The choir kicked in and the soloists stood up, the organ played, and the whole place harmonized, and somehow the hatred and rage melted away and were replaced by — I don't know. Something impossible happened.

We felt rage and love — at the same time. The holy ghost mixed together all our feelings, mercy and joy and hate and fear. Somehow the whole mess mixed and merged until all we could do was sing and dance, weep and shout.

The pastor said: Our King told us, "We must develop and maintain the capacity to forgive. He who is devoid of the power to forgive is devoid of the power to love." Are we devoid of that power? Are we devoid of the power to love? Choirmaster, we need Love today! You got any for us?

The pastor said: Our King told us, "I have decided to stick with love. Hate is too great a burden to bear." I have decided to stick with love. Choirmaster, we need help! We need LOVE today!

And the choirmaster did help. The choir helped. The organist helped. And somehow the entire church levitated. The entire church floated up toward heaven and took us with it.

The pastor said: Let Freedom Ring!

The pastor said: Join hands and sing in the words of the old Negro spiritual: "Free at last! Free at last! thank God Almighty, we are free at last!"

I have a confession. I cannot fully and accurately describe the New Pentecostal Freedom Church's memorial service for Martin Luther King, Jr. To give an adequate idea of that service I would need a pipe organ. I would need a rockin' choir with soloists that make you believe Aretha Franklin and Marvin Gaye are there in the church with you. I would need 200 ladies wearing huge colorful hats. I would need an aisle full of dancers and a congregation on its feet humming and swaying and calling out. I would need to be filled and inspired and lifted by the holy spirit.

Mercy, Mercy, Mercy!

Lord Jesus!

The King is Dead! Long live the King!

26

Naomi's Letters

Bobby Kennedy got murdered out in California when I was sound asleep. He was running for president, and a lot of people thought he could save America. Every day and every night, we were killing people in Vietnam. Maybe he could stop that. Every day and every night, white people were ruining the lives of black people. Maybe he could stop that too. He had long hair for a politician. It's amazing how much that seemed to matter. He recited poetry and read books and he had a lot of kids. He was young, still in his forties. When he spoke, there was a quality in his voice that could touch your heart. The terrible night Martin Luther King got shot, Bobby Kennedy appeared in front of a group of angry, frightened people. He looked sad and weary. He pushed back his hair and quoted his favorite poet, an ancient Greek who said: "In our sleep, pain which cannot forget falls drop by drop upon the heart until, in our own despair, against our will, comes wisdom through the awful grace of God." His brother John F. Kennedy had been murdered, so he knew plenty about pain and despair, about the power of the violent to destroy good men. Maybe he was wise. People hoped that was true. Maybe through the awful grace of God, Bobby Kennedy had learned wisdom. We needed someone like that.

I had a lab in advanced chemistry class. It was the very end of the school year, the last two weeks of the semester. The seniors were already gone; they were released from school 14 days ahead of the rest of us. Half our class was gone, including Epstein and Cooper. The teacher didn't seem terribly interested in making the rest of us, the juniors, work hard. He kept giving us what he called "fun labs."

I was fine at book learning. I could read my chemistry manual, learn the concepts and the definitions, answer the questions in the workbook, and do OK on the exams, but when it came to mixing concoctions of chemicals in beakers and test tubes, I was a disaster. What I did was hang out with one of the nerdy girls, let her do the experiments for both of us, and record the results. At least, that way, I did not break any more test tubes.

Our teacher had brought a radio to class because he wanted to listen to the news about Bobby Kennedy. Everyone knew he had been shot last night, but maybe he was still alive. We hoped he was. According to some reports, he was clinging to life. OK, they killed Martin Luther King, Jr. But MLK was a black man. Bobby Kennedy was a white man, rich; he was the brother of a president. No way, could he get killed. Probably he was on an operating table. The most brilliant surgeons in the entire world were saving his life. And then, right in the middle of the lab, came the news. Robert F. Kennedy was dead. Just like his brother, he had been assassinated. Whatever good he might have been able to do for our country was never going to happen.

The Democrats nominated Hubert Humphrey, the guy who had been LBJ's vice president. He was going to run against the Republican, Richard Nixon. Obviously, Humphrey was going to win. Who in his right mind would vote for Tricky Dick Nixon?

When summer vacation began, my mom said I could lay around the house for a week, but then I had to get a job. I had already scouted out the Spaghetti Ranch, but the cook took one look at me and told me to forget it; he had enough dishwashers. Probably by then, he was suspicious that I was the one who had invented the Game of Breakage. A girl I knew said she thought she could get me a job at the Dairy Queen.

In the week I had to fool around, I read *The Fountainhead* by Ayn Rand. I loved it. *The Fountainhead* is about a genius architect named Howard Roark who is thwarted at every turn by idiots. In his idle moments, he has sex with this hot masochistic woman who worships him. He builds a tall skyscraper with beautiful pure clean lines, but the idiots get involved and mess everything up. It was unclear to me what was so cool about a skyscraper that looked like an elongated brick, or why it was so horrible that the idiots wanted to add a few gewgaws to it, but it was Very Bad that they wanted to do that. It was just plain horrible. A crime against Art! A crime against Genius! When a guy is a genius like Howard Roark, obviously whatever he wants is Perfect. Finally, the architect gets so mad at the idiots that he blows up the entire skyscraper. Wow. He will not allow the idiots to mess up his beautiful pure design! Geniuses are like that. No compromise!

I was just the age to adore this novel. I felt that I too was a Genius. OK, my Genius had not yet fully manifested itself, but I knew it was inside me (somewhere) just waiting to emerge. Like Howard Roark, the architect in the novel, I was thwarted at every turn by idiots – *Mom, I'm looking at you.* All my ideas (many of them) were Great. I wished I owned a skyscraper because if idiots even THOUGHT about messing with it, I would love to blow it up! *Take that, you idiots!*

When I finished reading *The Fountainhead,* my brother Dean caught me up on events in our neighborhood. He said all the kids thought I was a snob because I never talked to them anymore and acted as if I thought they were stupid and beneath me.

207

I thought: *What's new?*

He said Micky and Ray and the Nazi weren't as mad at me as everyone else in our neighborhood because I had tipped them off about the drug raids.

"What drug raids?"

Dean said it was unbelievable that I didn't even know about the drug raids. "It's all anyone's been talking about!"

The sheriff had sent his two best drug cops out to Micky's farmhouse, but Micky met them at the door with a shotgun. He wouldn't let them in without a warrant, which they did not have, so they had to leave. He told them they better get off his porch fast or he was going to sic his German shepherd on them.

That was not all that happened. Three local drug cops came to visit the motel. They brought a drug-sniffing dog! Mr. Broom told them they could search the whole place, which they did. They had the dog sniff every single motel room and the office and the basement rooms under the motel. They even explored Mr. and Mrs. Broom's house, which was right beside the motel, paying special attention to the guest room, which until recently had been Ray Kavanaugh's bedroom.

"What'd they find?"

Dean said, thanks to my timely warning, the maids (Dean was one of the maids) had thoroughly cleaned Ray's old room after he moved out, so it was clean as a whistle. "We also cleaned all the basement rooms. We scrubbed the cement walls! That stupid dog ran all over the place sniffing everything and didn't even find a bottle of aspirin!"

"Ray still living with Micky?"

Dean said Ray had moved home again.

That surprised me. "He's living with Naomi?" Naomi was Ray's mother. She was OK if you didn't mind the religiosity and the racism. She made very tasty pork chops.

Dean said Ray and his sister Julie Ann were worried about the mental health of Naomi. "She's writing letters again!"

"Again?"

It turned out I had fallen woefully behind in terms of keeping up with the gossip about Naomi Kavanaugh. Since the death of her husband (an unsolved murder), she had become obsessed with Mrs. White, the mother of Tommy and Rose White. Naomi believed that her husband Red had been lured by Mrs. White. Seduced. This notion was stupid because Red Kavanaugh was the sort of man who chased every woman in skirts. Mrs. White was a black woman, a licensed practical nurse who went to church every Sunday, and was married to Mr. White. Red Kavanaugh had been a red-faced alcoholic with a beer belly and a receding hairline. Mr. White was tall and fit and handsome. Probably what had happened was that Red had made a drunken pass at Mrs. White and she had scorned him. And then told Mr. White about it. I felt this was probably the true story because Mr. White had had words with Red at Big Bill's neighborhood tavern. Red, even when drunk, had not had the guts to fight Mr. White. If he had, he would have wound up in the hospital.

Someone had burned down the Whites' house when they were away visiting their relatives. To this day that was an unsolved crime, but I had long suspected that if Red had not started that fire, then Naomi might have done it.

About a year later, Red Kavanaugh was found dead in his garage. He had a sofa and a radio out there. He would sit on his sofa and sip whiskey from a bottle and listen to a ball game on the radio until he passed out. One night, someone entered the garage, found Red asleep on the sofa, pulled a hammer off the wall, and used it to murder Red. That too was an unsolved crime.

Naomi believed Mrs. White responsible for the untimely death of her husband. This was ridiculous. The cops had looked into it and learned that Mrs. White wasn't even in town that night. That fact did not stop Naomi from believing her happy married life had been terminated by Mrs. White. The idea that Naomi had ever had a happy marriage with Red was also ridiculous. Not only did Red cheat on her every time he met a woman stupid enough to sleep with him, he occasionally beat her up. When Red was still alive, the cops many times had been called up by the neighbors because they heard her screams.

For a while, Naomi had carried a hammer in her purse. Julie Ann her daughter believed that Naomi hoped to murder Mrs. White with it. She carried it around with her in hopes of someday seeing Mrs. White out in public where she could be attacked. Then there had been a period when Naomi sent hammers in the mail to Mrs. White. It was never proved that it was Naomi who sent the hammers, but all the women in my neighborhood including my mom heard the story and believed it was Naomi.

Now, Dean said, Naomi was writing letters and sending them to the mayor and the police chief and the district attorney and the newspaper editor. According to these letters, Mrs. White was a dirty whore, a homewrecker and a murderer, probably the leader of an entire Negro crime ring. She should be in prison! If Mrs. White was not stopped, she would lead a huge army of angry black people and murder every decent white person in our town.

I had my doubts our town contained that many decent white people, but I said, "How do you know what she writes in these letters?"

Dean said he had become good friends with Julie Ann, Ray's little sister. Julie Ann was a fountain of information.

I didn't think Naomi's letters would be taken seriously by the town authorities because the White Family was famous. This was partially due to the fact that Rose their daughter had led a successful student revolt against the No Biracial Dating Policy at East High, but mainly it was because Rose's brother Tommy was the greatest football player our town had ever seen. He had led the East High team to the state championship last year when he was only a junior, and everyone believed he would do it again this year. According to the newspaper, Tommy was already being recruited by the coaches of major university football programs.

Dean said Ray had moved back in with Naomi and Julie Ann in hopes of keeping Naomi from completely losing her mind. He said when Naomi did not have her mind fixated on Mrs. White, she was fine. Completely normal. "She cooks and cleans and goes to church and everything like that."

"How's Ray doing?" Ray had been kind of unhealthy all winter.

Dean said Ray was going to a doctor here in town and his health had improved wonderfully. "He takes pills every day. Prescription pills for his heart."

"Who pays for that?" Ray didn't have any health insurance. He was too old to be on Naomi's government health plan.

Dean said he didn't know.

I wondered if it was Big Bill Ryan, Cathy's father. Big Bill loved athletes and Ray was the star bowler on Bill's bowling team.

27

Three Banana Splits

That summer, I got a job at the Dairy Queen. I was the only boy who worked there, and Patty Johnson (the girl who got me the job) and the other girls started calling me Flash because the coolest song that summer was "Jumpin' Jack Flash" by the Rolling Stones. The girls preferred "This Guy's in Love with You" by Herb Alpert. Patty and the other girls said the reason I liked the Stones song better than the one they liked was because I wasn't romantic like them. They said in general girls are romantic and boys are wild.

I said, "You mean stupid."

Patty Johnson and I were in homeroom together. Also, she was in the math classes I had to take from Miss Sweet. Sometimes in homeroom I helped her with her math homework, not that she really needed any help. It is possible she had a little crush on me and just pretended to need help. If Miss Sweet gave us a super difficult problem, chances are I never solved it. What I did was call up Calvin and ask him how he did it. Patty convinced Mr. Rossi to hire me against his better judgment. Normally, Mr. Rossi only hired girls, but she told him I was a genius at math and a hard worker.

Patty and the other girls loved Herb Alpert, but they loved Diana

Ross and the Supremes even more. They liked to pretend they were going to be a girl-group and would soon become Huge Stars, but in the meantime what they did was sing along with Supremes records like "Love Child." While they sang, they did lots of dance moves and gestures and tried to look sexy. It isn't that easy for nice white girls to look sexy, but they did their best. Patty got to play the part of Diana Ross.

Mr. Rossi told me he had a policy of hiring only girls age 17 or younger who had what he called "that girl next door" look. He felt that look went along with the corporate image of Dairy Queen which was wholesome.

"Right," I said. "Makes sense."

Mr. Rossi said, "Our concept is: Wholesome girls serving wholesome treats."

"I get it." It was 11 AM and we had just opened and didn't have any customers yet. "I know you usually just hire girls, Mr. Rossi. I really appreciate that you made an exception and hired me. I'm gonna work my tail off for you. I promise."

Mr. Rossi gave me a look. He did that a lot because he suspected me of being the kind of kid who isn't half as smart as he thinks he is, the kind of kid who uses sarcasm. If there was one type of person he hated, it was that kind.

Mr. Rossi said his Dairy Queen was a fun place to work as a first job. He said he was giving good work experience to the girls. He said girls today need work experience.

"Right."

"You used to work at that Spaghetti Ranch."

"Yes, sir. Last summer."

"They got a different type of environment there. What we have here is a family-type of environment. What they have there is more what I would call a party-type of environment. Here, I don't hire nobody over age 17, but over there they hire older than that."

I already missed the party-type environment of the Spaghetti Ranch, so I just wrinkled my forehead and tried to look as if I thought every single thing he said was super intelligent.

"Some of them who work for the Spaghetti Ranch have a reputation for using drugs, drinking, a reputation for wildness. We don't need that here."

"No, sir."

Fortunately, a car drove up, so I was spared having to hear again how I better not be bringing any of that Spaghetti Ranch type wildness into the Dairy Queen and corrupting his girls.

Our DQ had two windows, no inside dining. Mr. Rossi helped open up, but then he sat in the back reading the newspaper and listening to a religious broadcasting channel on his radio. He only came out to help us when there was a whole line of impatient customers dying for ice cream. People think that heroin is the most addictive drug, but if you ask me it is ice cream. We opened at 11 and it was slow until 11:15 and then, especially on hot days, it was fast pace and non-stop until we closed at 10 PM. Because people gotta have their ice cream.

Or soft serve. Mr. Rossi explained, "You're not actually eating ice cream when you order a cone, not at Dairy Queen. To be categorized as official government-approved ice cream, the minimum butterfat content must be 10 percent, and our soft serve has only 5 percent butterfat. Let's say somebody asks you, 'Is this REAL ice cream?' This is what you say: It's not ice cream, but it is delicious."

"Good one," I said.

"Say it so I can know you got it."

"It's not ice cream, but it is delicious."

"It's soft serve. It's almost the same but a little bit different and in fact better because not as fattening."

"Got it."

Mr. Rossi said the exact formula of DQ soft serve is a company secret kept in a vault somewhere. "It's THAT valuable."

The thing with soft serve is it is not supposed to be TOO soft. It starts out in five-gallon cartons and looks like milk. You pour the milk-like stuff into a machine, and the machine cools it down and makes it not exactly hard but stiff enough that you can serve it to the customers in cones.

An important part of the job is staying ahead of things by making sure there is always plenty of fresh, right-out-of-the-carton soft serve in the machine. That way, the machine has enough time to chill the soft serve and turn it into something that resembles official ice cream but is in fact a little bit better because less fattening.

If you fail to keep up, disaster awaits you. Pretty soon the machine is going to be running low. When you finally notice the problem and realize you got behind and pour in five gallons of new stuff, the new stuff is going to start coming out of the spigot before it can get sufficiently frozen. The soft serve is going to be too soft. For a short time, you can serve it to a customer and get away with it, but if you have a whole line of customers and every single one of them is ordering large cones, eventually the soft serve is going to come out in the form of milk. Just before that happens, a disaster will occur.

A customer comes to the counter and orders a large dip cone, butterscotch. You put three fat swirls on the cone, making sure you create the trademark Q on top of the third swirl, but the soft serve isn't cold enough. It's so soft, it starts to settle. When you turn the cone upside down and plunge the three swirls of flattening soft serve into the vat of butterscotch, the whole damn mess falls right into the butterscotch. Another scenario: the customer asks for a large cone. You make the thing, but the soft serve is too soft. Very gently and carefully, you slide the cone out the window but now the soft serve is starting to tilt. It is starting to resemble the Leaning Tower of Pisa. The suspicious customer takes it and immediately the Leaning Tower falls over and lands on their wrist.

Then you have to apologize and give them back their money and listen to their outrage because they want ice cream, not ice soup. They want ice cream right now! When I say ice cream lovers are addicts, this is what I mean. Don't tell an addict he or she can't get (unofficial) ice cream unless she waits fifteen minutes.

You have no option. You have to put out the This Window is Temporarily Closed sign and wait for the machine behind you to chill the soft serve before you can sell more cones. Eventually, when things slow down again, you are going to get called into the back by Mr. Rossi who will verbally abuse you and tell you how much money he lost for every minute the window was closed. He will ask you if you are intentionally trying to make him go bankrupt. Are you trying to ruin his business? Are you attempting to ruin the international reputation of Dairy Queen and drive customers to rival companies like, yuck, Tastee-Freeze?

I wanted to punch Wayne. I wanted to punch him in the mouth just to knock that stupid grin off his face. Cathy Ryan said it was not Wayne's fault. It was hot that day. It was super-hot. They were in his backyard by his pool.

"Wayne has a fucking pool?"

"In his backyard," Cathy said. "They have hardly any grass, just this big outdoor pool with a lot of cement around it."

"You and Wayne?"

"And Mary Ellen of course. I told you Wayne and Mary Ellen are dating."

I imagined Cathy Ryan in a bikini and Wayne looking at her. In my imagination I was punching him repeatedly in the face.

"It was so hot, and we were drinking iced tea. Wayne's mom made us an entire pitcher of sweet iced tea, but it was so hot. Jack, you know how hot it was! And then Mary Ellen said we ought to go out for ice cream, and it was so hot, ice cream just seemed perfect, the perfect treat for a hot day, and we knew you were working at the DQ, so naturally we thought: *Let's go see Jack!* And on the way there, we were talking about banana splits. I mean it was so crazy because Mary Ellen and I are dieting, but at DQ it isn't even real ice cream, which would be fattening, it is soft serve. I mean, you told me that, Jack. You explained how DQ soft serve is NOT fattening, so we started gushing about banana splits. I mean, Mary Ellen and I had not DARED to eat an entire banana split since FOREVER, since we were children, and it just seemed the perfect idea. Decadent! Of course! But non-fattening! And it was so hot!"

How could they know that in my world it had been a non-stop rush for three solid hours or that one of the machines broke down so we had only one machine that worked, only one machine making all that soft serve, which we were turning into cones as fast as we could because people gotta have ice cream! How could they have known that I got so busy I forgot to pour more cartons of soft serve into the machine even after Mr. Rossi yelled at me to do it? I was going to do it, but I got distracted by this one lady with three brats, all of them yelling different instructions at me, and she said I short-changed her, which was not true, so I forgot to carry out Mr. Rossi's order. Ten minutes later, Mr. Rossi himself poured in more cartons of soft serve but by then it was too late. It was already coming out of the machine too soft. It was getting softer and softer.

Exactly then is when I looked up and saw Cathy Ryan and Mary Ellen and Wayne at my window. I had been so busy, I hadn't even noticed them standing in line. I wasn't happy to see them. Oh great. They got to see me sweaty and hot and exasperated, wearing a stupid

DQ shirt with chocolate syrup smeared on it. Despite their good intentions about visiting me at work, I was not happy to see them, not even Cathy. Especially not Cathy. She was only supposed to see me when I had time to clean up and look cool.

Wayne more or less pushed Cathy and Mary Ellen out of the way so he could tell me what to do. He ordered THREE banana splits. Did he have the slightest idea how much soft serve that is?

I looked helplessly at Mr. Rossi and said, "Mr. Rossi, we have to close the window! The soft serve is coming out like milk!"

Mr. Rossi yelled at me, yelled at me like he was the master and I was his slave, yelled at me right in front of Cathy and Mary Ellen and Wayne. And Wayne grinned. Rich boys do not have to get summer jobs. Rich boys do not have to wear dorky uniforms and get yelled at by morons like Mr. Rossi. Rich boys can just lay around their pool with girls in bikinis.

That is how I managed to get fired from my summer job at DQ. I told Wayne to meet me behind the DQ where I was going to kick the shit out of him.

That never happened. I never got a chance to punch Wayne in the throat because right in front of my friends, Mr. Rossi fired me.

Yelling at a customer was against DQ policy. Employees NEVER yell at customers. Employees never CURSE customers. DQ employees – politely! — ask customers to please wait. They NEVER EVER EVER EVER THREATEN CUSTOMERS!

Cathy Ryan said, "I think you would like Wayne if you just give him a chance. You have a lot in common. He loves to read. He adores science fiction. He practically worships John Lennon."

In my imagination, Wayne was lying on the ground bleeding and I was kicking him.

28

The Viking

That summer I met a bunch of bikers, friends of Micky and Ray. These bikers were what was called dirty bikers, club bikers, outlaws. They roared around town on Harleys and wore "colors," denim jackets with the sleeves cut off. Their club name The Dark Boys was on a patch on their back. Beneath the patch was their biker nickname.

Micky and Ray were not members of the Dark Boys, but they were acceptable to the members for the following reasons: Micky owned a ten-year-old Harley. Ray rode a Harley that was even older than that. Also, Micky knew how to kill people with his bare hands because he had once been a member of the United States Marine Corps and spent a year in Vietnam before he and the Corps parted company. (Why exactly Micky was no longer in the Corps was somewhat mysterious.) Ray also had the kind of background that bikers respect; he had been to reform school and had jailhouse tattoos on his hands. Plus, he was a high school dropout.

The fact Micky and Ray were riding around town on Harleys was the number one thing that made them acceptable to the Boys. The Boys sneered at motorcycles made in Japan and called them "rice-burners." They approved only of motorcycles made in the USA, which meant Harley-Davidsons. Harleys are big and heavy and slow, but they make this deep throaty roar, which in the opinion of outlaw bikers is beautiful music.

That summer, Micky supplemented his drug dealer income by renting out his two extra bedrooms to two of the Boys. One of these guys was called Turd. The other one was called No Brain. Turd was called that because at a party he won a Gross-Out Contest. The concept of this game is to gross out everyone else, so players do really disgusting things until someone is declared the winner. One guy got a bloody sanitary napkin from his girlfriend and made tea out of it. Then, in front of everyone, he drank the tea. That seemed like the for-sure winner of the evening, but then Turd – he was not yet called that – fished a turd out of the cat box and stuck it in his mouth as if it was a cigar and smoked it. I don't think he in fact smoked it, but he pretended to light it with a Bic lighter and puffed on it until everyone at the party wanted to throw up. After that, everyone called him Turd.

I never found out why No Brain was called that. He did not seem stupid. He seemed big and scary.

Once Micky had Turd and No Brain living in his house, they had a lot of parties. Pretty much every weekend, lots of bikers and their girlfriends showed up. It was amazing to me how many pretty girls loved bikers. The bikers were not gentlemen. They were not kind. People say bikers are racist and sexist. In my experience, that was pretty much true.

On the other hand, they were funny. They were – some of them – excellent story tellers. They liked to tell stories about the time they punched a cop, or the time they got super drunk and roared down an empty highway at 2 AM and then a cow suddenly appeared in the middle of the road, or the time they were having sex with a stripper and their old lady came home so they had to shove the stripper out the bedroom window but the stripper had a big ass and got stuck in the window. Some of the bikers could tell a story that was so funny, it made people laugh until tears came out of their eyes.

One weekend, the Nazi and I were going to a birthday party at Micky's. The Nazi now had a driver's license. His dad had bought him a car, a Rambler station wagon with 100,000 miles on the odometer. There was a hole in the floor. If you looked down there while the Nazi was driving, you could see the highway. I didn't like to look down there and see that.

I said, "Does he still have the monkey?"

"It'll be locked up in Micky's bedroom."

"Did he get another parrot?"

"He replaced it with a ferret."

"A what?"

"Don't you know what a ferret is? It's like... a weasel. It's like... a tube of fur with beady black eyes and sharp teeth."

"Great. I guess it will be caged too?"

"He lets it run around loose! Last time I was there, the ferret tried to run up my pant leg. Oh my god! They like holes, you know. If a ferret sees a hole, it wants to go explore it! So, it sees my pant leg, and the next thing I know the damn thing is crawling up my leg! It's inside my pants, crawling up my leg!"

"That sounds horrifying."

"I'm slapping at it and hoping it can't get any higher than my knee, and Micky is yelling at me, 'Don't hurt my ferret! Don't you dare hurt my ferret!' He loves that ferret. He got on his hands and knees and dragged it out of my pants. I was never so relieved in my life."

"What about the tarantula?"

"I think it died or got loose or something."

I thought: *Oh great, it's crawling around in the walls.*

I started having second thoughts about going to this party.

The Nazi said since I had last visited Micky's farmhouse, they had re-modelled. They had built a bar in the basement out of plywood. The idea was, when people came over, they could go down into the basement and buy alcohol. The income produced from the bar would help Turd and No Brain pay their rent. (Both of them worked in construction but only occasionally, due to the fact they kept getting into fights with the other workers.)

I said, "But I don't have any money." Since I got fired from my DQ job, I had become a penniless bum.

The Nazi said not to worry; he would buy me a beer. He said this party was for The Viking, who was out of jail finally and having a birthday.

"Wonderful. That's just great. You could have told me that before we left."

I had met the Viking on one other occasion. I called him that because he looked like a Viking warrior. He was six foot four and had long yellow hair. So far as I could tell, he was completely out of his mind. At an earlier party that summer, I had seen the Viking pick up a guy – a big guy — and throw him up onto the roof of Micky's garage. At the time this happened, Ray was standing beside me. He told me that guy was lucky because the week before at a different party, the Viking had picked up a different guy and thrown him through the windshield of a car.

"Wow," I said.

Ray said the victim had been drunk and had passed out on the ground. The Viking had a rule. Guys who pass out at parties deserve punishment. The guy was passed out drunk lying in the grass behind the barn, so the Viking tossed the guy through a windshield of an old Ford that was up on blocks in the barnyard. The drunk guy woke up in a front seat with bits of broken glass everywhere. He had climbed out of the car and gone to get another beer.

Ray said, "It was beautiful."

I thought about these stories and told the Nazi I planned to keep away from the Viking.

"Just don't get drunk and pass out," the Nazi said. "Is my advice."

"Right," I said. "One beer, that's all I'll drink."

"And don't talk too much like you do. Don't bullshit everyone." It was the Nazi's opinion that I had become a bullshitter.

"I'll keep quiet as a mouse, don't worry. Is Ray gonna be there?"

The Nazi said Ray would be there, so we wouldn't have any trouble with the bikers. Ray and Micky would make sure we didn't come to harm.

When we arrived at the party, Ray was drunk talking to a girl. We found out from a different guy that the party had already moved into the legendary status because the Viking had thrown his birthday cake into the face of another guy, a visiting non-biker, and so terrified the guy that he had just wiped frosting off his face and left the party.

Why had the Viking done this?

Who knows?

The other bad thing that happened was that the Viking's girlfriend gave him a gun. Ever since, the Viking had been wandering around the party with his gun, pointing it at people.

I did my best to avoid the Viking and his gun. When he came downstairs to buy beer, I stayed out of his sight and went upstairs. When he came upstairs with his bottle of beer and his gun, I went downstairs into the basement.

The Nazi was in a generous mood, so he bought me a beer, and then two more. I was not really drunk but I was getting there. I decided three would be my limit. Unfortunately, after finishing the third bottle of beer, I needed to pee. The bathroom was upstairs. It was the only bathroom in Micky's farmhouse. I hated the bathroom because Micky and his housemates never cleaned it. I felt I could catch a lethal disease if I even touched anything in there, but it was the only bathroom, and I needed to pee.

When I got upstairs, there was a biker making out with a girl on the sofa, and two girls talking over by the front door but otherwise there was no one in the living room. There were people outside in the yard. Everyone else was downstairs in the basement. Then I sighted the Viking.

He was on the phone, blocking the kitchen doorway. The problem was, to get to the bathroom, I needed to go through the kitchen. What I should have done is go out the front door and pee outside, but there were people out there drinking and smoking and I didn't want anyone to see me peeing.

Unfortunately, my route to the bathroom was blocked by the Viking. He was on the phone, talking to a girl. He did not seem to have his gun. I looked to be sure. Nope, no gun. The phone was the kind that is mounted on the wall. It had one of those long curly cords. The Viking was sitting in a kitchen chair in the doorway, leaning back so the chair was balanced on its back legs. He was trying to convince the girl to come to the party. The problem for me was that he and his chair and his long legs were blocking my route to the bathroom. How was I going to get past him? The Viking, I am sure, was aware of me, but he didn't feel like moving out of my way, not for me, a non-biker, a punk who was still in high school. He kept yakking to the girl and pretended he did not see me.

By then, the summer between my junior and senior years, I was almost six feet tall and I had long legs. I solved my problem by just stepping over the Viking's leg. I could see I startled him by doing that; I could hear the surprise in his voice, but he was talking to the girl and he didn't want her to know that a punk with long legs had just stepped over his outstretched leg.

The Viking's birthday gun was in the bathroom, on top of the toilet tank. He must have used the bathroom before he got on the phone and left his gun in there. I thought about picking up the gun and examining it, but I was afraid if I did, I would accidentally fire it. I knew nothing about guns but was pretty sure I was not a gun-person. I was the sort of person who while trying to examine a gun accidentally shoots himself in the foot. I didn't touch the damn thing.

I washed my hands and exited the bathroom. The Viking was right where I had left him, still blocking the kitchen doorway, still yakking away to the girl. I noticed the remains of his birthday cake were now lying on the floor, a mess of cake and frosting and unlit wax candles.

I aimed myself at the Viking, moved fast, stepped right over his outstretched leg, and made my way back to the basement.

Downstairs at the plywood bar, the Nazi was talking to No Brain. No Brain was behind the bar, acting as bartender. He was explaining the family history of the other bikers who were in the basement. He said the one thing all bikers have in common is fucked up families. He pointed at one guy and said that guy's dad was a violent alcoholic. That guy beside him, his dad's in prison. That guy right there, he was raised in the foster system. Five foster families. Same deal with that guy there, except he kept running away so twelve foster families. That guy over by the steps, he has no idea who his dad even was.

While I was absorbing all this sociological information about bikers, the Viking appeared at my elbow. He shoved me out of his way and jumped up on the plywood bar. He sprawled out on it as if it was a sofa.

"Dammit," No Brain said. "Put that away."

The Viking aimed his birthday gun at me and told me to buy him a five-dollar bottle of wine.

I said, "Unfortunately I don't have any money."

The Viking looked at me with his cold dead eyes and aimed the gun at my head. He said, "I just told you to buy me a bottle of wine."

The Nazi said, "He hasn't got any money. Really! He's a broke-dick. I'll buy you a bottle of wine."

The Viking acted as if he didn't hear what the Nazi said. He kept the gun aimed at my nose. He was enjoying himself.

No Brain said, "Goddammit, Jerry." Jerry was the real name of the Viking. "Why do you pull this shit?"

The Viking said, "I said, I want HIM to buy me a bottle of wine."

There was something psychotic in the way he said it. I was unable to move or think, and I felt as if I needed to go pee again.

The Nazi got out his wallet and pulled out a five-dollar bill. "Here," he said, handing the bill to No Brain. "Give the birthday boy a bottle of wine. It's on me!"

No Brain opened a bottle of wine. "What you gonna do, Jerry?" he said. "Shoot him?"

When the Nazi was driving us home, he said in his opinion the Viking would never have shot me. No Brain would not have allowed it. In any case, I was still alive.

I felt this was because of luck.

Upstairs, while my life was being threatened downstairs, a biker had taken a girl into Micky's bedroom to use his bed. The biker and the girl had been getting hot and heavy in the bed and then the girl had screamed, "There's something in this bed!"

A minute later, the girl ran out of the bedroom, semi-dressed and barefoot, still screaming, and Micky's ferret was chasing her, nipping at her heels.

This occurrence caused so much noise upstairs that everyone downstairs surged up the steps to see what was happening. The Viking quit staring at me and looked away. We could hear screams coming from upstairs. Screams and laughter. No Brain looked at me and made a jerk with his head which I took to mean, *Get the hell out of here.*

"Here's your wine," he told the Viking.

I got out of the basement as fast as I could.

"Hey," the Nazi said, driving us back to town, "at least you're alive."

29

Harold and the Purple Crayon

One hot night in the middle of August, Ray decided it was time I dropped acid. We accomplished this rite of passage behind the motel. The Nazi refused to participate except as an observer because, he said, he valued his brain cells. Ray provided the acid, a tiny blue pill. "This is blue microdot, which is great. It's as good as sunshine, maybe better."

"OK."

"I'll take half and you take the other half."

I thought the pill was too small to divide, so I said, "What the hell? I'll take the whole thing." I was in a devil-may-care mood.

Ray said, "You sure about that, man?"

"Give it to me." I snatched the pill and immediately managed to drop it onto the driveway. We weren't sure where it rolled. Ray was in a panic as if I had dropped a diamond, and the Nazi said it was obvious I was a chicken and dropped it on purpose.

I found the pill by accidentally stepping on it. I pulled back my shoe and there it was. A little bit of it had broken off but otherwise it was intact. I picked up the pill, winked at the Nazi, and popped it into my mouth. "Goodbye, braincells."

Ray said he would consume the rest and swallowed the fragment. We looked at each other for a minute.

"Anything happening?" the Nazi asked.

I pretended all my brain cells were dying. I said every time another one died, it made a little scream which I could hear inside my head, and the Nazi said I wasn't funny.

Ray suggested we go to the bird sanctuary. He had some firecrackers. It was going to take a while for the acid to kick in. We might as well have some fun while we were waiting.

The bird sanctuary was at the edge of town, a square mile of woods with a creek running through it. It was the Nazi's favorite place in the whole world. He had a little notebook and kept track of the different species of birds he sighted when he visited it. When I went along, I would say things like, "Oh, look, a pterodactyl. Oh darn, you didn't see it. It was one of those rare red, white and blue pterodactyls."

It didn't take Ray long to get bored looking for birds, so we set off the firecrackers. He had a couple packages of ladyfingers and a dozen cherry bombs.

When we used up all the firecrackers, we got back in the car but before we got very far a cop in a patrol car appeared behind us and flashed his lights until Ray pulled over.

"Stay cool," Ray said. He rolled down his window.

The Nazi said the acid was going to kick in any second and the cop would notice because I would probably start acting crazy.

I said, "Over there, do you see what I see? I think it's a Giant Rabbit."

The Nazi said, "For god's sake, will you shut up?"

The cop walked up to Ray's side of the car and asked to see his license. Ray said he could not produce his license; he must have left it at home.

The cop said someone who lived nearby had heard kids setting off firecrackers in the bird sanctuary. Did we know anything about that?

Ray said nope and the Nazi said, "That was those other kids." Ray said, "Yeah, there were three little kids here. Don't know where they went though." I said, "I think one of them had freckles."

The cop made Ray step out of the car. I was in the back seat, and the Nazi kept stealing looks at me to see if I was still OK.

The cop made Ray come back to the patrol car with him.

The Nazi said, "Just stay cool. Everything will be all right. I think Ray really does have a license. Pretty sure he does. You cool?"

Ray came back with a warning that said he had to produce his license at the police station within 48 hours. He told the Nazi, "You gotta drive."

The Nazi drove us back to the motel. The cop followed us for a while and then disappeared.

Ray admitted maybe the blue microdot acid was no good, so we watched TV till it got dark and then went behind the motel to smoke a joint.

After a while, I said, "This is the best pot I have ever smoked." That's how we found out the acid was good after all.

We wound up in the kids' park that was across the street from my parents' house. I lay on my back on the merry-go-round, and Ray spun it so I could watch the stars spiral. I liked the spiraling stars so much I started laughing. I realized I could no longer talk but I could see into the future.

Ray and the Nazi did their best to take care of me and entertain me. It was as if we were little kids again enjoying the park equipment, the slides and the swings, except really we were young men at the very beginning of adulthood. And it was dark. The darkness and the starlight made the playground, a place I had visited or at least seen nearly every day of my life, seem strange and wonderful.

I would think: *Ray is going to say something.* And Ray would say something. I would laugh because it is funny to see into the future. I would think: *The Nazi is going to scratch his chin,* and the Nazi would

230

scratch his chin. I realized the blue microdot acid had given me a superpower. I could think something, and then my thought would cause the thing to happen.

There is a picture book for little kids called *Harold and the Purple Crayon*. Little Harold draws something like stairs, and then he climbs up the stairs. They have become real. He draws a star and then he steps off the stairs onto the star and floats away. I started to feel like Harold. My thoughts had the power to create the world.

I could not stop laughing. Maybe it was the pot, maybe it was the acid and the pot mixing together and killing my brain cells. Everything seemed funny. Hilarious. Pretty soon, my unrestrained laughter affected the Nazi and Ray. It transformed them back into little kids and granted them access to Pure Joy. Soon, they too were laughing.

I thought: *Ray will climb to the top of the big slide.* I giggled knowing he would have to obey my thought. I couldn't speak but I could giggle. Ray climbed up the slide's ladder. I thought: *He will start acting like a chimpanzee.* And Ray did act like a chimp. He held onto the ladder with one hand and swung loose and made monkey noises and scratched his arm pit, exactly like a chimp. Even the Nazi thought it was hilarious. Ray ascended to the top of the ladder and stood atop the slide. I thought: *He will turn into King Kong.* And Ray did it. He turned into an enormous hairy gorilla. I laughed so hard I had to sit down in the grass, and the Nazi sat beside me. He too was laughing. I thought: *King Kong will start dancing.* And Ray — covered with gorilla hair — started dancing like Fred Astaire. The Nazi thought Ray was so funny he had to lay back in the grass and hold his stomach.

I thought: *The power of my thoughts has become so great that, if I want to, I can do anything. Anything!*

I thought: *Ladies and Gentlemen, for your viewing pleasure, Ray will turn into a fat old toad.* And Ray – still tap-dancing on top of the big slide – did turn into a fat toad.

I experienced terrifying remorse. *I have turned my friend into a toad!* I realized if I looked at him again, even for one fleeting moment, my thoughts would make him die. I stood up and turned my back on Ray so I could not possibly look at Ray and cause his death.

"Oh-oh," Ray said. "Mood swing."

"What's wrong? Is he OK?" The Nazi got to his feet.

I made a sound, a groan, because I still could not speak actual words, and started walking rapidly toward my parents' house. It was after midnight, but I thought I needed to go home immediately or else I might cause the stars to fall from the sky.

Ray and the Nazi soon caught up with me. They took hold of my arms.

I said, "I have to go home." I felt frightened and ashamed. My thoughts had become too powerful. Who knew what I might do? I did not know how to stop thinking. *What if I blow up the entire universe?*

I stole a glance at Ray and was relieved to see he no longer resembled a toad.

The Nazi said they could not allow me to go home. "He'll wake everyone up. He's tripping his ass off."

And then a patrol car appeared.

Ray said someone must have heard us running around in the park in the middle of the night and called the cops. We hid underneath the triangle slide. I feared I would float up into the sky, so I sat between Ray and the Nazi and held onto their shirt sleeves. The patrol car drove into the school parking lot.

The Nazi was nervous and kept telling me to be cool, but I wasn't nervous. I had already seen into the future and knew no harm would come to us. The cop switched on his search light and swept the park with the light. I could read the Nazi's mind. He feared if the light ever touched us, something terrible would happen. I wanted to tell him there was no need to worry, but I could not speak. At last, the cop switched off the search light, got back into his car, and drove away. The Nazi was still afraid. He wanted to go home. He wanted to be home in his bed and safe.

I dipped into Ray's mind, and it was calm and cool. He enjoyed hiding from the cop.

We walked back to the motel. The Nazi said he could not let me into his house because who knows how crazy I might get – I might wake up his parents — so he unlocked a motel room for us with his passkey. "Don't make too much of a mess."

When we were alone, Ray asked me if I was OK. I told him he could go to bed. "I'll be fine." He didn't take his clothes off or get under the covers, just lay back on the bed and soon he was asleep.

For a long time, I watched colorful patterns form and dance on the ceiling: red triangles and yellow polka dots and dark green paisley shapes. I held out my hands and discovered I could make them turn blue. I made drops of blue appear on my fingertips, and then I made the drops run down my fingers until my hands were entirely blue, and then I made my fingers turn pink again.

I went into the motel room bathroom and examined my reflection in the mirror. It looked like me, but something was different. My eyes. They were old eyes, and I had a strange thought. My eyes were my eyes, but they belonged to a much older version of Jack DeWitt. He was far away, in the future, looking back at me. For a long time, I looked at Jack DeWitt, and Jack DeWitt looked at me.

Ray said when he awoke the next morning, I was curled up, asleep on the floor of the room. He made me get up before Mr. and Mrs. Broom could find out we had used one of the motel rooms without permission. Ray went home, and I slipped into the motel basement and fell asleep on an old sofa.

30

Pigasus

The summer and fall of 1968, I watched a presidential election unfold. It was the first election I cared about, and it did not end happily.

The first political event noticed by kids my age was the assassination of President John F. Kennedy. Boy, did that get our attention. JFK's vice president became president, a Texan named Lyndon Baines Johnson, nicknamed LBJ. He was loud and vulgar and ugly and did weird things like show reporters his appendix scar and pick up his beagles by their ears.

For a time though, LBJ was hot stuff. More powerful than JFK. That's what my dad said. JFK was better at being a myth, but LBJ knew how to run a country. He won a huge landslide victory against a conservative Senator from Arizona named Goldwater. LBJ's party, the Democrats, won big majorities in the Senate and House and, as a result, passed a lot of progressive legislation in a hurry. The civil rights laws, Medicare and Medicaid, Food Stamps.

But there was that damn Vietnam war.

LBJ didn't want to lose it. No way did he want to become the first American president to lose a war, especially a war with a poor country.

The North Vietnamese were little people who looked as if they never got enough to eat. People said an army of American cheerleaders could probably kick the crap out of them. They didn't even have an air force. The war with Vietnam should be a walk in the park. It would conclude five minutes after it began.

That did not happen. Somehow, despite our overwhelming military superiority, the war did not end. The North Vietnamese just kept fighting. We kept bombing them. They kept dying – thousands, tens of thousands, hundreds of thousands of them – but they wouldn't quit.

Americans began to weary of the war. We watched it on TV. Machine guns fired, bombs fell, tracer bullets flashed across the dark skies, helicopters roared toward distant horizons. More and more Americans came home in body bags.

We murdered half a million of them. It didn't seem to matter.

The war dragged on and on. It was embarrassing. The greatest Navy and Army and Air Force in the entire world was not up to the task.

We beat Hitler! Now, we could not beat this poor Asian country most Americans could not find on a map. What had happened to us?

We need more troops! More helicopters! More tanks! More bombs! More aircraft carriers! More fighter jets! More missiles!

We didn't exactly lose, but we never won. That North Vietnamese Army refused to surrender! Didn't they know we were the freedom-loving Good Guys?

The war dragged on.

LBJ kept sending more troops. The idea was if you got drafted and sent over there to risk your life, you only had to do it for one year. Then you could go home. In order to maintain hundreds of thousands of troops over there, more and more young Americans had to be sent. They had to replace the soldiers who got to go home. The total number of Americans sent to Vietnam kept getting higher and higher because we still were not winning.

To sustain this project, America had to draft young men. When you turned 18, if you were male, you were required to sign up with the Selective Service. Soon after you graduated from high school, you were vulnerable. Any day, you might get that letter telling you it was your turn to show up at the induction center.

Party hard, kids. Tomorrow, you might be dead.

As a result, boys my age followed this election carefully. It mattered to us. If LBJ won another term, the war would continue.

Our hero was a Democrat named Senator Eugene McCarthy. He bravely ran against LBJ in the primaries. Everyone said LBJ was the most consequential Dem in the White House since Franklin Roosevelt. He'd won a huge victory against Goldwater. LBJ was unbeatable! McCarthy didn't care. McCarthy was the Peace Candidate. He looked like a college professor. It turned out he wrote poems. The Peace-loving Poet vs the Texan Warmonger. We did not have any trouble picking out the guy we wanted to win.

LBJ stumbled in the early going. The first big primary contest was in New Hampshire. LBJ won but not big. McCarthy got way more votes than anyone expected. LBJ was embarrassed. Maybe he was a loser? Despite all that progressive legislation he got passed, maybe he'd lost his mojo.

That damn war!

One Sunday afternoon that spring, LBJ appeared on TV and shocked the world by saying, "With America's sons in the fields far away, with America's future under challenge right here at home, with our hopes and the world's hopes for peace in the balance every day, I do not believe that I should devote an hour or a day of my time to any personal partisan causes or to any duties other than the awesome duties of this office — the presidency of this country."

I was sitting on the floor of the Nazi's living room watching this speech on TV. "What did he just say?" I was petting the Nazi's dog Betsy.

"Accordingly, I shall not seek, and I will not accept, the nomination of my party for another term as your president."

I yelled so loudly that Betsy got scared and ran into another room.

LBJ, the war lover, was going to – GIVE UP?

Was it possible? Could we run our hero Eugene McCarthy? Could we run on platform of Peace? Could we end the war?

For a few days, for a few weeks, for a month or two, that outcome seemed possible.

Hubert Humphrey, LBJ's vice president, announced he would run. He was a plump guy who smiled a lot. People said he had a lot of good points, but as far as we were concerned, he was compromised. He didn't have the guts to say the hell with the war. He said what we needed to do was "de-Americanize" it. Slowly, we would "educate and train" the South Vietnamese until they could take over the war. Then, we could go home.

We thought this policy was stupid. As if the corrupt bastards in the South Vietnamese government could win the war the entire American military could not win.

Then Bobby Kennedy pushed back his long hair and said he was running. A lot of people liked Bobby. Some people loved him. But he drove the McCarthy supporters crazy. Our hero does all the hard work, challenges LBJ, scares and depresses LBJ, drives LBJ from the field – and then is supposed to step aside so Bobby Kennedy can win the prize?

The Kennedy fans said, "Yeah, OK, our guy took his time, but he can win. The Republicans are going to run that damn Nixon. You want Nixon to win? McCarthy will lose. You want that? Vote for Bobby!"

Bobby Kennedy won the California primary. A lot of people loved him. He was a winner.

And then, he got shot in the head.

This is the kind of talk a kid could hear in every school cafeteria in America: *Assholes are running the world, man. Whenever the peace party gets too big, whenever it challenges the war party, the peace party leader must be eliminated. First, they got John Kennedy and then they got Martin Luther King and now they've murdered Bobby. Know what happens to heroes who love us ordinary people, who champion the poor and fight for peace? They get murdered by the war mongers and racists. The Pigs! The pigs are in charge! Down with the Pigs!*

That summer in late August, thousands of protestors descended on the Democratic convention in Chicago.

Chicago was run by Mayor Daley – The Boss. He looked like a human fireplug. The mayor demanded and got the Democratic National Convention for Chicago because he wanted to show the world how cool his city was – Chicago, the City of the Big Shoulders, Hog Butcher to the World!

Unfortunately, Mayor Daley's Big Project was in trouble. The press was not interested in Chicago's wonderful restaurants and gorgeous lake front. They didn't care about Chicago's symphony, its opera and ballet, architecture, world-class museums, thriving theater scene, and colorful ethnic neighborhoods. The press was interested in hippies. Mayor Daley's city was going to be overrun by protestors, bums, radicals. That was the story the press wanted to cover. Hippies vs Cops!

Mayor Daley played right into this scenario. He said nothing was going to mess up the Convention, not in Chicago, not on his watch. He would surround the Amphitheatre with barbed wire and thousands of cops. Not those wussy liberal cops they have out in California. Chicago cops! The world would see who was really in charge of Chicago. And it's not a bunch of bums!

The protest leaders included serious anti-war people, aging leftists, middle-aged lawyers wearing suits, radical priests, socialists and pacifists and vegetarians, but it was two long-haired hippie clowns that won my 17-year-old heart, Abby Hoffman and Jerry Rubin. They headed up something called the Youth International Party, nicknamed the Yippies. Abby and Jerry had a gift for grabbing headlines with ridiculous threats and street theater. They held press conferences to announce they were going to send in teams of hot hippie chicks to seduce and brainwash the convention delegates. They threatened to pour gallons of LSD into the Chicago water supply and turn on the entire convention. They were going to invite the most famous rock stars in the world to Chicago and stage a free Festival of Life that would compete with the Convention, which was a Festival of Death. Since none of the guys running for president was worth a jar of warm spit, they were running their own candidate for president, a pig named Pigasus!

"This is one pig that doesn't pretend to be something it's not."

"What are you Yippies going to do when you get to Chicago?"

"We're gonna sing and dance and fuck in the streets, man! We're gonna stop the war! Yippie!"

When 10,000 protestors arrived the week of the convention, Mayor Daley lost his mind. For four days and nights, the press got exactly what it wanted, Cops versus Protestors. The Battle for Michigan Avenue!

"Peace Now! Peace Now!"

"This is an illegal demonstration. You will disperse to your homes immediately."

The cops were so covered up in riot gear, they hardly looked human. They carried clubs and wore helmets; they issued threats through bullhorns and swung their clubs and fired off rounds of teargas. The protestors sang and shouted and refused to disperse. Sometimes clouds of gas drifted right into the Amphitheatre and choked the delegates. 700 people got arrested. 200 hundred cops got injured. God knows how many protestors got clubbed. Temporary medical facilities had to be set up to treat the injured.

"The whole world is watching! The whole world is watching!"

"Pigasus for President."

Pigasus got arrested.

Inside the convention, the peace plank got defeated. The Democratic Party would not promise to end the war.

Hubert Humphrey, the "happy warrior," defeated Eugene McCarthy. Peace lost. War won.

In November, Richard M. Nixon won the presidency. He presided over the greatest bombing campaign in history. Another million people died.

My entire generation learned that sometimes the good guys lose.

31

Senior English

My problem was I did not own a typewriter. How was I going to type a 10-page research paper for Senior English? I was going to have to ask my mom for the money. My mom's policy was she would give me the money when it seemed necessary, but first she would give me a lecture. On this occasion, Mom told me I was irresponsible. She said I was the sort of boy who lives in the moment without a care for the future. I was like the grasshopper in the story of the Ant and the Grasshopper. Did I know that story?

I said, "Yes, Mom, I know it." I did not say it out loud, but I thought it would be much better to be a grasshopper able to hop into the air and spread your wings and fly than be a boring ant.

Mom gave me enough money to buy a used typewriter, a portable. Unfortunately, I had a second problem. I did not know how to type. I was the only student in Honors Senior English who did not know how. This was because I had not taken the typing class my sophomore year when all the other smart sophomores took it. It had sounded to me like a boring waste of time. I could have signed up for the class my junior year, but I would have been a junior in a room full of sophomores, which would have been beneath my dignity.

My third problem was the assignment. It had a whole bunch of steps. Step 1: Read the book. I accomplished this step, but it wasn't easy because the book I chose *The Fire Next Time* by James Baldwin is a tough read. It is not a novel. The first half is a long letter that Baldwin wrote to his nephew. This letter is difficult to read because of the vocabulary and the length of the sentences. It contains so much information about the Baldwin family that is shocking and also so much hardcore information about white people — bad stuff we did, bad stuff we think, bad stuff we almost certainly will go on doing — that I found it difficult to believe it was a real letter. I tried to imagine I was Baldwin's nephew when this huge letter arrived in the mail. How many postage stamps would you have to put on a letter like that? How many letters do you get that have titles? The title of this so-called letter was *My Dungeon Shook*.

The dungeon that shook was the United States of America.

The second half of *The Fire Next Time* is another huge essay that has to do with Christianity and Black Muslims. It turned out, when he was a kid, little Jimmy Baldwin was a preacher. The whole idea of a kid preacher blew my mind. I tried to imagine being a kid like that, in front of a congregation, waving a bible, stomping my foot, shouting. Impossible. But Little Jimmy Baldwin had done it. No problem.

I felt James Baldwin was smarter and more talented than me. Much smarter and much more talented. Compared to him, I was a mental midget. Mental midget was an expression my friend Calvin liked to use. He would refer to people he didn't like as mental midgets. I often thought that, compared to Calvin, I was a mental midget. If I was a midget compared to him, what was I compared to James Baldwin? A little ant. How was I supposed to write a 10-page essay about Baldwin's thoughts? It would be like an ant attempting to write about my thoughts.

I amused myself by imagining a little ant hopping up and down on the space bar on my portable typewriter, trying to push it down. "Need help, little fella?"

Also, I was a white boy. Thinking about my color made me nervous. I would look at the color of my hands. They were not actually white but sort of pink and tan. I would think about all the horrible things people with hands the same color as my hands had done and were still doing to black people.

I thought about how weird these terms were, black and white, as if we were talking about people who were as different as black and white. Opposites. My friend Eugene was not in fact black. He was brownish. The palms of his hand were mostly pink. The same was true of Rose White and her brother Tommy. I thought about how pathetic it was that I only knew three black people my age. And I didn't even know Tommy that well.

I told my teacher Mr. Ball I was feeling daunted and might be unable to write my 10-page research paper. He laughed and said it happened to him too, this feeling of defeat. He said it happened to all smart people. He said this feeling is called the dark night of the soul, and everyone like us has to experience it, but then we come out the other side and write a really great 10-page research essay. He said I needed to do the steps he recommended in the assignment. I should start by writing The Mess. Just write down my random thoughts as fast as I could, write whatever popped into my head, do not worry about spelling or grammar, just write as fast as you can until you've covered a couple pages with messy handwriting. Then, step two, come back to it later, read over what you wrote, The Mess. Look for the Good Stuff, the stuff that got you excited. Underline the Good Stuff. Expand the Good Stuff. Focusing on the Good Stuff and nothing but the Good Stuff, create your Topic and then your Thesis Statement. Assemble your Research Materials. Create an Outline. And so on. When I did all these steps, my Dark Night would dissipate. The sun would come out. Mr. Ball assured me I was going to write a fantastic 10-page research essay. He had confidence in me. And then he showed me the door because he had to talk to the next kid in our class who was also experiencing a Dark Night.

I decided to focus first on my typing problem. My mom bought me a book called *Learning to Type: The Touch Method*. It was a spiral-bound book with thick pages and lots of pictures. I propped up the book on the kitchen table and looked at it while I attempted to learn how to move my fingers in the proper way. I was pretty good with my thumb movements but awkward with my little fingers. If a letter was in the middle of the keyboard, I was much more likely to hit it successfully with my index finger than if it was on the flanks of the keyboard and I had to hit it with my pinkie. The shift keys gave me problems. Also, I had trouble not looking at my fingers as they blindly groped for the right keys. Sometimes, my mom would observe me at the kitchen table, practicing my typing skills. "You're cheating again. I can see you looking."

I would press my lips together to avoid saying a bad word to my mother.

My other problem was love. Cathy Ryan occupied all my spare thoughts. It is difficult to write a 10-page research essay about *The Fire Next Time* by James Baldwin when you keep thinking about a girl. My thoughts about Cathy Ryan were not just sex thoughts. I thought about her taste in books. She was trying to get me to read a collection of weird and funny short stories called *Come Back, Dr. Caligari* by Donald Barthelme. She said stuff like, "You should take surrealism more seriously." I thought about her taste in music. She loved a jazz guitarist named Django Reinhardt. She said he was a gypsy and only had two functioning fingers on his left hand. She was into a Brazilian bossa nova singer named Antonio Jobim. Like a normal person, she loved the Beatles (especially George Harrison), but she also loved Lighting Hopkins and Sarah Vaughan. Her favorite singer of all time was Billie Holiday. When I told Jimmy Levine at the record store about Cathy's taste in music, he said she had an "old soul." He said some people do not really live in the Now like the rest of us. They drift around in time as if they are just visiting the Now, and will soon go back to the Past, their real home.

I hoped if Cathy Ryan ever went back to the Past for good, she would take me with her.

Calvin told me I was making a bad mistake putting off the work on my 10-page research essay. He said no one can write a research essay the morning it is due, especially if he has to type it and he is not very good at typing. He reminded me about footnotes. He said footnotes were invented by the devil.

I promised Calvin I would get to work on my essay, but in fact, I spent all my free time listening to records and thinking about Cathy Ryan.

Our essays were due the week before the big East-West football game. Everyone in our class turned in their essays, 10 pages long, typed and double-spaced. I turned in my essay, which was only two pages and hand-written. I slipped my essay into the pile when Mr. Ball was distracted talking to another kid.

A week later, the day of the Big Game, Mr. Ball handed back our essays.

Racism, an essay by Jack DeWitt

What I have learned about racism by reading African American writers like James Baldwin, the author of The Fire Next Time.

Every color of person has been enslaved at one time or another. Here in our country, the good old USA, we have our own type of racism based on our special kind of slavery — whites owning blacks.

American racism was invented by white slave owners who wanted to feel good about the fact they were buying and selling human beings. The slave owners described their own skin as "white," and said white skin is a "race." A superior race. They called people with dark skin "blacks." Whites told themselves that the white race is a master race, but the black race is a slave race. God (old white guy with a white beard) actually wants whites to buy and sell blacks, said the slave owners. Their pastors assured them they were right about all this race bullshit.

Slave owners, the men in the family, had sex with their slaves. This was never supposed to be discussed in public, but it went on in most slave-owning families. The result was "mixed race" children — sometimes called mulattoes, quadroons, or octoroons. Whites pretended it is possible to have a percentage of "white blood" and another percentage of "black blood." White owners sold their own mixed-race children. Let me repeat – WHITE OWNERS SOLD THEIR OWN KIDS! You can't get more depraved and morally lost than that!

Black families were destroyed on a regular basis as family members were bought and sold. Whites liked to say the broken families proved blacks sucked at family values. Slave-owning whites were really great at blaming the victim. Black slaves were not allowed to go to school. Even northern whites liked to say uneducated slaves were stupid. White slave owners did not pay their slaves, and then said their slaves were obviously lazy because they did not eagerly work for free.

One thing you can learn by reading the black writers like James Baldwin the author of The Fire Next Time is how evil the whites became in order to justify the buying and selling of human beings. "Respectable" white people who carried their bibles to church every Sunday picnicked with their kids beneath trees from which swung the bodies of lynched black men. They enjoyed doing shit like that.

246

After the North won the Civil War, slavery in America ended. This is sort of true. But racism just rolled on and on. The Jim Crow South emerged and the Northern whites like the ones right here in our town started practicing segregation.

Black people can live in our town but only if they live in the crappiest neighborhoods in the North End. For the most part, all the good stuff in our town is run by white people for the benefit of white people. The whole white system is designed to make sure blacks have high unemployment. That way, we whites can go on telling each other that blacks are lazy.

Right here in our town there is plenty of racism. Just look around and you will see it. The high school on the east side of town is "half black." Our high school, good old West High, has only one black student and only one black teacher. Supposedly we are the "good" side of town. "West is Best. East is Least." Banks won't make loans to black people, so it's near impossible for black families to buy houses or start their own businesses. Most businesses won't hire a black man except for crap jobs like washing dishes or picking up garbage. Unemployed men develop alcohol problems or smoke pot and wind up in jail. Poverty pisses them off and who can blame them? Whites like to say black poverty proves they are right when they claim blacks are inferior, but whites are the ones who cause the poverty. If you look up hypocrisy in the dictionary, you will find a picture of a white person.

Facing a whole bunch of white resistance, black people have been organizing, rallying, complaining, marching, and protesting. This is called the Civil Rights Movement. This movement is the most thrilling example of heroism ever witnessed in the history of our country. There are many great leaders like Martin Luther King, Jr.; Malcolm X, Medgar Evers, and Rosa Parks, not to mention great writers like James Baldwin the author of The Fire Next Time. Tens of thousands of black people — preachers, teachers, cleaning ladies, maids, moms, dads, and little kids – are participating in this great movement. They are the bravest and best people in our country.

Whites love the concept of white superiority. We eat it up like ice cream. This is the way it is in our town. Racism is our favorite kind of bullshit. We love white supremacy with all our hearts and will fight hard to preserve it. And like I said, we run everything, the banks, the courts, the jails, the jobs, the schools, everything.

Martin Luther King Jr said, "The arc of the moral universe is long, but it bends toward justice." Maybe when I am old and senile and living in a nursing home, goodness will prevail, common sense will carry the day, and we white people will give up our whiteness and quit being so stupid and creepy.

It doesn't seem likely though, does it?

On the back of my essay, Mr. Ball wrote:

JACK, YOU MAKE SOME GOOD POINTS HERE AND THERE BUT THIS IS NOT A SATISFACTORY RESPONSE TO THE ASSIGN-MENT. THIS IS MORE LIKE A HANDWRITTEN JOURNAL EN-TRY THAN A PROPER TYPED RESEARCH PAPER. ASSIGNMENT ASKS FOR 10 PAGES NOT 2. YOUR TITLE IS OVERLY BROAD AND INDICATES YOU NEED TO NARROW YOUR THESIS. DON'T USE INFORMAL EXPRESSIONS LIKE GOOD OLD AND WAY BACK. AVOID SENTENCE FRAGMENTS. AVOID SWEEP-ING GENERALITIES. DO NOT USE PROFANITY EVER! USE PROPER CITATION METHODS! YOUR ESSAY DEPENDS TOO MUCH ON YOUR PERSONAL OPINIONS. YOUR CLAIMS NEED TO BE SOURCED. DID YOU EVEN READ THE ASSIGNMENT IN-STRUCTIONS? WHY ARE THERE NO FOOTNOTES? ENDING IS WEAK AND PESSIMISTIC. WHERE IS YOUR BIBLIOGRAPHY???

FRANKLY, JACK, I'M DISAPPOINTED.

GRADE F.

The F was underlined.

32

Looters

"Jesus Christ," I told Calvin. "You watching this?" He was studying his program. We were on the West side of the field. Our team's players were being announced and running out onto the field. The crowd around us was cheering every player.

I could see Mr. and Mrs. White and Mrs. White's mother. They were in the stands on the other side of the field, sitting where they usually sat right up front and on the aisle. Rose was in her wheelchair on the field at the end of the players' bench.

While the players were lining up for the National Anthem, a crazy woman attacked Mrs. White. The crazy lady sprawled over Mr. White and tried to hit Mrs. White with something. Other East parents were sitting behind and beside the Whites, so they got involved. Mr. White shoved the crazy lady so hard, she sprawled on her side on the steps. It was hard to see because a whole bunch of people, in fact everyone sitting close to the Whites was on his or her feet. People were yelling and shoving. Mr. White had his arm around his wife. The crazy lady disappeared beneath a pile of black ladies. All the East fans in that area were on their feet, screaming.

By the time two security cops arrived, three large black ladies were kneeling on top of the crazy lady, holding her down and occasionally punching her. The cops made them get off and led away the crazy lady.

"That's Tommy White's mom," I said.

"Shut up," Calvin said.

Everyone in the stadium stood up for the Star-Spangled Banner.

"A crazy person just attacked Mrs. White," I said. "I don't think she's hurt though."

Calvin never heard me. He had his hand over his heart and was singing the Star-Spangled Banner.

The game was not a thriller. We kicked off to East. Tommy White caught the ball on the ten-yard line and ran it down the field forty yards. Everyone on my side of the field sat back down. I told Calvin that Slim O'Malley was here. Slim was our quarterback from last year. He had graduated and was now married to his girlfriend, who appeared to be pregnant. He didn't play football anymore. The injury he had received in his last game was what they call "career-ending." People said Slim was now working at the factory on the assembly line.

Two plays later, East scored a touchdown. By halftime, they were up 21-0. Tommy scored two of the TDs. After halftime, we got close enough to kick a field goal. That was our only score. The final score was 28-3. The whole last quarter, East played its second string.

Calvin and I did not go straight home. We went to an open-all-night restaurant, ate chilidogs, drank Coca-Colas, and talked about this and that until after midnight.

When I got home, my dad was up listening to the radio. He said, "There was a riot downtown."

That stopped me in my tracks. It was weird that my dad was still up. Usually if anyone was going to stay up till I got home, it was going to be my mom. My dad went to bed every night of his life at 10 PM.

"What do you mean, a riot?"

Dad said he had stayed up because he was afraid I might have been involved.

"Nope," I said.

Dad said the East fans after the game marched downtown, where they rioted, broke windows and looted stores. He said, "Someone got killed. Someone named Tommy."

Westside people said it was a tragic accident. No one's fault. We have to support the police. They have a difficult job. Anyone can make a mistake. The Tommy who got killed wasn't Tommy White. It was a different Tommy. There had been a report that it was Tommy White, but that was a mistake. It was chaos down there. Hundreds of black kids on the loose like that. Out of control. Drunk. Yelling. Windows got broken. A record store and a clothing store and a liquor store got looted. The mob poured across the Fourth Street Bridge. Who knows what a mob will do? The police station is right there on the other side of the bridge. The cops had information a mob was going to attack their police station. It was impossible to know for sure what happened. It was a riot situation. All bets are off in a situation like that. The cops couldn't just stand there and let an entire mob attack their station. No wonder they had to use tear gas. 25 arrests were made. More businesses could have been looted that night. It's lucky only one person got killed.

The Tommy who got killed was a big black guy, 25 years old, unemployed. One conviction on his record, an OWI. The cops told him to lie down on the ground, but he kept coming. He moved his hands in a way that suggested he might have a weapon. One cop fired, and then the others fired. Cops are trained to support one another. You have to respect that.

"It's a shame. A damn shame," my dad said the next morning. "But at least it wasn't the other one, the football player."

My dad said there was talk that next year's East-West game might get cancelled. "Obviously the city council has to do something. We can't have riots."

I tried calling Rose White, but the phone kept telling me I had reached an inoperable number.

Tommy White distinguished himself the following week. He organized a memorial service at his high school for the other Tommy and convinced the principal to allow the students who had permission slips from their parents to attend the other Tommy's funeral.

The day after the funeral for the other Tommy, there was a picture of Tommy White and his coach on the front page of the paper. They had their arms around the other Tommy's mother. The caption said FOOTBALL COACH AND STAR PLAYER ASK CITY TO REMAIN CALM.

Tommy's coach, a white man, made a speech at the funeral. He didn't know the other Tommy, but he said we need to love one another. We need to forgive. We need unity. A boy from East High School who had a great voice sang Sam Cooke's "A Change is Gonna Come," and everyone at the funeral, white and black alike, broke down and cried. Eight men, four white guys and four black guys, carried the casket out of the church. Tommy White was one of the pall bearers. The paper said 200 people were at the cemetery.

The Sunday newspaper included a special section with lots of photographs, a tribute to East High's Championship Season (their fourth). The section was titled *Triumph and Tragedy*. The Tragedy part included photos of the stores that got looted, one of which was the record store where my friend Jimmy Levine worked.

Jimmy said there is no accounting for the taste of looters. All the Motown records were stolen which made sense but also all the Herb Alperts.

"Wow, looters like Herb Alpert. Who woulda thunk?" Herb Albert was a smooth jazz guy who did covers of popular songs. His albums always had photos of sexy girls on the covers.

"None of the Beatles."

"NONE of the Beatles?!" I was shocked.

"They took most of the Stones records though. All the soul records. The Temps and the Miracles and Aretha. Every record. None of the jazz except Herb Alpert. None of the classical or the show tunes. But, get this, they cleaned out ALL the gospel records, including the Mormon Tabernacle Choir."

"Wow."

"My feeling is that a lot of mamas are going to get a gospel record for Christmas."

On the back page of the tribute section, there was a brief article titled ATTACK ON WOMAN. The article described how, in an incident unrelated to the East/ West football game, the mother of a player on the East High School football team was attacked by an unnamed woman with a history of mental illness. That woman, who had used a hammer in her attack, had been detained and was now under her doctor's care. The article said the mother of the team member had not been harmed.

"My idea, it was Naomi all along."

The Nazi didn't say anything. We were in the motel basement. The Nazi was in a bad mood because he was worried about Ray. After the incident at the football game, it was generally agreed that Naomi needed more supervision. Her daughter Julie Ann needed help taking care of Naomi, so Ray was living at home again. Permanently. The Nazi wasn't happy about the new situation. He said the real problem wasn't Naomi. It was Ray's health. He said if I could see Ray, I would know how serious the situation was. Since Ray didn't have any medical insurance, the Nazi and his dad drove him a hundred miles to the state hospital because they were the only hospital in our entire state that would care for an uninsured person.

Betsy the dog was comforting the Nazi. She had her chin resting on the top of his shoe and every now and then she made a little whimpering noise.

I didn't believe Ray was dying. He was a force of nature. It was impossible. He was not even twenty years old. As usual the Nazi was over-reacting.

I said, "Naomi heard the rumor about Red and Mrs. White. For years, she had been putting up with his shit. Red cheated on her, drunk all the time. He beat her. She puts up with it, but this? No way. I have serious doubts the rumor was true. Have you seen Mr. White? I bet if Red made a pass at her, she laughed in his face. Red flirted with her. Mrs. White told him to get lost, and then she told her husband about it. That was why Mr. White got into a thing with Red, and how did that go? Red backed down. He didn't have the guts to fight Mr. White. Then – what? – two days later, Red made a scene in Big Bill's Tap. Called Mr. White the n-word but still didn't have the guts to actually fight him. I think Naomi heard about that. In her mind, that little incident proved it was true what she heard about Red and Mrs. White. It wasn't, but once Naomi got it into her head, she couldn't get it out. Red was cheating on her. OK, he cheated on her plenty but always with white women. That, she had to put up with, but not this. Red cheating on her with a black woman? No way! Day after day, she broods about it and gradually loses her mind. She has to do something. Who can help her? No one. She's gonna have to take care of business herself. One night, she goes over to the Whites' house and flattens the tires on their car. She keys the word NIGERZ on their car door. But it doesn't work. They don't move out. She sets the clothes on their clothesline on fire. That doesn't work either. She goes for broke. When she hears they're out of town, their house unguarded, in the middle of the night, she goes over there, breaks in, pours gas all over their kitchen, and burns down their house."

The Nazi didn't say anything.

"It was all Naomi. And that time, it worked. They were forced to move out of the neighborhood. But there's still a problem. She still can't let it go. She's not the downtrodden passive little mouse she used to be. She's different now. For the first time in her life, she knows she's capable of scary levels of violence. Now, every time Red slaps her upside the head, she gets a look in her eye. She waits her chance. One night, when he's passed out in the garage, she goes in there, takes a hammer off the wall, and –. "

The Nazi was playing with the dog's ears.

"It was Naomi; it was her all along."

Betsy was making noises.

"She got rid of Red, but she still could not find peace. A black woman had wronged her and got away with it. Finally, one night, Naomi went to the football game with her hammer, and –."

The Nazi rolled his eyes.

"Tell me I'm wrong!"

Betsy barked at me. The Nazi touched her nose with his fingers.

"You know! I know you know. Tell me, goddammit. Am I right, or am I right? It was Naomi."

"Quit talking so loud. Betsy doesn't like you talking so loud."

Betsy stood up, came over, and licked my hand.

The Nazi looked down at his dog. "You gonna eat dinner with us? If you are, we better tell Ma."

33

A Presentation by Jack DeWitt

I had to give my *The Fire Next Time* presentation on Friday, seven days after the other Tommy's funeral. I had prepared, practiced. My mom had heard me give my speech three times. It was almost exactly ten minutes long. She said I needed to work on my eye contact and hand gestures. I had my collection of notecards. I had a thesis: *Baldwin's masterpiece is timely and important.* I was going to describe who James Baldwin was, the impoverished Harlem neighborhood where he grew up, the titles of his other famous books, the awards he'd won. Then I would describe the two-essay organization of *The Fire Next Time.* I was going to describe the thesis of each essay, summarize the main points, and explain why the ideas in the book were so important. I would mention the glowing reviews the book got as evidence of how important it was. In my conclusion, I would summarize my sub points the way Mr. Ball told us to, and then conclude with a final restatement of my thesis. I was going to say *Thank you* when I finished, so the class would know it was time to clap. And then I would say, "Any questions?"

I had received an F on my research paper so if I was going to get a B in this class, or even a B minus, I was going to have to nail the presentation. The principal was going to be there. He was attending all our presentations. We were the Honors Senior English class, so he was honoring us with his presence. Lots of times, when a presenter asked the class afterward if anyone had a question, the principal would raise his hand and ask something, so the presenter had to be prepared for that.

I got up in front of the class, clutching my notecards. I looked out at the class. I could see Michael and Calvin grinning at me. Eugene Masterson, the only black kid in our class, looked as if he had a sinus headache. Mr. Ball had his clipboard on his lap and was already writing something on my score sheet. The principal was sitting there in the back right beside Mr. Ball. He gave me a little nod as if to say, "You got this, kid."

In that moment, I lost my way. My prepared speech fled right out of my mind.

Afterward, when Calvin was driving me and Michael home from school, Calvin said it was like watching a person vomit out the contents of his unconscious mind. Michael said it was the greatest speech he ever saw in his life. Calvin said, in a way, it was wonderful, but of course I was going to get another F.

Michael said that was what made the speech so great. "You failed to do ANY of the assignment. You didn't even tell us what the title of the book was."

Calvin said, "I liked the part when you told us to raise our hands if any of us were racists, and no one stuck up his hand, and you said we were all liars."

Michael said, "You said all white people are liars and murderers."

Calvin said, "You said if there really is a God, he's gonna come down from Heaven and kick our asses."

"You actually said asses," Michael said, "with the principal sitting there and everything. *Kick our asses*. It was great."

"You said white people are thieves and murderers and deserve to die."

"You said every single white person is a racist, and we all deserve to roast in hell."

"You said a white lady can attack a black lady with a hammer and get away with it, can burn down a black person's house, nothing happens, but if a black guy is just marching down the sidewalk after a football game, he gets murdered by cops."

"That was when the principal lost it."

"I guess he doesn't think he deserves to roast in hell."

I did not recall saying all these things. When I had stood up there at the front of the class and looked out at them, my ears had started to ring. My face grew hot.

I remembered that my hands got sweaty, and when I looked down, my notecards were lying on the floor. I remembered that, when I quit talking, I forgot to say thank you, and no one clapped. I just stood up there in front of them and felt miserable and didn't know what to do. And then the bell rang.

Before anyone could move, the principal stood up, strode to the front of the room, and told everyone to stay in their seats. He went to the door, opened it, and told the two kids out there they could not come in yet. He told them, "Tell the others. No one enters this classroom until I am done." He shut the door in their faces, turned around, and told the kids in our class to stay in their seats. They would be late to their next class, but he would take care of it. He told them he could not let them go, not until he told them what he had to tell them, that the United States of America is the greatest country on earth.

I can't remember what else he told them, but it took ten minutes, and by the time he released us, the bell had rung again, and there was an entire class of students out in the hallway, waiting to enter our room.

Michael said, "The whole time, while the principal talked, you just stood over by the door with your shoulders slumped."

"You looked like your dog just died," Calvin said.

"I wish I had a movie of that class," Michael said. "Because it was beautiful."

34

Big Bill's Announcement

I had to accompany Cathy Ryan to her dad's Christmas party, which was held at the Knights of Columbus Hall. She was anxious and moody even before we got there. I was wearing a sport coat and tie, and Cathy was wearing a dress. Her friend Mary Ellen was also with us, and Mary Ellen's boyfriend Wayne. Wayne was a guy I didn't like. He was good-looking, fit – on the track team. No pimples. Cathy liked him. She and Mary Ellen had known him since they were little kids. Cathy and Mary Ellen transferred to West, but Wayne still went to the Catholic school.

The hall was all fixed up with colored Christmas lights everywhere. A swing band was on the stage at one end of the room, playing WW2-era tunes. Every few songs, the bandleader worked in a holiday standard – "Jingle Bells," "Baby, It's Cold Outside," that sort of thing. The hall swarmed with middle-aged people in suits and dresses. The usual crowd of Bill's friends was there, the mayor and the city council and so on. Mrs. Department Store was standing beside Bill, wearing a glittery dress that displayed her entire back. She was super happy, laughing loudly at every little thing he said. I had heard someone say she had gotten a great divorce settlement from Mr. Department Store.

Lots of couples were dancing, holding one another close. A mob of thirsty people was in front of the open bar.

Cathy sent me to the bar to get her a glass of chardonnay, which I did not really want to do because what if the bartender asked to see my ID? Cathy said this was not going to be a problem. Also, I thought Cathy was already drunk. She didn't need any more wine in her bloodstream. She said she could not possibly spend two hours at this stupid party without being drunk. Mary Ellen said Wayne should go with me because she too needed a drink. Wayne pushed his way up to the bar, and I stayed on his heels. We got four drinks and carried the drinks back to the girls. They were sitting at a little table. Cathy took the glass of wine from me and drank all of it. "Thank you," she said. Wayne set down his drinks and asked Cathy if she wanted to dance. To my surprise, she did. She and Wayne deserted us. Mary Ellen and I sat at the table, sipping our drinks. I was never sure if Mary Ellen liked me, and I had no idea what to say to her. I didn't like watching Wayne dancing with Cathy.

Mary Ellen said, "He's a better dancer than you."

I said, "You wanna dance?"

She said, "God, no."

We watched them dance. Mary Ellen said they had both attended Madame Somebody's Dance Academy. It was hard to hear her sometimes because the band was loud.

I said, "Did you go there?"

"Don't be stupid." Mary Ellen's father owned a dry cleaner's, which to me seemed pretty good. My dad was a tool clerk at the factory. I watched the dancers for a while and wondered how much money was in this room. I thought about how in other cities, New York for example, there were people ten times richer than Big Bill and Mrs. Department Store. Maybe a hundred times richer.

"Hokey pokey," I said. "I know how to do the hokey pokey."

Mary Ellen sipped her drink, watched Cathy dancing with her boyfriend.

I worked on my rum and Coke.

At midnight, when everyone was drunk, Big Bill went up on stage and said something to the bandleader. The music stopped and the crowd quit talking to see what Bill was going to say. Bill called out to Mrs. Department Store and a couple guys helped her get up on the stage. She stood beside Bill and he put his arm around her. Bill said he had an important announcement, so we all needed to shut up. He said it was a beautiful night and we were beautiful people. He said he loved each and every one of us. He told us he had always been lucky. Lucky in business and lucky in love.

Cathy said, "Oh my god. Shoot me in the head."

Bill reminded us of the death of the love of his life, his first wife Catherine. Everyone got real quiet, remembering the car accident. Bill said after Catherine's death he descended into a dark and lonely place. A bad place. Bill said sometimes God is not done with us. In our dark nights of despair, God sometimes sends us an angel.

Cathy looked as if she wanted to murder someone.

Bill said *How do I love thee, let me count the ways* was his favorite love poem. He pulled Mrs. Department Store close and kissed her on the cheek. He said he could not even count how many ways he loved her. He said she was the little angel that God had sent him. The crowd cheered. "We're gonna do it!" Bill said. "Me and this gorgeous angel right here, we're getting hitched!"

Later that night, Cathy dropped me off at my house. I hadn't been able to borrow my dad's car that night. She got out of her car and walked me to my door.

"I need to tell you something," she said.

Ten minutes later, I was inside my house. Cathy Ryan had just broken up with me.

35

I Love Paris

For the wretched people like me who live in the Midwest, early January is tough because the holidays are over. You never got the presents you were hoping for. The days get so short you feel you're in danger of living in constant darkness. You're getting up in the dark and coming home in the dark. There's a foot of snow on the ground. The air's so cold, if you go outside for even five minutes, the little hairs inside your nostrils freeze solid. When you step on snow when it's sub-zero, under your boots the snow squeals – as if you're hurting it somehow. Driving is scary. Lots of fender-benders. You clutch your steering wheel so tightly, your hands cramp. Then there is the deer problem. Deer walk right into town looking for food. You turn a corner at night and right there in front of you is a deer, looking more beautiful than you will ever be in your entire life. According to my dad, the beauty of deer is dangerous. A driver sees one, swerves to avoid running into the elegant creature, stomps his brake, spins off the road into a tree, and dies of head injuries. My dad said it is better to drive right into the deer than to crash into something hard, like an on-coming car. If you crash into a deer, your car may get totaled, but at least you won't be dead of head injuries.

That January, as usual, I had a feeling the sun was moving away from us and probably would never come back. Bad things were coming our way, getting closer and closer.

When school resumed after Christmas break, Cathy Ryan was nowhere to be found. I went by her locker and was shocked to see another girl opening it. I found Cathy's friend Mary Ellen and asked her where Cathy was. She said, "She dropped out. She didn't tell you?"

I said, "She's not answering her phone. I haven't talked to her in a week. It's like she's ignoring me or something." I hung my head and said, "She broke up with me."

Mary Ellen said, "She gets like that when she's in a mood."

"Because of her dad getting engaged?"

"Who knows?"

"Do you know why she broke up with me? What'd I do?"

Mary Ellen said I should go see Cathy if I wanted to talk to her.

"I can't believe she dropped out." In my mind, it was crazy to drop out of high school. School was boring, stupid, irritating. No argument. Everyone knew it, but you still went because if you dropped out it was as if you signed up to be a loser forever. You might be flipping hamburgers for the rest of your life. Probably your situation was different if you were a rich kid. A rich girl like Cathy Ryan could just drop out of high school and it had exactly zero impact on her future.

Mary Ellen said she and Cathy had had a fight. She wouldn't say what it was about.

It took me two days to borrow my dad's car. I knocked on Cathy's door and Big Bill opened it. I found Cathy upstairs in her room.

It did not go well. She told me we were still friends, but I could no longer just drop by. I had to call first and get her permission.

I went to Ray for advice. He knew more about girls than anyone else I knew. Also, he and Cathy had something in common now. Both of them were dropouts.

Ray said, "What's she doing?"

We were sitting in his bedroom at his mom's house. Despite what the Nazi told me about Ray's health, he didn't look that sick, but I noticed all his ash trays were gone. He was trying to quit smoking. Instead, he was chewing on a toothpick. He said he had to have something in his mouth, or he felt weird, so it might as well be a toothpick.

I told him, "She listens to records and draws pictures of her mom. And drinks wine. She won't talk to me."

"I told you rich girls are high maintenance. Is she going to a shrink?"

"I think she's taking pills."

"Dump her."

"I need you to tell me how to get her back."

Ray smiled. "You're in love, aren't you? Don't lie."

"Yes, no, I don't know."

"I know what your trouble is. It's obvious."

"What?"

"You're pussy-whipped."

"Shut up."

Ray said love is OK for girls. They like it. But a guy, especially someone like me who never even had a girlfriend before, that guy is gonna get pussy-whipped. "You got addicted to the love and now you're going through withdrawal."

I squirmed.

"What you need is another girl." Ray said he could fix me up if I wanted.

"I don't want another girl. I want Cathy back."

"You're what I call lovesick. When a lovesick guy gets dumped, he goes crazy and wants to kill someone. He wants to murder the girl and her new boyfriend. Then he wants to kill himself."

"She doesn't have a new boyfriend. Quit saying that."

Ray reminded me about this guy we knew who got dumped by his girlfriend for another guy. The poor bastard got so low afterward, he took an overdose of pills trying to kill himself and wound up in the mental ward at the hospital. When he got released from the mental ward, he drove his car straight into the side of the girl's house. He and his car wound up in the girl's living room. No one got hurt, but he did kill the girl's dog.

Ray said, "Look me in the eye. Don't turn your head. Does she have another guy or not?"

I squirmed and lied. "No way."

I didn't want to tell him, but I had a desire to kill her friend Wayne. Wayne and Mary Ellen had officially broken up. This happened right after Christmas. After Big Bill's party, Cathy broke up with me. A couple days later, Wayne broke up with Mary Ellen. Now, Wayne was frequently over at Cathy's house. He didn't have to borrow his dad's car because he had his own car. His parents gave him one.

I hated rich boys who owned their own cars. I hated it when I went over there and found Wayne already there. I especially hated it when he and Cathy talked French. Both of them had been taking French lessons for years. One summer, their parents took them to Paris just to improve their French. I hated it when they talked (in English) about their friends that were still going to Catholic school, people I had never met. They had lots of topics like that, stuff they knew that I could not possibly know anything about.

Cathy said Wayne was one of her oldest friends. I didn't need to worry because they were just friends. She said I was cute when I got jealous.

Ray said I was stupid to be still going over to visit Cathy Ryan. He said when you get dumped, you should hate the girl. This is the sensible reaction. You hate her guts, and you avoid her as if she's the plague. He said going to visit your former girlfriend and seeing her with another guy is like going to the store and buying a bottle of cancer.

And drinking it.

I liked to daydream about ways Wayne might accidentally die. For example, Wayne is walking along talking nonstop about something stupid like he does, and he accidentally falls into an open manhole. Or maybe he is driving his car. The brakes fail when he is on a bridge and he slides right off the side of the bridge into the river, through the ice, and no one finds him or his car until spring.

I knew these fantasies were childish. And wicked. Only a lovesick person like me would even have them.

Ray said he had his doubts Big Bill would in fact marry Mrs. Department Store.

"Why not?"

"Just a feeling."

Ray changed the subject and started talking about the new band he was trying to form, a blues band. He said he was working on a new song called "It's a Bummer to be a Drummer in the Summertime." He said all he had so far was the title.

While he talked, I imagined another way Wayne might accidentally die. A giant python could be living unnoticed inside the walls of his house, getting bigger and longer every day. One night when Wayne is sleeping, this giant reptile oozes slowly and silently out of the wall, finds Wayne snoring in his bed, curls itself around him, and squishes him to death.

Every day I called Cathy Ryan, but she never answered her phone. Finally, I talked my dad into letting me borrow his car. All the way over, I practiced what I was going to say to her. *Are you my girlfriend or not? Did I say something, do something? Are you mad because of that time I said you were drinking too much? Are you mad because your dad is marrying Mrs. Department Store? Are you into that goddamn Wayne now? Well, it's either me or him. Choose!*

What if I got tears in my eyes? What if my voice got weird? Was Cathy Ryan the sort of girl who would like that or not? Maybe if I delivered an ultimatum, it would just make things worse. Maybe she needed more love, not anger and ultimatums.

When I got to Cathy Ryan's house, Ray was in the driveway just about to start up his Harley. He waited when he saw it was me. "Jesus, is that your car?"

"My dad's. What you doing here?"

"Leaving. I had some business with Big Bill."

"OK."

"You're here to see her, aren't you?" He laughed and then kicked the starter on his Harley and roared away – like a commercial for that Steppenwolf song, "Born to be Wild."

I knocked on the door. Pretty soon, Big Bill opened it. Instead of motioning me in, he came out onto the porch, which scared me a little. I took a step back.

"Hello, Mr. Ryan, is Cathy here?"

"She didn't tell you?"

"Tell me what?"

"That she's in Paris going to art school? She left last week."

I opened my mouth to say something, but nothing came out.

Bill said, "Sorry, kid. I'd invite you in and offer you a stiff drink, but I gotta go."

"Right," I said. "Thank you for telling me."

A week later, I got a postcard from Paris. There was a picture on the back, a watercolor self-portrait of Cathy Ryan. At the bottom of the picture, she had written, "I love Paris in the springtime." In the picture she looked sad and gaunt. There wasn't any return address.

36

The Last Time I Saw Donald

The wedding of Big Bill and Mrs. Department Store was announced in the newspaper. The article said they were honeymooning in Hawaii. I wondered if maybe Cathy came home for the wedding, so I hitchhiked over to her house. This was the summer I discovered hitchhiking. All I had to do was stand at the side of a busy road and stick out my thumb. Pretty soon, someone would stop, usually someone young in a VW Beetle or a microbus or a pickup truck. If a middle-aged guy driving a big new car pulled over, that usually meant a driver who wanted more than I was willing to offer.

No one answered the doorbell at Cathy's house, and I noticed mail had piled up in the mailbox. Big Bill must have gotten so excited about his honeymoon that he forgot to stop his mail when he flew off to Hawaii.

"Jack DeWitt?" someone said behind me.

I turned around and found Donald Simpson the Second. I put up my hands in case he wanted to fight, but nope. He was holding hands with himself and did not look dangerous.

"She is gone."

"Paris, right? Art school."

"You were hoping against hope to find her here. I am sure you dream of her."

"I thought maybe Big Bill's wedding…."

"She did not attend her father's nuptials."

"I guess that art school keeps her busy. Did you want something, Donald?"

"She broke your heart, as I knew she would."

"Well."

"She leaves behind her a trail of broken hearts."

"I don't know if I would say — Well, if you say so."

"Wayne's heart is broken into a million little pieces, as is mine."

"Wayne's got a broken heart, huh?" I forced myself not to smile.

"He yearns to fly to Paris, but his parents won't let him."

"Some parents are like that, I guess."

"Men like us, men with a hole where once was our heart, we are ghosts."

"Not really following you, man."

"Still alive and yet not alive. Dead to hope, dead to love."

"I gotta go, Donald."

He drifted away like a ghost. A tiny one wearing a polo shirt and Bermuda shorts.

My Draft Card

That summer, soon after my high school graduation, I sent back my draft card. I sent it to the chairman of my draft board, but nothing happened. No one knew I did it but my mom, and she wasn't sure. I included a letter explaining that I was against the war. It was full of high-handed pretention, I have no doubt, but what can I say? I was young. On the backside of the letter's envelope I wrote, "This will numb your numbers minds." I attached my letter to our mailbox with a clothes pin. An hour later, I checked. My letter was gone, so I figured it was on its way to my draft board. A couple days later, my mom confessed. She couldn't stand it. In her mind, she had committed a sin, and she had to confess. She had my letter. She showed it to me. It was still unopened. She had seen the letter pinned to the mailbox and stolen it. "I didn't open it. You can see I never opened it."

I called her a thief. I snatched the letter out of her hands and marched to the nearest corner mailbox, opened its little door, and threw in my letter. What had I done?

Except for my mom, no one else even had a suspicion. Neither of us told anyone else. A month went by. Nothing. Two months. I went off to college, a little church college in Seattle, the only institution of higher education in the entire country my parents were willing to pay for.

In mid-March, two FBI agents came to see me. I was in my dorm room reading a novel by Kurt Vonnegut. My roommate, a guy named Al, was laying on his back on his bed listening to a Simon and Garfunkel record.

There was a knock on our door. I looked up and said, "Will you get it? I'm reading."

Al jumped up and answered the door. I noticed he got all serious the moment he saw who was out there. Al turned around and said, "There are two men here. They want to see you."

I got scared. "Who are they?"

"They say they're FBI agents. They have badges and everything."

Two middle-aged guys wearing suits came into my dorm room. One of them asked my roommate if we could have some privacy.

Al said, "Yes, sir!"

When Al exited, one of the FBI guys closed the door. The two agents stood there, looking at me.

I said, "You wanna sit down?"

One FBI agent sat on Al's bed. He was about three feet away from me.

The other FBI stood over by the door with his arms folded, watching me.

The guy sitting on Al's bed did all the talking. He said the FBI office out in my home state had contacted them. "You sent back your draft card?"

"Yes, I did."

The FBI guy explained that it is a felony to do that. He asked me if I knew what a felony was.

I said, "I think so."

The FBI guy said, "It's five years in a federal penitentiary is what it is. And a five thousand dollars fine."

"OK." I was trying to absorb this information.

The FBI agent said fortunately I could still take back my card. "What do you say?"

I startled him by stating I was never going to take back my card.

The agent again explained about the fine and the five years.

The agent over by the door said, "Don't be a damn fool, kid."

I said, "No thanks."

The agent on the bed said, "You sure about that? We want to be sure you fully understand the consequences."

"I understand."

The FBI agent pulled out a little notebook and a pen and asked me if I wanted to make a statement. I said I had already said everything there was to say in my letter.

"What letter?"

"I wrote a letter to my draft board."

The agent by the door said, "It's in the file."

By the time the two agents exited my dorm room, I was famous because my roommate had run from door to door telling everyone else on our floor that the FBI was in our dorm room arresting me.

Another month went by. By then, the story of the FBI agents had circulated through the entire college. A lot of kids didn't believe it. They said I was just making up the story to get attention.

I did get plenty of attention. College girls told me I was cool. Guys told me prison was probably going to be tougher than I realized. They had never experienced prison themselves, but they were pretty sure it was tough. One of my professors told me to hang in there. He said he too was against the war. "But is this the best way to fight it?"

In November, two U.S. Marshals came to my sociology class and arrested me right in front of my classmates. I guess they wanted to make an example out of me.

I spent two hours in a holding cell. I noticed some of the prisoners who had been in the cell before me had managed to scratch their names on the wall. They must have used their fingernails.

When I saw the magistrate, he said he could make this go away, but I would have to enlist. I couldn't just take back my card. That door was now shut. I could enlist in the Army or the Marines. The Navy and Air Force were not options, not for the likes of me.

I said I didn't want to enlist. My bail was set at $500, but I only had to come up with 10% of that, $50.

When I got back to my dorm, I was a celebrity. Girls I did not know hugged me. Other girls, especially the ones who had an older brother in the military, told me they did not like me anymore.

I had to drop out of college and go back home to the Midwest for my arraignment. My parents were shocked. My dad got mad at my mom for not telling him about the letter I sent to my draft board. He said he would take out a loan to pay for my lawyer. He wanted to know if I was sure I didn't want to enlist. He said he had served during World War 2. He reminded me that his little brother had died in the war. I told my dad I was going to get a court-appointed lawyer.

My arraignment was in a federal courthouse fifty miles from my hometown. My mom drove me down there. I didn't meet my lawyer until the day of the arraignment.

My mom and I met with my lawyer in a little room in the federal courthouse. He said he didn't like this case, which I took to mean he did not like me. He did not like it that I was wearing blue jeans and a sweatshirt. What was wrong with me? My mom said she had told me to wear a suit and tie, but I had refused. My lawyer said the judge would take one look at me and decide I was a deadbeat.

I said, "I want to plead innocent."

My lawyer said I could do that. That was my right. He said all that would happen today was the judge would take my plea and set the date for my trial. He said, when we got to the trial, he would make some kind of lame speech about the war, how it was bad, but it wouldn't make any difference. "They have all the evidence. They have your letter. You've already confessed." He looked my mom in the eye and told her, when I got sent to prison, I would get raped. He said it would probably happen the first night. My mother began to weep. My lawyer said I would also lose my right to vote.

I wanted to punch my lawyer in the mouth.

At the arraignment, the judge set the date for my trial. It was only three weeks away. That whole time, waiting for my trial to come, I felt sort of funny about everything, as if life – my normal life — was no longer real. My parents, my brothers and sisters, my friends no longer seemed real. When I looked at myself in the mirror, I did not look like a real person.

Two days before my trial, my lawyer called me up when I was at home. I had just gotten out of bed. When the phone rang, I was sitting at the kitchen table, eating a bowl of Cheerios. While my lawyer was talking, I was wiping milk off my chin. My lawyer was angry. It took me a minute to figure out what he was saying. The reason he was angry was the charges against me had been dropped.

It turned out my lawyer was in favor of the war. He had done his duty during World War 2, and he hated draft protestors like me.

The lawyer who had represented the prosecution when I was at the arraignment was a young guy, probably just out of law school. His boss, the U.S. Attorney for our district, had looked over a list of upcoming cases and noticed my case. He called in his young assistant. "What's this case?"

The assistant told him.

"It's a crime to send back your card?"

"A felony, sir."

"We're sending a college kid to prison for this?"

"What do you want me to do, sir?"

The U.S. Attorney got on the phone and called up another U.S. Attorney, a friend of his. "You ever put a college kid in prison for sending back his draft card? No, he didn't burn it. He just sent it back to his draft board. You never did?"

After the fourth U.S. Attorney told him nope, the U.S. Attorney for my part of the country decided he did not want to do it. He had no desire to be the first U. S. Attorney in the country to send a college kid to prison just for sending his card back to his draft board. He told his assistant to pull the plug, so the young lawyer called up my lawyer and told him the news. They were dropping the charges.

When I got off the phone, my ears were ringing. A miracle had happened.

Sometimes when you are young, you do something wild and dangerous. (It probably helps if you are white.) You get away with it. You get caught in the Stream of Life, and you almost get swept right over a cliff, and then it turns out your enemy the U.S. Attorney isn't such a bad guy after all, and the guy who is supposed to defend you hates your guts.

Life is hard to figure out.

That winter, I returned to college. And my friend Ray died. His rheumatic-fever-damaged heart slowly gave out. His feet and ankles swelled up. He lost all his energy, his inner fire. I didn't go back home for the funeral, but after it was over, I called up the Nazi. He told me, at the visitation, Ray's biker friends tucked full cans of beer into Ray's coffin.

37

The End

My senior year of high school, the Beatles released the White Album. Right at the end of 1969, they released *Abbey Road.* I listened to the songs on those albums a million times.

Motown ran out of geniuses eventually, but not before giving us Aretha Franklin, Smokey Robinson, the Temptations, Mary Wells, Martha and the Vandellas, Marvin Gaye and Tammi Terrell, Al Green, Stevie Wonder, and the Jackson 5. Motown and the Beatles transformed the world.

Big Bill's marriage to Mrs. Department Store only lasted seven months.

Naomi Kavanagh started talking more and more to the pictures of the Virgin hanging on her walls. One day, soon after Ray died, she carried a hammer into the police station and asked the police to arrest it. She told them it was the Hammer of Satan and had murdered her husband.

The world often got dark and threatened to stay that way, but then something nice would happen.

I made up with my parents after the U.S. Attorney decided not to put me in prison. My mom wept and said she was a bad mother, and I said no, you are a great mother. I am a bad son. My dad said I was a fine son. He was proud of me. At least some of the time. He said God had given me a good brain; he figured sooner or later I would learn how to use it.

The government instituted a draft lottery. I got a high number, so I never did have to go to Vietnam. Three million people got killed over there, but eventually the Americans quit dropping bombs and went home and the war ended.

Nixon won a second election. That was the first election I got to vote in, and my candidate George McGovern didn't win. Some people called him Saint George because he wanted to end the war. Nixon won and he won huge – 49 out of 50 states.

But then he got exposed for his crimes and had to resign.

Ricky Fox got his picture in the paper standing behind a table piled high with bricks of marijuana and stacks of money. His dream of wearing a cop uniform and driving around in a patrol car came true.

Little Grimm got pregnant the summer after high school, but I never found out who the father was. She kept the baby.

I found out why my friend Michael was so mysterious, why he would never stand up for the Pledge of Allegiance. He was a Jehovah's Witness.

I lost track of my friend Calvin. After we graduated from high school, I never saw him again.

My brother Dean finally started growing. After high school, he gave up shoplifting, went to college, got married, and became a pastor. No kidding. People will surprise you.

Epstein and Cooper went off to college. Rothstein got into Harvard. I don't know what they did with their lives after that. I never saw them again.

Eugene Masterson got a degree in accounting. He married a white girl and they had three kids.

Rose White became a lawyer in Illinois. One time I was in a hotel in Chicago. I found her name in a phone book and called her up. She didn't recognize my voice and sounded surprised when I told her who I was. She said she was doing fine. We ought to go out for a drink. Unfortunately, she was pretty busy. I never talked to her again.

During the 1960s when I was growing up, my mom had an appendectomy and a radical mastectomy and a hysterectomy and a thyroidectomy. She had Meniere's disease and false teeth and hemorrhoids. She suffered from anxiety and depression. When she was not in the hospital or recovering at home, she taught Catholic school children about world geography and American history. Because of that, there was enough money to send me to college.

The Nazi made a huge amount of money in the stock market but then lost most of it. He sold the motel.

Cathy Ryan got married to a French artist who made statues out of junk, but the marriage didn't last. After her divorce, she moved to California and started writing me letters. We wrote one another a lot of letters. There is something about letters. You can't touch the other person. You can't kiss them or interrupt them. I used to study her handwriting and the little pictures she drew. She had beautiful handwriting. I read each one of her letters a hundred times. I found out about love by reading and writing letters.

In the 1980s, Cathy and I got married, and now we are growing old. It is the 21st Century. I feel as if I accidentally wandered too far into the future. I belong in the Past.

Cathy has been on the wagon for many years. She wears hearing aids. She turns them off when I lecture her about current events and books. She says that helps her concentrate.

The Nazi told me I was wrong about who burned down the Whites' house. It wasn't Naomi. He said it was Ray and Micky. Mostly it was

Micky. Ray just carried the can of gasoline. The Nazi said he didn't think Micky was really all that racist and didn't do it because he hated black people. He just wanted to do something exciting that night.

There was a lot of anger floating around in the 1960s. People did crazy things. But sometimes they did beautiful things.

On July 20, 1969, men landed on the moon.

It was the best of times. It was the worst of times. It was Motown and the Beatles, Martin Luther King and Malcolm X. Draft cards on fire. Pot and acid. Assassinations and hippies. "LBJ, how many kids did you kill today?" It was napalm and Nixon and body bags and the Summer of Love. It was Ray Kavanaugh and Tommy White and Cathy Ryan. It was the Sixties.

And now it was over.

THE END